THE END OF DYING

A Novel

by

Mignon Holland Anderson

Mignon Holland Anderson
October 20, 2001

To Lois -
one of the
sweetest friends I'll
ever know. God bless
and keep you,
always -
Mignon

AmErica House
Baltimore

First printing

ISBN: 1-58851-019-0
PUBLISHED BY AMERICA HOUSE BOOK PUBLISHERS
www.publishamerica.com
Baltimore

Printed in the United States of America

Acknowledgments:

To dear, good friends . . .

Brenda O. Anderson
William B. Branch
Raymond K. Brown
Richard Oliver Butcher
Uriah H. Carr, III
Uriah H. Carr, IV
Sandra Hart Christian
Susan Harrington
Chester M. Hedgepeth, Jr.
William P. Hytche
Richard C. Keenan
John Oliver Killens
Roy Lynn Piepenburg
Dolores Richard Spikes
Jackie Thomas
Martha C. Zimmerman

to my dear friends and agents . . .

Beverly A. Nason
&
Willie E. Nason

and to my family . . .

Averill Vernon Anderson,
my Son;
Nora Carr Anderson Kelley,
my Daughter;
Michael Bradford Kelley,
my Son-in-Law;
Lael Michael Kelley,
my Granddaughter;
and to Mom and Dad,

Ruby Vivian Treherne Holland Lynk
and
Frank Bernard Holland, Sr., deceased

my unending appreciation . . .

All My Life I've Remembered . . .

I was ten that summer
when my father took me by the hand
as he helped me from his car
and walked beside me toward the post office.
Dad was tall, brown, handsome, kind.
We came upon the Post Master
near the Cheriton, Virginia, Northampton County, U.S. Post Office
door.
His five-year-old son walked beside him.
My father spoke, "Mr. White."
"Turner," came the reply.
Dad ignored the salutation discrepancies
(I don't know if he hated them more than I),
and spoke with interest of White's son.

"What a fine looking boy, Mr. White. He has
surely grown tall since last I saw him."

Mr. White smiled proudly, and looking down
upon his boy, spoke to his upturned face.
"Son, say hello to Turner Allen."
The boy looked surprised and glanced my father's way.
"I don't want to speak to no ole coloured man,"
he said, and looked my tall, grown father straight in the eye.

Mr. White colored red, as deep a red face
as I had ever seen.
He sputtered for a second, then said,
"Good-day, Turner. Good-day."

Again, my father took my hand.
I could not see his face as we walked,
but I knew what he knew—
that a little white boy had kept the promise of his people
to do what they could, even through a child,
to make my daddy, in the real world,
in my eyes, less of a man.
Still, in my eyes, the kept promise did not truly matter.

There was too much love in my daddy's eyes for me,
and he was too tall, too brown, too handsome, too kind
to ever be less than he truly was . . .
But I don't know if my daddy knew,
I truly don't know if he knew . . .

There were no lynchings on record in Northampton County, Virginia, in recent years, yet many black men, women, and children suffered a lessening and a shortening of their lives due to the insidious, as well as overt racism which, even today, lives among its people. And most knew about the open murder by a mob of 2000 whites in 1933 of George Armwood, in Somerset County, Princess Anne, Maryland, some sixty miles north. No one was charged after Mr. Armwood was dragged, from the jail, beaten, stabbed by members of the mob, dragged down the street by a rope around his neck, hanged from a tree near a local judge's house, and was then dragged back up the main street, where his unclothed body was doused with gasoline and burned beyond recognition in front of the Courthouse. He was alleged to have sexually assaulted a 72 year-old white woman, the accusation of rape based entirely on unfounded rumor.

It is in memory and honor of those black citizens of Northampton County, and the DelMarVa Peninsula as a whole, who were and are, on one level or another, victims of white supremacy, that this fictional exploration is written.

All names and events are purely fictional. Where the real names of places appear, no persons or events, as depicted here, actually existed or occurred. Any similarity or facsimile, thereof, is purely coincidental.

Mignon Holland Anderson
January 20, 2001

Dedication:

And

For EMMETT TILL,
and the well over 6,000 other
African American
men, women, and children
lynched in the United States of America
by white Americans since 1619 . . .

LONG AFTER

June 1, 1998.

Oh, my dear Lord in Heaven.

It is finally told.

I sat with her over morning coffee, a kind woman, a novelist and poet who listened with her heart—a place of old understandings, comfortable, clear-sighted, soothing and stark sometimes in the pain that from her own life, lingered, just out of sight.

Our friendship was serendipitous. She and her family bought the house next door and I took her a pie to say hello and welcome. She was my sister from the moment my eyes took in her face as she stood framed by her front doorway.

I had just turned fifty; she was a few weeks away from fifty-four. Like me, she was light-skinned and culturally, experientially, and genetically African American—black in the pit of her soul, yet also genetically Native American [Cherokee and Powhatan for me, Lakotah (Teton) Sioux and Cheyenne for her] and European (several of those countries that preyed upon the black and the red with such ferocity). And like me, hers was a family that had been entirely American, in all its aspects, for well over nine generations.

One morning, after months of sharing our thoughts about what it was to grow up coloured, Negro, Black, and finally African American, I began telling her what I hadn't shared with anyone since I was ten years old. I needed to tell somebody. My parents and my brother knew some of it, but not the parts that happened to me when they weren't around. Their closeness to me made me not want to tell them, as though telling them would bring them sorrow because I had let so much time go by without letting them know the whole truth.

Not one day had passed that I didn't want to tell somebody, but first I had to let myself remember, and I didn't have the strength to let myself fully do that until my lastborn gave birth to her first child. I don't know why that grandbaby was the key to giving me the courage to review those days from so long ago, but as I held that little one, I knew that I had to let myself remember and to understand what was hiding inside of me. Being free of hiding from myself seemed the best gift to give from a new grandmother to so young a grandchild. And then my new neighbor arrived and I had a friend like no other.

So, I told her . . .

Carrie Marie Allen

PROLOGUE

May, 1959.

It was not quite evening. The waters of the Chesapeake were calm. There were inevitable tracings of foam and scum between the larger waves coming in and the smaller ones rebounding from the beach out to sea, but for early May, it was quiet, and the light breeze blowing landward was unseasonably warm.

In variations of light sand and driftwood, the shoreline carved its shape against submerged green-black beach grass and water. A short distance to the south, a string of slim fishnet poles struck out beyond the shallows, vertical still sentinels, seeming to move, yet unmoving in their stand against the tide. They could be seen to bend almost imperceptibly, on occasion, under the weight of perching sea gulls as they lurched forward into flight. Scattered in jagged ribbons, trails of orange-red light stretched from several miles out, across the rippled surface of the water, up to the bottom of a giant sun, like some ethereal wake made of liquid fire.

"I never get enough of that old sun burning up the bay," Turner said. "I used to get chastised by my father for looking at it for so long when I was a boy oystering on his boat." Turner sighed and shook his head in mild consternation. "Poppa would tell me, whenever I spoke of how sacred a thing the sun was, that he had given up Indian Way and the sun was just to show him his work between the dawn and the fall of night. He couldn't admit it, but he really hated changing the way he did."

Turner gestured toward a place on the sand for Stella to sit. They had walked far enough down the shore and it wouldn't be long before they would have to start back home. He sat next to her, tossed their shoes a ways off and leaned back with his head in her lap. Stella played with the short soft hair at his temples and smiled. Turner was more relaxed on this late afternoon than he had been in many months. His father's death two years earlier had left him thoughtful to the point of his often being morose, a disposition foreign to what she had known of him since their first meeting, when he was a cheerful boy of fifteen.

"I guess folks wondered about Poppa. He sounded so tough with me sometimes. Actually, he was gentle and even tender on occasion. Turning away from his heritage broke something inside of him. I see him whenever I see or smell the Chesapeake." His eyes scanned the great expanse of dark green water as its soft, whispered roar lulled the coming dusk and the briny smell of it filled his nose and lungs. He could almost see his father standing behind the men on the dredges of his skipjack, as they hauled in oysters at the stern of the boat, the mast empty of sail behind him and his skin weathered a reddish brown by wind and sun and the salty waters of the sea.

"He didn't mean that, I don't think," Stella said.

"Didn't mean what?" His voice was soft and always compelling in its timbre. He seemed so much more like himself this night. Turner closed his eyes. His wife's hands were soothing on his temples.

"What he said about giving up Indian Way. I mean, not in his heart. He still saw the value of it in his heart?"

"Poppa meant it. He lived and died that way from twenty-five on. If a reservation Indian leaves home, a half black one at that, he either dies or he becomes a white man. Poppa lived physically, but inside of himself he died, and he lived that death with the hair of an Indian and the features and brown complexion of a black man. In his own eyes, he became a nigger."

"Oh, Turner." Stella hated that word—the ugliness of it. She could almost taste the hatred spread between the letters as they slid through the clenched teeth of all of those who actively hated black people. "Your father was a man; not a nigger."

Turner smiled ironically. "Yes, he was a man. That I know, but Poppa didn't know it after awhile. After the grieving set in, he didn't know."

Darkness moved closer. The colors of things faded until everything was a display of blacks and grays and dusky whites. There was a slim trace of first quarter moon slipping up from behind the woods and over their heads, all hushed over by the constant breathing of the sea. As they grew quiet, each one thinking, the breeze picked up and white caps showed here and there, making small waves increase their height as the wind rushed beneath their tops. They spit foamy showers of salt sea in protest and commenced to crash against the shoreline.

The low hiss grew to a bounding roar and the pines behind the beach moved en masse in answer. It all stirred a restlessness in Turner, which for a time had gotten harder to define with every passing day. For most of his life he had been aware of a tension, sometimes as sudden in its rising as the Chesapeake's sudden squalls—argumentative winds, calm to gusty within an infinitesimal span of time. He was getting very tired of struggling against all of the racism, which confronted him on all sides. It was enough to simply fathom the riddles of how to be a husband and a father and how to make a living amidst the promise of one day growing old. Why this added circumscription of his mind and heart, of his body and very soul? He was as bound in the center of the least among the whites and their condemning eyes as was the Eastern Shore to the waters of the Atlantic and the Chesapeake Bay. He lacked the means to sail across to any permanent freedom. His father had died from this state of being with a little prostate cancer thrown in.

"God, Stella. It's 1959. I'm 50 years old and most of the people I meet still don't believe I'm really a man, either because they're white and racist or because they're black and oppressed of mind. I can feel that killing me, like it killed Poppa."

Turner closed his eyes and wiped his hand in a slow stroke down and across his weary face, as though to erase or at least to ease the weariness. He took a slow, deep breath and looked out again across the now rolling black-green waters.

"Black clouds over there," he said, pointing towards the southwestern-most horizon. There was no cloud cover anywhere else in the sky, except for that one dark patch, and it was spreading its influence, changing shape, broadening, and coming on.

"Won't be long before that'll be here. We'd better go." Turner sat up and pulled her closer.

"No. No . . ." Stella said. "A few more minutes." Stella hugged him, her bowed head resting on his shoulder in the growing wind and dark, wondering what of significance, if anything, she could say. She had never heard him talk this way before. He often talked to her about things that bothered him, but tonight he seemed so much more vulnerable in his openness, and strangely calm despite the meaning of his words. She thought of what Turner had told her just the day before, when he came in from removing two bodies from the Seater-Wharf fire. The initial call had been to pick up only one man, a friend: Charley Finney.

Charley's wife, Marie, was there. She watched and waited until they found her husband in the charred hulk of the oyster house. It was ironic to all who saw it how that old building had burned down right over tons of water, all around and underneath. "He never talked to me, Turner," she said. "Much as I loved Charley, I never knew what he wanted except for guessing, like all that water so close to the fire and no account at all. How can I live with that, now that he's gone?"

Turner had looked away, pausing to weigh his thoughts before he spoke. "His life has passed, Marie. You can't change whatever you did wrong. Maybe ... Maybe it's a lesson for both of us. You have to tell people what you think when you have the chance." He paused, weighing. "Maybe you should have told him," Turner said. "He couldn't change if he didn't know he needed to. Maybe he didn't know." His words had seemed harsh, though he hadn't intended them to, so he had hugged Marie and held her for a few minutes while she cried.

They found another body in the wreckage. Somebody said the man was JoBoy, a migrant worker from down Georgia someplace, but nobody knew his real name. Since the Sheriff, Luke Haskins, had almost nothing to go on, Turner placed him in a special box in the vault house, the body covered with lime to keep the odor down. This kind of procedure was one of the things he hated most about being an undertaker. It might be weeks before he got an authorization to bury the man. But oddly, the only thing that Luke seemed concerned with initially was making sure the victim wasn't white.

"Are you all sure this fellow's a coloured man?" Luke looked earnestly into the face of each person, his right hand resting on the butt of his pistol. The men nodded and repeated, as one, each in his own words, that the unidentified man had been new and had just been hanging around the place when the fire broke out, and he was coloured.

Luke had turned to Turner. "You understand that if this here corpse is white, I'll have to call a white undertaker?"

"His skin's burned to nothing, Sheriff," Turner said. "What the hell difference does it make?" Turner had walked away, clicking his teeth in disgust, and had gathered up the remains, leaving Luke to stand alone on the dock to ponder Turner's uppity show of nerve.

Bits of sand suddenly flew in a gust and stung their faces. Turner moved as though to get up, but Stella gently held him, her arms still tightly around him, her head still bowed against his shoulder. Her thoughts were suddenly so clear. That was what Turner was doing. He was telling her in ways he had never chosen before, telling her plainly, about the silent fears inside of himself, at least some of them, so that she might better understand and help him, like Marie never did for Charley because Charley never knew to help her. A feeling of admiration rose quietly in her heart. It took a great deal of courage to talk about such things, to admit such things.

"You can't let racism kill you," she said, breaking the silence. "You can't anymore."

He could barely see her in the failing light and didn't want to turn on his flashlight and disturb the intimacy, which the darkness under the moon had sealed.

"What do you mean?" he said. "How can I stop it from chewing up my guts? It comes straight at you and from behind you all at once. It has so much more . . . so much more tenacity . . . than I do."

"No. You've seen it," she said. "You've recognized it. Even if you can't stop it, you can harden yourself to it. You can try." She wasn't sure. "Can't you? Can't we, together?"

"No." Turner held a serious expression for a moment, and then chuckled to break the tension. "No, indeed. Racism mutates like bacteria. Not tolerance; killing it is the only way. But your optimism is wonderful." He turned and held her, his mouth kissing hers, lingering, as he squeezed her closer and moved his hands across her back. A tenderness warmed in her. Except for the sand and the wind, the growing chill and the coming rain, supper to be served and the children alone long enough for one evening, and the Washington family due to come to pick out a casket... Oh, Jesus, there were so many things for which one could make exceptions. Right now she wanted to lie down, right here on the beach in her husband's arms, and never move until the heat was gone from between them out to sea, sure to come again, sure to be welcomed again, and again loved away. All the tired days and the fretting days struggling into years. Nights of crying. Money scarce and good friends robbed and cheated and lynched and disappointed into Glory and gone. Turner made up for it all. He was one sweet dream that had come true for her. Lord, if she should ever lose him . . . ?

The moment passed. He looked through the moonlit darkness into her eyes. "I'll try. With your help, I'll try. I don't want to die of bitterness. I've been consciously working on it for months now—turning away the bitterness one minute at a time. Racism is a disease as surely as cancer or diabetes. Railing at disease won't end it. Gramma said it in her very wise and eloquent way. 'You must apply yourself to remedies and remain sweet in the heart, or life will choke you with itself'. Huh?"

They smiled at one another and he wiped at the tears he couldn't see that he knew were falling in soft rivulets down his wife's face.

"You ole soft-hearted thing, you," he whispered. She kissed his mouth with a soft, sweet kiss.

They stood, and holding hands, took one more lingering look at what were becoming the quarrelsome waters of the Chesapeake. The black cumulus clouds were almost overhead and as they turned back down the beach, the first heavy gusts full of gritty sand blew angrily around them. They had just begun the trek through the adjacent pines when they were met along the woods path by their son, M.T. His small flashlight bobbled in the darkness, and when they saw his face, it was filled with anxious excitement.

"Daddy!" the boy shouted. "Momma. It's Carrie. She fainted!"

"What? What Happened?" Turner aimed the beam of his light against M.T.'s chest so he could see his face without blinding him.

"She's all right. Miz Rosie and Chug are with her. She came to." He was breathless from running.

Turner took M.T. by the arms. "Explain, son. What happened?"

"It's Shorty King. Doc Reynolds just called and told me on the phone. I told Carrie and she looked real funny in the face and then she fainted." M.T. took several deep breaths. Turner let go of his arms and returned the light beam to his chest.

"Son, for God's sake, tell me. What did Doc Reynolds say?"

"It's Shorty King. Doc Reynolds said they found Shorty King dead in his bed at home. Shorty King's dead! Dead from all the drinkin'. Doc said the house was full of every kind of empty whiskey bottle on God's earth. He's dead and gone, Daddy."

Turner reached out to Stella and pulled her to him, both of them leaning against one another, eyes closed as though exhaustion had suddenly descended on them. Neither had ever wished Shorty King dead, but now that he was, it was a relief. Their prayer had been that Carrie would survive Shorty's impact on her life, intact. That she would grow up whole and unscarred by all that he had precipitated.

It was a year now since the trouble had started with Shorty King. They had hoped it was over months ago. They thought even now that it was finally over; that they knew and understood the significance of this ugly little man's death.

But they didn't know. They couldn't begin to know. Only their daughter, Carrie, knew.

Chapter I

June, 1958: One year earlier.

The storm was beating up against the outside of the house like it wanted to get in. The house was strong; built by her father and made beautiful inside by her mother. Carrie lay cuddled up to her favorite pillow on her bed in the darkness of her bedroom, both comfortable and vaguely ill at ease. Her father was out in that storm picking up the body of a dead man. It seemed to her that it was an odd thing being the daughter of an undertaker.

Most of the families who called the Allen Funeral Home lived in Northampton County, a few in Accomack, among the many forests, creeks, and back country roads of the Eastern Shore of Virginia.

Sometimes he took her with him on calls. Going with him at such times was like living a mystery. People were different, strange, soft, their eyes cast down or glistening wet with tears and hurtful expressions. People were always standing around in motionless bunches, the men with their hands in their pockets, their shoulders hunched, or they were seated, their elbows on the tops of their thighs, hands quietly wringing one another, shoes spread wide as they looked down, waiting for her father to come and to go quickly; everybody staring blankly with expectations of something they knew not what, talking in whispers, in little knots of three or four, heads nodding to whatever was spoken like there was some conspiracy of understanding. There was a warm, yet foreign cohesion among the people, witnesses all to the ending hour of a human life, which would one day be their own. She couldn't have explained this to anyone if her life had depended on it, yet for four years now, since she was six or so, she had made such calls with her parents, mostly her father, and deep within her she knew these things, these ways among grieving people, to be true.

Whatever her father said seemed acceptable at such times, a kind of last judgment. He was the one who knew what to do. He had a kind of power which made him remain all the taller in her mind. She saw this same power in her mother on those occasions when her father wasn't there. They both carried with them a knowing authority, which she assumed without thinking would one day be a part of herself.

19

When her parents worked together, they worked in unison, her father in charge of the removal, her mother caring for the family, both quiet masters of knowing what to do and to say to put the bereaved family and the situation at ease. Each one did what worked out best for the other. Carrie had a strong feeling that this was what marriage was supposed to be; especially when she heard some of her friends talking about the fights between their parents at home. She had no way of knowing that she would soon be at the center of an argument that would threaten to tear her parents apart. Nor could she know how many of the people she loved would be dead by summer's end.

The rain splattered the windows and the roof and washed over her consciousness. Before she knew it, she was asleep and dreaming about going to Capeville School. It was a vivid dream in full color, with all of the sights and sounds and smells of the real world, as if she were really at the school bus stop just down the road.

And so falling asleep, Carrie dreamed about being at the school bus stop, back a few months ago in January .... somebody was cooking. Collard greens and pork chops or something like that. It was Mr. Pat. Pat's Place was open and cooking odors were swarming from the exhaust fan, a warm aromatic flow of air mixing with the cold just outside the store where the children stood.

"Here dey come!" Joe Joe shouted. All of the children, cold and shifting back and forth on cold-numbing feet, were standing in front of Pat's Place, waiting for the coloured school bus to come take them ten miles south to Capeville. While just across the main highway from them there was a large brick schoolhouse, just like their raggedy school, but in excellent repair, with a playground full of new swings and slides, which they, by law, could not use.... "Here dey come, one by one," Joe Joe crooned, this time more softly.

They heard the hum of them first, and then yellow school buses full of white children suddenly came into view along the highway from north and south and turned into the main driveway of Cheriton School. They were new, a bright clean undented, unscratched, unused yellow, all with heaters that worked and seats that looked unsat upon. Not one white child had to ride without a seat. Not one rusted hole was anywhere in the floor where icy breezes might blow upon a white child's feet.

"Here dey come. One by one. Fat and yellow and rich and new —- for everybody—but you. Here dey come. One by one."

Joe Joe was always making rhymes, standing with Carrie and Beanie and Susie and M.T. and Georgia and Shirley and Birdie, all of them cold, some of them hungry, looking with an angry, subdued puzzlement at the white-only schoolhouse five hundred feet across the road, and all of those beautiful new school buses. Of all of the buses that carried children to Capeville, only one was brand new. The kids who were assigned to ride that bus were almost celebrities; their privilege was so rare.

It wouldn't be long before there would be enough seats on the coloured buses. December had been unusually mild, but now the cold of January was beginning to set in with a long-term purpose about the depth of its chill and the ferocity of its winds. Colds and flu and aches and pains and pneumonia here and there would soon make room. Wearing blue jeans instead of dresses would only help some of the girls not to get sick. Soon there would be seats to spare, despite the fact that some ten children always had to stand the last seven miles of the trip to Capeville during the warm months of the year.

Georgia, a second grader, pulled her wool cap down over her ears and asked a question out loud which each child older than herself had already asked time and time again.

"Why we gotta go to Capeville when Cheriton School is right 'cross the road?"

"Because you black, girl. Why you think? Jes' 'cause you jes' in the sucund grade don't mean you gotta be stupid," Joe Joe, feeling his power as a fifth grader, answered with his hands on his hips.

"Hey," Georgia said, her eyes narrowing. "I don't play that. I ain't black, now. You watch your mouth. And I ain't stupid, neither. You watch your mouth, boy. I is coloured."

"Joe Joe laughed. "Well, coloured, then."

"White people ain't no betta than being coloured," said Beanie. She kicked at the dirt and watched the white children climbing the wide steps into the white school. Some of them were probably as poor as she was, but across the distance, stepping from those buses and walking into that well kept building, they all looked rich and brand new from head to foot. Beanie's father cleaned the floors there. She knew from him how nice it was inside there.

"Damn," said Joe Joe. "White sho' is betta the way it comes out." He leaned close to her face, his lips drawn into a mocking grin.

"Ohhh, you said a bad word," Susie said.

"Yeah. White is a bad word. You betta believe it." Joe Joe did a dance step in front of Beanie and Georgia. "You one dumb couple a nigger girls to be thinking they ain't no betta than you."

M.T., Carrie's brother, was the oldest and tallest among the children and the only seventh grader. He grabbed Joe Joe by the collar of his thin coat and turned him around, bending over a little to look him directly in the eye.

"You don't use bad words around here, Joe Joe. Especially bad words about us. You say the N word one more time and I'm gonna hit you so hard you gonna think your ears were born on your behind. You got that straight?"

There was an explosion of laughter, some of the kids repeating what M.T. had said, obviously impressed with M.T.'s cool delivery. Joe Joe stiffened and pulled away. He wiped his hand nervously across his mouth. He wasn't about to tackle M.T. Not for anything. Carrie covered her mouth, laughing. Georgia looked over at M.T. openly, as though she'd been rescued by a saint, while the other girls shared secret glances of appreciation and shrugged their shoulders at Joe Joe. They all knew that M.T. had spoken for them—even for Joe Joe. M.T. turned to Beanie.

"It's not that they're better, Beanie. My daddy says it's the law and white folks own the law like practically everything else."

The wind stopped howling for a moment and then came on in a blast that slammed a heavily-leaved tree limb hard against the side of the house. Carrie awoke suddenly, startled out of her sleep. She looked around, got her bearings, eased back onto the bed, full length, and turning over on her side, went back immediately to dreaming.

Carrie used to like riding the school bus, even in the cold, but her feelings had changed early in the spring of this school year. It was a warm, spring-feverish, lazy kind of afternoon. All of the flowers were budding, some blooming, and the breeze brushing by her face from the bus windows was so soft that she began having trouble keeping her eyes open. She had chosen to sit on one of the two seats at the very rear of the bus. There was no one left back there to talk to and she wasn't allowed to change her seat, so she swiveled around to look at the vehicles behind the bus. In a few minutes she would be at her bus stop and it was embarrassing to be caught sleeping. Somebody always made fun. "Wake up, little baby. It's time for da baby to git off the bus, now." It was usually Joe Joe.

Her bus rounded the long curve at Bay View and quite unexpectedly, a bus carrying white children pulled into the traffic immediately behind. This same thing happened again the next day and then on the next. It wasn't always there, but when it was, it made her skin crawl. There was a boy on the white bus who picked on her. She hadn't told anyone about it and none of her gang had noticed because she was usually alone walking home. She and M.T. were the only two who lived back down the highway past where the bus had come, and since M.T. was sweet on Susie, he always walked her home before running after Carrie. By then, if the white bus and that boy were there, the teasing he did had already occurred.

The first time it happened, she stepped from her bus like always, and after yelling good-bye to Beanie and Georgia, she turned to walk home. The white kids had their windows down. As she neared them, a red faced boy with sandy hair and blue eyes leaned through a window and shouted, "Hey, little nigger, you got something up your funky dress for me?"

Carrie didn't know who he was talking to at first, so she just kept walking, but when he said it again, she looked around behind her. Four or five other white kids yelled, "Nigger." She looked back into their eyes to stare at them, her face beginning to burn. It took a great deal of effort to stand there and to look them directly in the eyes. The white boy raised his middle finger in the air and kept calling her a nigger while the others laughed. His mouth was ugly, forming the word, the word coming fast but his mouth seeming to move in slow motion, red and wet, slinging accusations.

The word nigger caught her in the chest like a physical blow, taking her breath, making her mouth open in shock and a sickening comprehension of something absolutely hideous. She sensed that because she was coloured, she deserved what the boy was saying about her, offensive as it was: vile and wrong as it was. It was the way things were. She felt a shame, as though she had done something very wrong and was being punished.

Yet it wasn't true! She knew it wasn't true! The bus drove off and she watched it until it turned the corner up by the two "white" brick churches. From where she was standing, instead of driving down a street between the two buildings, it looked as if the bus had literally driven into the two churches, its occupants safely protected by all of the well-dressed respectable white families who went there each Sunday.

"I'm not a nigger." Her voice was weak and breathless as she whispered under her breath and fought not to cry. She had walked home that day looking back over her shoulder, feeling less than she had been the day before.

Everyday now, after school, there that white bus was, along with the boy and his long middle finger.

"I'm not a nigger." My mother said there's no such thing as a nigger. It's a slave word and coloured people aren't slaves anymore and slaves weren't really niggers either. Those white trashy dumbbells must need their brains fixed to keep on calling me a nigger every afternoon. "I'm nobody's nigger!"

It had become a dreadful, despicable process. Staring out of the back of the bus at Bayview curve, wondering if the white bus would be there waiting to turn onto the main highway. Taking a deep breath when it wasn't there, losing inner composure when it was. Seeing it come along behind. Stalling about leaving her seat. Finally running straight for Pat's Place and pointing at penny candy or cookies she didn't really want so the bus would leave and she wouldn't have to pass it, walking home.

"Carrie." Stella called from the kitchen. Carrie sat up out of her sleep. She was glad to be awake. It seemed impossible these days to think about anything else but that school bus. The room was cold, but she was sweating. Before she had fallen asleep, she had been looking at an album of her favorite pictures—photographs taken over the years by members of her family. She hadn't realized until now that she'd fallen asleep holding the one she liked best. The one with the hunters was all crumpled in her hand. She could tell in the dark because it was the smallest in her collection. There wasn't another like it anywhere. Granddaddy Lawrence had loaned it to her. Most of his brothers were dead now and they were all together in this one picture, all of them dressed in hunting clothes, shotguns over their shoulders and rabbits and wild geese strewn at their feet with their best hunting dogs sitting and lying here and there by their sides. nigger...nigger.

"I'm not a nigger."

She dropped the picture, picked it up again and smoothed it out as best she could. She wiped her nose and mouth across her sleeve and stood in the darkness. The rain was still pouring down. There should be a great flood by now. The world outside was surely floating. ...that picture was old. ...it couldn't be replaced. ..."I'm not a nigger."

"Carrie."

"Yes, Momma."

"Fixing baked chicken with dumplings and candied sweet potatoes and fresh broccoli. Come help me. M.T. made the salad and tea."

"OK."

Carrie took a look out of the window to see if there was a flood. A great bunch of oak leaves wiped across the glass from the end of a tree limb, and when the wind bent the limb down and the lightning flashed, she saw that just a little way from the house, Mrs. Lukus's outhouse was still sitting pretty on the low ground of the old lady's back yard. There had been some worry on her father's part during the heavy rains in April that the outhouse would wash off its foundation. Turner had suggested to Mrs. Lukus that he would gladly relocate and rebuild the structure for her on the higher ground in her back lot—not only to help her, but to move what for him was an eyesore. But Mrs. Lukus had insisted that eventually she would have the work done herself, and in the meantime, it was kindly none of Turner Allen's business. Carrie could unmistakably see large puddles all around it, glistening in the light coming from her back yard. There was no doubt that Mrs. Lukus would get her feet wet if she went to the outhouse anytime soon. The old lady never seemed to remember to wear boots.

Carrie sighed. It was June second, and the weather was acting like March and April. In a way she had been glad to see the storm and she was disappointed not to see a flood. There were only three more days before school would be over for the summer. If there were a flood, she wouldn't have to go to school anymore this year. She wouldn't have to ride the school bus home.

Laying the damaged photograph on her dresser in the darkness, Carrie headed for the kitchen. It seemed like it had been an awfully long time since her mother had last called her name for supper.

Chapter II

Carrie had the money she needed. Every school morning when the teacher asked each student to give a quarter for a hot lunch, and six cents for milk, from first grade to second to third to fourth, she had no difficulty meeting the price. The cost would go up in the sixth grade because they gave more food to the older kids. Carrie often wondered how the people in the kitchen arbitrarily chose the 6th grade as the point of departure from little meals to bigger ones. Some kids in the fifth grade were bigger and older than kids in the seventh. It sure was strange.

Beanie had six cents some of the time. Like many of the children, she brought a slice of bread or a roll; sometimes a fresh piece of fruit or a hard-boiled egg. There were days when she had nothing and went hungry. She wouldn't accept food or money from Carrie.

One time a year ago, Beanie had saved her milk money for a week until she had enough to buy a hot lunch in the cafeteria. That plus a penny she had found on the ground gave her thirty-one cents for lunch and milk. Beanie was very excited about it. She'd never eaten in the lunchroom before. There was a stigma attached to eating in the cafeteria out of a brown bag, and Beanie was too proud to undergo such an ordeal. Mrs. Whatchamacallit in the kitchen started the mess about how uncouth it was to eat from a brown bag in the big pretty cafeteria.

Carrie and Beanie sat together that day. Beanie gulped the hot food down so fast that she was sick when arithmetic period came around. She had to leave the room for almost an hour. When she returned, Mrs. Brown let her rest in the special rocking chair at the back of the room, until she felt better. Beanie sat and rocked, legs dangling, her toes tapping the floor in unison when the chair rolled forward, and kept her head turned toward the closet and away from the other children. She just sat still and rocked. After awhile, Carrie pretended to need a handkerchief from her jacket. She opened one of the closet doors and peeked over her shoulder to see what was wrong with Beanie. Her eyes were set in a fixed stare at the floor and a slow fall of tears dripped secretly down her cheeks. Carrie eased closer.

"I'm gonna bring my lunch tomorrow, Beanie," she whispered. "We can sit all by ourselves and have a picnic under the maple trees down by the ball field."

Beanie didn't respond.

"Heck, Beanie. I nearly puked myself. Mrs. Wilson's spaghetti looks like dead worms swimming in blood."

Beanie brought her hand up over her mouth to smother the sound of a laugh. Carrie giggled, rather pleased with herself, and returned to her seat. Although Beanie never ate in the cafeteria again, she and Carrie enjoyed many a lunch together out on the grounds of the school, and their friendship deepened to the point where they were practically inseparable during the school day.

Carrie's hair was long and straight; "good hair" folks called it. Her eyes were hazel, sometimes more green than gray, more blue than green, depending on the amount of light and what she was wearing. Her complexion was an olive tan during the late fall, winter, and early spring. But when the weather turned hot, her skin baked bronze. Carrie was happier with her summer coloring because she felt more at ease among her playmates. But even so, she was still very light-skinned.

As her life grew longer and she learned more about living, it seemed to her that "good hair" and light skin were a badge of honor of some kind. Some members of her family, especially her mother and her mother's sister, Claire, were always telling her at the slightest opportunity that coloured folks with straight hair were better off. Straight hair was prettier and more manageable and a mark of fine breeding, and to have light skin was to be fair and lovely.

Sometimes, Beanie would give Carrie's long braids a gentle appreciative tug, her eyes always, and sometimes her voice, saying, "I wish I had yo' hair. It sho' is pretty and long." Her eyes would look upward, self-consciously sometimes, for a split second as though she was trying to see the short four or five braids of super curly black folks' hair on her own head. It was puzzling to Carrie that even Beanie seemed to agree, most of the time, with her mother and aunt's values. It didn't make sense to Carrie. She had no words to express how wrong it seemed to her that Beanie or any other coloured person should feel that they weren't as good looking simply because their hair didn't look like white folks' hair. And brown skin was smooth and so soft looking.

She had asked Earl about that and he had explained it so clearly. He said that white people had done a great job of brainwashing almost everybody to think that if you didn't look like them, you were ugly. And every Negro person had to struggle against such thinking. Earl was a college man, now—a graduate college, law student man, in fact. He seemed to know everything. Yet the difference between Carrie and Beanie had a way of surfacing that made painful divisions in their friendship. The second day after the storm brought the worst of these. Halfway through the late afternoon recess, they tangled over what began as a minor disagreement. They were participating in a chase game.

"You're it, Beanie, not me," Carrie yelled.

"I ain't it, neither," Beanie shouted back. "You think you so smart, telling me what to do." Beanie placed her hands on her hips and leaned forward. "You been telling me what to do for days now. Well, you ain't my boss. You hear?"

The two girls circled each other, like the boys had a way of doing, and glared, waiting for somebody to make the first move. Carrie was hoping it wouldn't come to a fight. She was mad enough, but she didn't fight very well. She'd done a lot of wrestling for fun, but her parents got on M.T. so much about fighting that she had mostly avoided it.

Accusation came into Beanie's eyes as she focused on Carrie's eyes, hair, and complexion. She raised one of her hands in front of her face, examined her own dark coloring in the bright sunlight and then poked her finger into Carrie's face, screaming.

"You white yella-ugly white thang." Her hands went out for both of Carrie's pig tails, and before Carrie could veer away, Beanie yanked with all of the power in her seventy pounds of weight.

It was on from then on out! A viciousness burst from both of them beyond prediction, accompanied by curses, screams and name calling, rolling in the dirt, biting and kicking.

"Damn! Them girls fights badder then the boys."

"Git huh, Beanie. Beat huh yella butt."

The other children quickly formed a milling ring of noise around the two as they fought. Beanie feinted to her left, sprang at Carrie and spit as she lunged from the ground toward Carrie's waist. Spray scattered mostly into the air. Carrie sent a shower of spit back, some of it blowing into her own face. The two pushed and pounded one another, falling in a sprawled mass of flailing arms and legs, regaining their feet and slugging it out hit for hit, as hard as they could make their fists fly.

It seemed to Carrie that everybody was yelling encouragement to Beanie. She felt the hollowness of alienation in the thick of the fight, wondering why she didn't belong. She was a nigger to white people and yella to Negro people. It was as if she was a stranger who was merely tolerated wherever she went.

Beanie pushed off and laughed. "Bet yo' ole momma slept with the policy man." The gang burst into derisive laughter, some of them punching each other in fun at the joke. Carrie lost all restraint at that. She charged into Beanie with every ounce of determination she could find, hitting, kicking, biting, swinging, beating Beanie left and right and everywhere she turned. Words rushed out of her; words she knew better than to use.

"Nigger. Beanie, you black ugly nigger." Tears started down Carrie's face, tears of shame as well as anger, and mixed with the dust, turning her gray as she shouted and fought and tumbled with her friend to the ground.

Carrie felt a strong hand grip her along the back waistband of her blue jeans. She was pulled violently to her feet and shaken so hard that all the trees in the yard danced and jiggled. Beanie grinned at her in triumph. She knew Mr. Grant had heard what Carrie had shouted.

"Stop this! Do you hear me? Stop your fighting!"

Mr. Grant shook Carrie hard again, as though he secretly enjoyed the impatient anger that showed on his face. Carrie was still trying to secure a hold on Beanie who was on her feet standing unaided beside Mr. Grant, a look of defiance and victory on her face, now. Not a tear stained her dusty face. There was blood at the corner of her mouth, and the dingy dress she was wearing was torn from top to bottom, but she was miraculously composed. A sudden new layer of shame crept over Carrie and an even deeper anger. Beanie's momma would be sewing for days to fix that dress. What the devil was she crying for if Beanie wasn't?

"Now." His teeth were gritted shut, his voice menacingly low, as he looked hard, first at Carrie and then at Beanie. "You children should be ashamed of yourselves. Especially you, Carrie Allen, with your upbringing." Carrie glanced sullenly at the sky and then she squinted at Mr. Grant, showing a rudeness unusual for her.

"Don't you squint all sassy-like at me, child. Now, you go straight to Mr. Martin's office and wait there for me." Mr. Grant was such a prissy little man. Quite out of character, Carrie now glared at him. She had been taught carefully not to show disrespect to any adult, so it was with surprise, even to herself, that she cast such a disparaging look in Mr. Grant's direction. He saw the look and shook his hand at her as she walked dejectedly toward the school. She was almost there when Joey Tucker and Mable Smith poked out their tongues at her.

"Little yella shit." They laughed. They were Beanie's cut buddies. They always took up for her. But then, usually, so did she.

"We'll git you, girl, for beating on Beanie. Yo' daddy ain't no big thing. Gonna beat yo' butt."

Carrie turned on Mable who was closest. "You put a finger on me and I'll embalm you myself. Put you on my daddy's table and pump all the blood out of you you got." Mable backed off. Carrie had her, and they both knew it. Mable was scared to death of dead people, dying, and undertaker Allen. "You too, Joe stink." Carrie started to turn away when she heard footsteps running up behind her. She swung around just as Beanie came up almost into her face, with Mr. Grant coming at a run behind her.

"You think you so bad and all. Your ole daddy gonna die one day, too. Jest you live and wait. Big Turner Allen gonna go to glory in his own death wagon one of these days!"

She had thought many a time while standing beside her father in the morgue that if other people could die, so could her parents. Death was such a vivid thing in her life that the thought of her parents dying was a kind of ongoing painful expectation that part of her mind worked constantly to avoid. Carrie stopped moving for a moment. She could see it as plainly as day. Her father, her mother, lying dead in their morgue with clean white sheets covering them and the whole neighborhood waiting at the door to get a last look. She lowered her head and a flood of tears started down her face. She gritted her teeth,

31

balled up her fists and swung at Beanie viciously, her hands landing blows for which Beanie was totally unprepared. Joey and Mable jumped in to pull Carrie away, just as Mr. Grant, who seemed to run at a snail's pace, finally arrived. Carrie wrestled and squirmed as they pulled her back, and Beanie, gripping a bloody mouth, stood back, astonished at Carrie's fury. "You don't have a right to talk like that," Carrie screamed. Tears streamed down her face. "He'll never die. You hear! My Daddy will never die."

Carrie turned away and ran to the steps, catching a glimpse of Mr. Grant trying to catch up from behind. She rushed down into the basement past several older children into the girl's bathroom. The place stank, some stalls worse than others. Ugly words were written all over the walls and the names of girls and boys were chiseled here and there between the curse words. Carrie leaned against the wall and shuddered as an aching kind of sorrow stole up her back and joined the throbbing in her head and neck. She didn't like to fight. She had always been afraid to fight, not because she might get hurt, but because she would have to face her father and mother. She shouldn't have let herself get into this kind of mess. Damn Beanie!

So what if her momma looked white. Stella said she had prayed when Carrie and M.T. were on the way that they would be at least a little brown so the going wouldn't be so tough among coloured people—so Negroes wouldn't call them white and yellow like they used to call her when she was coming up. Her momma seemed proud of that wish about having brown babies, and M.T. was good and brown. But then, too, Stella wanted them to have straight hair. Even if she had been darker, Carrie still had the hair to contend with. All of a sudden she wasn't sure what her mother wanted and what was best: straight hair like white folks or brown skin like coloured folks. Looking like both sides made it hard to belong. Maybe Earl could help. He was due home from law school soon to work for her father for the summer.

Carrie reached toward the commode for a piece of tissue. Her nose was running and so full of mucus she could barely breathe. She blew hard and looked down into the bowl as she threw in the paper. Hanging from the edge of the seat and dangling down into the water was the longest, biggest round worm she had ever seen in her life. Every time it touched the cold water below, it half curled up again.

There were traces of brown matter on it that stained the water whenever it touched. Its long body alternately grew big around and then shrank to an unbelievable thinness. It kept pulsing like that. There was another worm all curled up in a ball down in the bottom of the toilet.

Carrie pushed out of the stall, nearly tripping herself. Some poor kid sure enough had a bad case of worms. She imagined having those things crawling around inside of her and going to the bathroom and seeing them come out, and she gagged. She entered another stall just in time to lose her lunch. By the time she reached the principal's office, she was so tired and numb that she wasn't afraid of the punishment from him, which was sure to come.

Chapter III

It was a long road to walk. The ragged old school bus was well on its way north toward Cheriton. She could hear a popping sound coming from the exhaust as Mr. Bayley took his foot off of the accelerator to make the curve into the town. She was relieved that there was no one to yell at her about niggers; neither white kids nor Negro. The meanness of the fight seemed way behind her in the distance someplace, and the white school bus hadn't been there today. There was just herself and the stretch of sandy highway shoulder and a walk along its distance, one long country mile or so to her front yard.

Her sneakers were over a month old now. They were tan and gray with dirt and sweat and a few drip spots from an orange popsicle. Carrie had hoped to keep them clean for a longer time. She sighed, feeling defeated.

Then she spied the water in the ditch; deep ditch, shallow water, running a fascinating current into culverts under unpaved driveways. Patches of thick weeds blocked the swift flow here and there with long slender fingers of bent green. The water ran clear and looked sweet to the taste. It sparkled so that it made her want to drink, though of course, she knew better.

Carrie sat on the edge of the ditch and dangled her legs over, a glum dull dread hanging all over her. A car passed. Then another. Swoosh. Swoosh. New York tags. Virginia. A big diesel truck rocked her with hot blown wind and road grit. She looked after the great big painted oranges on the trailer's side and rear and noted the Florida license plate. That truck would go straight up Highway 13 to Wilmington and then onto the New Jersey Turnpike into New York City, some three hundred miles away. As much as she loved her home, for an instant, she longed to be a stowaway on that truck.

Untying her shoe laces, Carrie removed her shoes and socks, eased her feet down into the ditch and smiled, delighted with the coolness tingling up above her ankles. The bottom was sandy, the grass soft a step or two in either direction. She leaned against the ditch bank and watched her brother.

M.T. and Susie. True love. Maybe it was. A striking change had come over him since September when he said girls gave him the purple creeps. He was kinder now to everybody and even polite. It had first become obvious to Carrie during the October Festival that M.T. liked Susie a lot. He actually spent his money to buy her ice cream. There had to be some power in Susie for which Carrie had not given her credit. Carrie wondered what it was. Susie was only twelve years old, just two years older than herself. What could she have learned in just two years that Carrie didn't have the slightest inkling of at ten? M.T. was a changed boy.

He was on his way home now, walking down the side of the highway toward her with Susie safely delivered to her mother's door where she could have easily walked all by herself.

He would be surprised to find his sister in the ditch. Lord, he had big feet these days, just to be twelve years old. From where she was standing, watching them plop down, they were huge. She hadn't noticed how fast he was growing. He would be grown and gone soon, like Earl Lionel Togan. The sorrow of that coming day swept over Carrie. Lord, have mercy, if only she didn't have to go home. Her Daddy would know about the fight by now.

"Hey," M.T. said.

"Hi." M.T. probably knew about the fight, too. If he did, it probably wouldn't be long before he'd be harping on it.

M.T. paused at the culvert and watched Carrie's feet diverting the fast water.

"Ever build a dam?"

"Huh? I don't know."

"Want to?"

Carrie looked up at him, squinted and frowned. "Guess so."

"Good." He quickly removed his shoes and socks and joined her. Cars swooshed by. Georgia plates and a bunch of Virginia. One Alabama. There was a sweet breeze blowing and the sun was July hot rather than the milder temperatures of early June. The weather had been crazy. Just two days ago that storm had roared and rained up and down the entire Eastern Shore of Virginia like it was the fall hurricane season. The next day had been exceptionally hot like today, drying up the puddles almost immediately. Carrie didn't care much about the weather for tomorrow, the last day, but school would be over after that, and as always, she hoped the summer would be all sunshine. Normally she would have been overjoyed that school was about over; especially not having to face that bus, but this mess with Beanie had fouled up everything. Her father would probably make her stay in the yard all summer.

Carrie hadn't been paying much attention to M.T. He had just finished carefully arranging his book bag above the culvert and had unwrapped something from a paper bag. He turned to Carrie and gently placed a peppermint stick between her teeth.

"Eat it or hide it from Momma 'til after dinner."

Carrie smiled despite herself and gripped the candy with her teeth so that it stuck out of the side of her mouth like a cigar. She bent down with M.T. as he scooped handfuls of sand into a wet mound near the grass and weeds and away from the culvert.

"See, you build up dirt and then you reinforce it with sticks." He looked around. There was a good supply of debris strewn carelessly. "Bring me the crate." Carrie bit down on the candy, not so lonely now and grateful to her brother, and did as he asked.

They played for almost twenty minutes, but nobody can build dams forever. It was getting late. They had already stayed much too long. If they didn't get home soon, they would be in trouble for that and Carrie's problems would be compounded. So, a deepening dread in her, Carrie walked beside M.T. very slowly toward home.

"I've been in lots of fights," M.T. volunteered, trying to comfort Carrie and let her know that he definitely knew. "Daddy didn't say much."

Carrie nodded.

"He might say something about you calling Beanie a nigger, though."

Something in her stomach dropped like a hot stone.

"You heard, huh?"

"Everybody at school. Light-skinned calling dark-skinned niggers is bad news. You know."

"Yeah, I know. What's a nigger anyway?"

"Us. You and me. Colored folks. Negroes."

"Shoot," Carrie bristled. "I'm not a nigger. We aren't niggers." She sighed, confused yet again about who she was and where she fit. Yellow seemed to her an uglier word than nigger, and yet she knew deep in her heart that it wasn't. According to Earl, the word nigger went with all of the ideas that had made Negroes slaves and anybody who said it was adding to all of the troubles coloured people already had.

"Well, now," M.T. said, exasperated. "Nobody's really a nigger. That's what Daddy said. It's just that white people like to call us that and when they say nigger, they mean everybody coloured."

"Not just dark folks? Light-skinned, too?"

"Coloured. Anybody who isn't white. You should know that by now. Of course, they've got a bunch of other awful names for Chinese and all the other coloured folks. White folks don't like anybody but themselves. Half the time, they don't like themselves, either. They're really hard to understand."

"But Beanie called Joey a nigger the other day and the whole school didn't talk about it, and if we're all niggers, what's the difference in me calling Beanie a nigger and Beanie calling Joey one, and if nigger's a bad word, what we doing calling people niggers in the first place?"

M.T. put his arm around Carrie's shoulder. "I don't know," M.T. sighed in frustration. "You betta ask Momma or Daddy."

They walked the rest of the way thinking their own thoughts. Finally, M.T. broke the silence.

"Don't worry about Daddy. Just explain." M.T. winked and left her at the back porch steps. She entered the house alone and walked straight to her room, hoping no one would notice.

Turner found her lying on the rug at the foot of her bed. He sat beside her and rested his back against the footboard. Carrie jumped when he reached out to touch her.

"Hard day?"

"Yes, sir." Carrie was hoarse from crying.

"Why have you been crying?" Conversations with his children were nowhere as easy as he had thought they would be before they were born. In those childless days he had thought that his children's problems would be like clay in his hands; something he could mold and form into a shape of his own making. How wrong he had been. How naive. He asked again.

"What are you crying about?"

"I don't know."

"Why did you jump when I touched you? I never hit you." He smiled.

"Daddy."

"Well, a spanking here and there, but always with a warning in advance." They laughed. Carrie sniffled and took the tissue he offered. "What's worrying you?"

"Nothing much." Carrie looked into her father's face and was afraid, not of a whipping, but of his disapproval. His opinion of her was critical. He never really spanked her as hard as his eyes could look when he was disappointed in her.

"Tell me about school today."

He knew. Mr. Martin had called, the stinking old buzzard. No. That wasn't true. Mr. Martin was nice. The fight wasn't his fault. Why didn't her father just say that he knew, and she was wrong, and get the whipping and the lecturing done? Carrie chewed on her bottom lip and swallowed, her throat dry.

"You mean the fight?"

"Yes."

"Well." She could feel herself beginning to cry, and she swallowed again, fighting it. Turner waited without helping her. "Daddy. I'm sorry. We got in a fight. It just happened. We whipped on each other. Beanie—Well, she said something mean to me and I said something mean to her." Carrie sighed, heaving her shoulders, and prepared herself for the bomb to drop. Mr. Martin had probably already told, anyhow. "She called me yella and I called her a . . . a nigger." She said the ugly word softly and felt immediately better for having made confession.

Turner reached for Carrie's hand, pulled her to a sitting position and leaned her against him, tucked under his arm. He didn't say anything for awhile, his thoughts very sad over the fact that every Negro child had to learn the same painful lessons anew, generation after generation. There seemed no innovative way to save them from the ugly hatred of racism, from the repetition. The world around Carrie was teaching her that she was inferior for being a Negro, yet somehow special for being a light-skinned member of her race. How could a child know with certainty who he or she was or how great her value, without an inflated and false sense of self among her darker brothers and sisters? It had been almost four years since the school desegregation case before the Supreme Court. It represented such a fundamental change, such hope, and he was grateful. Surely Thurgood Marshall deserved Sainthood for his brilliant efforts, yet in reality, very little had changed in the midst of the turmoil, even though that young minister down in Alabama, Dr. King, seemed to be making progress. Palpable progress was going to be slow, so very slow, and in the meantime, children's lives were being misshapen. Turner involuntarily shook his head, as though he was saying no to something only he could see.

"Carrie," he said, squeezing her shoulder gently to reassure her. "You have a right to exist as you were born. All of the people in the world share this right. You're fine and beautiful as you are. So is Beanie." He sighed, changed his position a little, feeling a rising frustration. He wondered if his words would mean anything. There was so much to say to so young a child.

He went on, his voice soft. "There is a beauty in every complexion, dark and light. The word nigger can never be used in a good or humorous way. No Negro, and no white person for that matter, but especially no Negro, should ever use it, in anger or in jest, because it makes the word legitimate. By that I mean that using the word nigger as a name for someone for any reason makes the word lawful and genuine and reasonable and right somehow, and its ugliness should never be graced with such dignity. Do you know why you called Beanie a nigger, today?"

Carrie thought about it for a minute or so. "I didn't like her when she called me yella. I hated her guts. I wanted to make her feel bad, like she had done to me."

"Yes, but now you feel just as bad or worse because you know you did the wrong thing. Right?"

"Yes, sir. But I was so mad with Beanie. She hurt my feelings in front of everybody. She said something awful about Momma. She said that white insurance man, you know, Mr. Waller; she said Momma had, she said. She made it sound like I was his and everybody laughed. I just couldn't help it. I know it was wrong, but . . . I didn't know what else to say. Momma says that most light-skinned coloured people are better than dark people like Beanie. I thought about that, Daddy. Momma says we're not supposed to let other people know we think that. I couldn't help it. I shouldn't have said it. It was a secret and now I don't even know if it's true."

She looked up into her father's face, more confused than she had ever been. He was looking up at the ceiling, his eyes closed. He didn't say anything.

Carrie stared, not knowing what else to say. She was tired. It had been a long talk. A whipping might have been better. She turned her face into her father's shirt and cried softly. Maybe Beanie would never be her friend again. Why should she want to be? There was something awful about the word nigger that didn't come close to being called yella.

Turner struggled to compose himself. He had hated the racial prejudices within his race almost more than those that came from whites. Of course, he knew that all of the trouble had initially come from whites, but sometimes Negroes sure helped to keep themselves in conflict. Stella almost never talked about her feelings. She was one of the most beautiful women he had ever seen, and in practically every place in the world she would have been thought a white woman. He hadn't realized that she was teaching these things to the children. How could he not have known? They had been married for fifteen years. They had talked and shared so many things. How could he not have known? Turner shook his head again and again, a soft and rising tension pulling at the base of his neck and down his back, almost to the point of agony.

"Carrie," he said, wiping at her tearful upturned face with his hand, his hand as gentle as his voice. "It isn't wrong to be angry momentarily and it's sometimes impossible not to feel hatred for a short span of time. What's wrong is holding on to anger and hatred. What's wrong is hurting someone else because of those feelings. Some words can't really be taken back. You and Beanie are both members of the Negro race. And you're friends. You should both be proud and you both must work together to make the word nigger and the word yella words that people will one day stop using. Do you understand me?" His voice was pleading and so soft that it seemed a wonder that she could hear his words at all.

41

"Yes, Daddy."

"Negro people have been badly mistreated in this country, even in Africa, and I believe with all my heart that one day we'll find a way to get things straight. We've been brave and we've done wonderful things to make this country better; to make the world better. I want you and Beanie to always be proud of who you are. You must! You must, Sweetheart. Tell me you understand." Carrie had never seen his face so full of hope or of pain. She could not know the measure of his disappointment in her mother. She was too young to know how much he was fighting not to scream out his anguish at the top of his voice because he was even more disappointed in himself. How could he not know?

Carrie nodded, "I understand, Daddy," and looked up at her father's face. He was looking away now, toward her open window where the oak tree leaves were dancing to a light breeze. It was as if he was looking for answers way off in the distance, but Carrie didn't know that, either. She surely loved her father. She wanted to say, "Thanks for not whipping me or being angry or yelling," but she couldn't quite get the words out. Instead, she reached up to him and hugged him hard around his neck and cried softly as he hugged her in return. Even so, there was something she didn't understand that she didn't have the energy to ask. Why was it that white people hated Negro people so much, and why was it that Negro people couldn't seem to stop white people from bothering them all the time? What was wrong with white people if Negro people weren't the ones who were wrong? Somebody was surely wrong. What was she going to do about it? For the first time in her memory, she felt a genuine hatred for white people somewhere building slowly in her consciousness. They were the problem. Not fighting them was the problem.

Her father squeezed her softly in his arms and wiped away her tears as she grew quiet and sleepy from all of the worry and crying.

Chapter IV

He stood there, alone and uneasy, barefooted, his toes rubbing a crying sound off the hardwood floor. No pajama top. The bottoms short and comfortable; a little baggy as he preferred them. His hair was tussled and his left thumb rubbed nervously against the side of his index finger. The bedroom window was open to the night's summertime and its dark, sweet honeysuckle breeze, warm and so quiet in its whispers that he could hear his own insecurity moving in the pit of his stomach.

"You've got to change your thinking, Stella. It's wrong what you think, now."

The mood and the feeling between them now was so strange for them. There was usually harmony, something they consciously cherished. The bedroom with Stella there was more home than any other place in the world; but not tonight. Not now. Maybe the harmony had been only seeming. Maybe they harmonized because neither probed nor searched the other very deeply, leaving a falsely comfortable illusion.

He hesitated and then spoke slowly, measuring his words. "What you think and what you've been teaching the children is dangerous." He had to say it. Had to.

"What I think? Well. What right do you have to tell me what to think?" Her voice was angry but controlled.

He turned to look at her. Even now, his heart melted when he looked at her. There was a grace about the way she was made: her complexion creamy, a slight tinting of rose in her cheeks, just right; her hair dark brown, heavy and straight and luxuriantly long, braided now into a rich rope down her back; five-foot-five; slim and curvaceous; a warm, sexy woman so often full of laughter and fun. Like no one else, she had satisfied him. Yet his work, the pace, and the needs of the children had worn away at their time together, and now, at this moment, he realized how lost from one another they had become. As he looked at her, he felt his desire rising to cool his anger, so he turned back to the window again, not wanting to lose the edge that had made the beginning of this delicate conversation possible.

Stella was hurting. Angry. Accused. Uncertain. She watched her husband's back, noted the fine sculptured lines of his silhouette as he turned toward her for a moment and then turned away again. She almost smiled, bitterness mixing in, as she thought of something her mother had told her when she was seventeen.

"Be sure, Stella, my dear child, that you never marry an ugly man. For any number of reasons you will regret it. He must have substance in his personality and values, of course. These in the long run are the most important, but in his physical beauty will be a mainstay far greater than you might imagine." She had looked at Stella's father's picture at that moment and had nodded knowingly. "On many a night," she continued, "when your father and I had disagreed ourselves into a burning resentment, and we went to bed side-by-side that way, unable to resolve our anger before retiring, yet determined not to sleep separately, I looked over at him in the dawn hours. So often, I would find myself awake and restless while he would be sleeping like a baby. And I would see how fine he was. So good looking. There were times when that sight held me from doing something foolish. Never marry an ugly man, for when you're angry and you look at him and he's ugly, you'll be much more inclined to say, 'it's over'."

She had done as her mother instructed. Her choice had been literally fabulous. He was tall; six-foot-two, broad shouldered with a physique like a Greek God's statue. His hair was straight and black, his skin bronze, his eyes black with the look of eagles in them. And he had always been considerate. He had never lorded his power as a man over her. Yet he was undeniably the head of their household. How could he attack her like this about opinions she was convinced he also shared; or at least had shared with her when they were younger? Despite his good looks and all of the positive images that came with them, she felt the strangest kind of alienation rising in her. It had a physical presence, which almost made her feel ill.

The room had grown silent. An answer to her question had come immediately to his mind, but he had thought better of it, not wanting to speak too quickly or callously.

"Stella, we both owe it to one another to straighten each other out when it looks like the other is going wrong. I'm not trying to tell you what to think. I'm only suggesting that you need to change one aspect of your thinking."

"Semantics," she said. "I'm a grown woman, Turner. I can think for myself without any urging from you." Her voice dropped. "I have a right to my own thoughts."

Turner took a deep breath, trying to stop himself from the beginning of a slow and dangerous burn. "I understand why you think like you do. I've thought that way myself, but it's been some time ago. The way you're thinking is wrong, pure and simple. What's more, you know it's wrong. That's why you don't talk much about it except to the kids, who don't know what to say back in defense. You've got to change!"

The ill feeling in her mounted. "Now you wait one minute!" Stella took a step closer, her hands making fists.

"OK. Maybe I'm saying it the wrong way, but don't you see what I'm saying," he interrupted. "You've got Carrie thinking she's better for having "good hair," light skin, and green eyes. You and Aunt Claire both. That's lies. That's the same crap the white man's been saying about all of us. You think it makes any difference to him whether you're a light nigger or a dark one. You're a nigger to him, just the same."

Stella flushed. The word stung her, Turner calling her that. Her anger flared, matching his.

"I'm not anybody's nigger, Turner. Nobody's on God's earth. And it does make a difference being light. You know it does. Our lives prove that. We're respected by white and black alike, more because we're light. People speak to us special. Nice. They say, 'There goes Turner Allen or there goes his wife or his pretty children.' You go into the stores and they take time to talk to you. They don't treat us like niggers. They show no real respect for dark folks. When you need a bank loan, just by our looks they trust us more. Looking like we look helps us to live halfway decent. You know that. And I want Carrie and Morgan to have the same advantages and to recognize it for what it is." Her fingers closed tightly around the bedpost at the foot of the bed and her eyes glared at him defiantly as she stepped nearer.

He turned back to her. All this time he had been directing his words at the window in an attempt to control an anger so deep and so volatile that he was afraid of it. It lay near the base of all of his insecurities about his identity as a black man in a society whose power had struggled from the beginning of his existence to denounce, to avoid, to strangle, to just plain destroy his manhood. He walked to her, looking her in the eyes, and took her gently by the shoulders, holding her so that she had to look back at him.

"Stella, that's not the whole truth. You know that. Dr. Reynolds is as dark as a Negro can be. The Bryce family, Sylvester was dark brown and so were most of his people. The same for the Shepherds. They make a whole lot more money and carry a whole lot more weight than we do. The Johnsons and Wilsons are not wealthy, but white and black people listen to them because they have a dignity about who they are that can't be denied, even by a bigot. I could go on naming ordinary black people who are dark and fine and far from ordinary. The Togans, Earl and his folks, would be tops on the list. It's more than just complexion. It's standing up and making something of whatever opportunities come your way and then passing that on to your children. So few of us have been given even the smallest chance to make it, no matter how hard we've tried, light or dark."

"Sure, there are exceptions." Stella backed off a little. His hands on her upper arms were like steel bands. "But you forget that Sylvester Bryce's mother looked like a white woman, and from the rumors, was the daughter of Dr. Borough of Bridgetown, one of the richest white men in the Tidewater. White people are easier on us because we look more like them. This is America and they rule America. I'm an American and I mean to live here as best I can."

Turner bent close to her. "We are niggers to them, Stella! Otherwise, why is it we can't sit down in Jacob's restaurant? Why do we have to sit in the balcony of the movie house and enter by the back door? Why are you, Stella, am I, Turner, when we call them Mr. this and Mrs. that? Why are our children in segregated schools? You tell me that! Who are we really with our highfalootin' high yella? And damn it, why should we want to be with them when we know how wrong and cruel and ugly 'decent' whites are when it comes to us?" His voice had become loud and strident.

Turner could feel his anger rising like pressurized steam. And he knew it wouldn't do. M.T.'s bedroom was just on the other side of the wall. He turned away and struggled to calm himself.

Stella lowered her head. "All right. There are things we still can't do, but we're safer. And we still get a helluva lot more respect. We're coloured, but that's better than being so black you disappear when the sun goes down, and you have to stand in the shade so the white man can have the sun."

"Oh, for Pete's sake, Stella. Listen to yourself. You're making excuses, hiding behind an illusion as false as me thinking I could be President. But worse than that, you're seeing yourself and other Negro people with racist eyes. Black people aren't ugly, but you imply it. You just plain say it.—You believe it. We're God's children as surely as white people are. Think, Stella. Think, for God's sake. You and I both see black people naked on our morgue table everyday. Some of the most beautiful people God ever made lay there, their lives over. And too many end up there because of racist whites."

Stella turned around and walked to the bed. Her mouth was drawn with tension. She sat down, trembling just a little. It had been a long, difficult day. When the call had come in from Mr. Martin at the school, she had feared a face-off with Turner was coming. Something had told her that they would have to discuss what Carrie had said to Beanie relative to what she had been teaching Carrie. She was amazed all of this hadn't come to light long before now.

Turner came over to her and sat beside her on the bed. He lowered his voice even further. "White people don't really care about us, anymore than they care about any other coloured folks. 'Good hair' and light skin don't mean a thing when you get down to it, except that he's managed to set us against one another, fighting our own little battles of racism within. We are all encouraged to hate ourselves, to be bigots for the racists. You've got to see that. We need unity if we're going to survive. We have to love ourselves."

Stella rubbed her hands together in her lap. She pressed them hard together, rubbing as though she would erase some part of herself. Her robe was open at the knee. She pressed the fair flesh about her knee and watched the pink of blood rise. Wouldn't there ever be any real lasting peace? She had been so poor as a child. Came up on her father's little farm, working in the dirt every day from five years old on up, trying under his stern hand to dream of something better. But even so, her family had been treated better by whites than many a dark-skinned family in the same financial bind. And Turner was saying she'd been thinking wrong all of her life. He didn't have the right to intimidate her for believing what she'd been taught, and what she had seen all of her life to be true. She felt so tired. Tired of it all, down to her backsides.

Turner spoke more softly. He could see the spiritual fatigue in Stella's eyes.

"Stella, white people don't know how to exercise the principles of their own proclaimed morality among coloured people. They espouse some fundamental and extraordinary concepts of decency, all of the egalitarian principles upon which the best way of life for any nation has ever existed, but they don't know how to implement them among anybody different from themselves.

"It's like they have some kind of sickness. I know that racism exists all over the world: that other racial groups give each other hell. But the white man's peculiar technological genius combined with his hatred of dark-skinned people makes him the most dangerous SOB on the planet, and I can't just pretend the danger away.

"Black people are black people, light and dark, straight 'good hair' or curly tight. Don't you know your great grandmother was raped to bring light color into you? And don't you know that white men sold their children and their lovers to the highest bidder at the Eastville auction block?"

"Stella sighed. "Yes. Much of what you say is true."

"Much of it?"

"Well, I guess . . . all of it." Her voice was subdued. "But given a choice between sweating and being whipped half to death in his fields, or cooking his supper in the big house, I'll take light skin and pots and pans any day, because you know we'll never be free of the white man. He'll always be on us, so we'd best take advantage of whatever we can." Her last words were shouted as she threw her head back in desperation. She thought of the children asleep and caught herself.

"I don't see any better way out, Turner. Honest to God, I don't."

"Stella, you've got to listen to me. You can't let this thing continue in you like this. It'll destroy you, and if it ruins your life, it will ruin mine and our children's." He wiped his hand absently across his sweating face.

"Trying to please the whites won't make us safer. But even if it would, you can't live without self-respect. You can't shuffle and feel worth a damn. And what about your people? What about their safety? They can't hide behind being light-skinned, and it's their birthright not to even have to think about such a thing. You can't turn your back on your responsibility to them. The white man doesn't want you, except to use you. If you turn away from your own people you'll be all alone. You'll have nobody."

"You're right!" She turned on him suddenly, passionately, so that he sat back, startled. "You're damn right. But it's the other way around. Negroes don't want me! It's been happening ever since I was a little thing of a child, and I couldn't help it. Black folks look at me and see white folks. They call me yella, mustard coloured, shit coloured. They don't accept me! So why shouldn't I cling to the people I favor so much? Why shouldn't I? I see how the folks at church look at me when they think I'm not looking. I came up among them. First time there was a disagreement, and it was just like Carrie and Beanie. They call dirty names just as mean as nigger."

Tears came to her eyes. She shook her head in a sorrowful rage. Turner reached toward her, but she pulled away. He was silent for a long time. The muffled sound of her crying filled the room, quietly unnerving Turner all the more. He felt like someone trying to balance on quicksand, feeling the momentary pretense of something visually solid beneath his feet just before sinking.

"I know what you're saying," he said. He touched her hand, but she pushed his hand away. He shook his head. "I've felt the envy and the hatred myself, but I found out why. It was because I hadn't accepted my own blackness. Stella, we don't look black on the surface, but according to the law, according to our culture, according to our conditioning and our history, we are as black as night. If I wasn't sure about being black, how could other Negroes accept and trust me? They were unsure of my loyalty because of the way I looked and because I wasn't sure of my value among them. As soon as I got my head straight, and black folk knew where I was, they knew I was black. That we're all brothers."

Stella closed her eyes and clenched her fists. "Why did you marry me? Tell me, what did you marry me for?" The room rang with her voice. "Why not someone darker with kinky hair? Do you want me to believe you didn't think about having straight-haired babies and running your hands through all of this straight grass on my head? Are you telling me that never crossed your mind? That you didn't want your own children to look like you and your parents and their parents, where everybody in your family was a mixture of Negro and white and Cherokee or some other Indian blood?"

The questions and their implications smacked him between the eyes. He could have sworn he heard a flat hand across his face. A stupid pain rolled down his face from the back of his head. Stupid from having to talk about hair and complexion to his own wife. Lord, it was absurd and horrible.

Turner rose to his feet and began pacing. He thought of his conversation with Carrie; thought of the many times he had spoken with his own parents about what constituted good looks in a Negro person. There had been an undeniable bias away from looking African; had been and still was in their minds, as best he could tell. Somewhere along the line, he had begun to change, to move away from this bias against African attributes, but it was clear that the change had taken place after he had chosen a wife. This rankled his conscience bitterly on this night when he had so clearly chosen to be the one in the "superior" moral position.

He stopped in front of Stella and looked down at her tenderly. She was beautiful; would have been anywhere in the world. And he had chosen her because of her beauty and her substance as a person. Yet he was making that very thing seem ugly.

"I don't have to tell you that I was a victim of words and prejudices coming up, just like you and everybody born Negro in this country." Turner deliberately went down on his knees before Stella, and reaching up, took her hands into his as she looked into his eyes. He gently pulled her down to her knees and sat back on his haunches so they were the same height, looking straight across at one another.

"We were taught," he said, "even dark-skinned people were taught, that kinky hair is bad hair. The straighter the prettier. The closer to looking white, the prettier. My own father taught me to have less respect for the Black and the Indian in me than the white, God rest his soul. It's drilled into our heads, so we're stupid with shame ... Sure ... I was taught just like you to marry someone with your looks, and when I saw you at Hampton Institute, standing on the steps of the library with the wind blowing your hair all shiny and long, I knew that you looked the way my wife was supposed to look. You were and you are beautiful, just the way you are. But that's not the only reason I married you.

"I fell in love with you, a person, a personality, and I've fallen in love with you many times since without a thought to your hair or complexion. God bury me if I'm that shallow."

Stella felt herself giving way to the pleading look in his eyes, but she wasn't ready or willing to let things go just yet, if at all. She tried to stand, but Turner wouldn't let her. The look on his face, the tears welling in the corners of his eyes, wouldn't let her.

"Please, sweetheart. I need your help. Morgan and Carrie need both of us to give them a strong, wholesome view of their own worth. All I'm saying is that we've all got to change the evil put into us about ourselves. You've got to help me, or more than likely, my efforts alone won't be enough. The children will end up confused and negative about their own identities. Neither of them look white, so they'll hate part of themselves all of their lives. We can't let that happen!"

Turner caressed her face and hair briefly, his hand brushing by with a sad touch; perhaps it was a slight trembling in his fingers, which in that small moment made her feel her heart would break. Then he was up and gone, like he didn't have the strength to remain in the room with her any longer.

There was more pain inside of her than she thought she could stand. So, she had been trained to think the wrong way—not to want a dark man with kinky hair. She had been taught to see these as imperfections. And she had seen so many lonely, hurting, pitiful little black children, mistreated, given no opportunity. Not to want children with kinky hair was the only way to protect her own children from being born with what her folks had convinced her was a powerful handicap. That's the way it had been with her parents. Somehow, she had always known it was wrong to think that way, for this entire philosophy had always been whispered or spoken quietly like a guarded secret only among those of like mind. Nobody had ever insisted that she change, and her own pride had to survive when somebody called her yella or white. And the damn rednecks left her alone. She was allowed to be respectable; someone under the protection of decent whites who would not stand for her or members of her family to be treated on the same level as ordinary Negroes.

What Turner was saying seemed right, but all these years? How could she change after all these years? She didn't feel like changing, no matter what right there was in changing. It would take such vigilance.

It was three hours before Turner came to bed. Stella pretended to be asleep, but lay restless and sadly empty. There was nothing inside of herself she could think of to say, and this frightened her.

Turner looked at Stella lying beside him in the semi-darkness, feeling a tenderness for her born of a love he carried deep in his heart. He wanted her in his life, and he was more than strong enough to help her to see. There would be no defeating him in his house.

He moved closer, held her, hoping that as was the case, she would not resist. They fell, ever so slowly, into a restless and fatigue-laden sleep.

Chapter V

Carrie managed to miss the school bus on the last day of school. Her father drove her. He was well aware of her reticence to go at all. Carrie was worried that Beanie would still be angry. Turner reminded her that Beanie was probably just as worried about her in the same way.

Carrie was very late, so she ran straight to the fourth grade room and took her seat beside Beanie just in time to stand again to recite the "Pledge of Allegiance," hand over heart, and eyes on the flag, which was faded by the sun. Next, everybody had to sing "My Country 'Tis of Thee." Then they said the "Preamble to the Constitution." In September, Mrs. Clark had said that America had a fine and wonderful Constitution and each child was to learn and repeat the Preamble every school morning for the rest of the year. In addition, Mrs. Clark had read the Constitution to the class, Article by Article, off and on throughout the year, so everybody would know what their rights were.

As soon as Mrs. Clark turned to write on the blackboard, Carrie took a moment to catch her breath, putting all of her things away except her writing tablet and pencil. She stole looks at Beanie out of the corner of her eye, hoping to see some sign of friendliness. Much to her dismay, Beanie smiled at her and handed her a note.

Eyes on the teacher; her back was still turned. Carrie's fingers unraveled the note, as she kept an alert lookout for Mrs. Clark. Mrs. Clark was known to have eyes in the back of her head. Carrie read the note stealthily.

"Hope your daddy don't never die." Carrie looked over at Beanie and then down at her desk because she was afraid she was going to cry. A feeling of thankfulness spread over her, but she wasn't able to look at Beanie until a second note came. "Earl got home las' night."

Carrie wasn't able to get the story straight until recess. Earl Lionel Togan had arrived home by Greyhound bus the night before. That's when she ceased to hear much of anything for the remainder of the school day. She and Beanie literally frolicked the day away since they were both overjoyed to have made up with one another, and the latter part of the day was taken up with the class end-of-the year party.

Earl Lionel Togan was home, and he had said to Beanie's mother, cross her heart that Beanie would fall out dead on her stomach with her

53

eyes rolled back if she was lying, that he sure was going to go see Mr. Turner Allen the next evening after supper to pay his respects, and to let him know he was ready to work at his job for the summer, and that meant this very night. No fooling!

All the way home on the bus, under the noise of the other children, Carrie excitedly planned what she would do for Earl's first visit. She wouldn't ask him to wait for her this time. Maybe on his next visit. She was still nervous about asking him because marriage was very important and she didn't want to rush him or anything. He might say no if she didn't handle it right.

There was no more school for three whole months, so Carrie was determined that she was going to stay up as late as she had to tonight in order to see Earl. She was going to wear a dress instead of blue jeans and put on some of her mother's Chanel # 5 perfume: A little rouge on her cheeks for color, maybe.

The breezy holes in the bus floor, the noise, the heat, the usually long ride, all passed Carrie by as she made plans. The bus stopped and jerked and started and turned and backed, and strained in first gear every time the driver tried to double-clutch it. Finally, Beanie nudged her and said, "We here."

Carrie moved off the seat like an explosion had gone off under her and when her feet touched the ground she was running. She was going to bathe in her mother's bath oil and bubble powder. Maybe she could wear her hair down over her shoulders instead of in braids.

Beanie yelled good-bye. Carrie spun around, laughing from a happiness way down deep inside, and waved. She saw M.T. walking off with Susie again. He sure liked that girl. Said he planned to marry her when he was grown. If he felt about Susie the way she felt about Earl, she could understand all the walking he was doing.

There were seven cars waiting behind Carrie's bus while the children piled off. Carrie ran by them, and then she saw the white school bus dead ahead. It was just coming to a halt in the line of traffic. She was almost up on it now, and she didn't want to waste her time by heading back to Pat's Place. She ran forward a little faster and braced herself for that red faced white boy. Sure enough, he stood up at his window, lowered it down to halfway, which was as far as it was designed to go, stuck his big head out sideways (there wasn't enough room the normal way) and opened his skinny red lips.

"Hey, yella nigger. Got somethin' up your funky dress for me?" He raised his middle finger in the air beside his face and stuck his tongue out lewdly at her.

It was all in slow motion. The entire day had been that way: more like dreaming than being real. Carrie saw his face and his mouth and felt the words hitting her so that an unaccustomed rage flared in her head as though something had exploded beyond her control. She opened her bookbag, took out her notebook, dropped the bookbag into the dirt, found a good grip and rushed the bus. It was starting to move off. She jumped up as high as she could out of her run, and catching the red face by surprise, she slammed the flat side of the notebook dead across the boy's nose. He screamed and cursed and the bus driver slammed on the brakes in a screech, which threw the boy against the back of the seat in front of him. Then he tumbled down to the floor between the seats, his scream high-pitched and full of pain.

Carrie backed off, picked up her bag and backed up involuntarily, like somebody was pulling her back. She couldn't take her eyes off the now empty window. She hadn't realized what she was doing until she felt the impact of his nose on the notebook. She wouldn't have done it for all the world if she'd thought about it first. He was screaming and crying, and when he climbed back up to the window, his face was as red as a tomato all over. Blood was trickling down his nose under his hand where he was holding it, and he had the most shocked look on his face. Carrie felt a surge of triumph. She shouldn't have done it, but she had and she was mighty glad. But her opportunity to enjoy her victory lasted only for a few seconds. The bus driver opened the door and jumped off the bus. When his feet touched ground, Carrie turned and ran, looking back as often as she could. Fear made her turn repeatedly to look over her shoulder as she ran.

The driver raised his fist at her, shouting, "Come back here, you little nigger."

Carrie ran like crazy down the side of the highway, hoping he wouldn't come after her. People started blowing their car horns, so the driver gave up, got back into the bus and drove away. Carrie slowed to a walk, out of breath, sweaty and a little weak with fright. She turned around, walking backwards, and watched the bus as it traveled slower than usual on its way toward the two "white" brick churches. She was praying the bus would just plain disappear.

M.T. left Susie when the trouble started. He and several of the other children stared, amazed at what had happened, and then M.T. bolted in a run down the side of the highway to join his sister as she continued to walk backwards toward home.

"Hey, I saw what happened," he said, panting. "You sure fixed that boy. And Shorty King was somekinda mad. Whooeey, you sure fixed him, but hitting a white kid . . . If you think fighting Beanie was tough . . ." He immediately saw the fear in Carrie's face and refrained from completing his thought. Instead, he took her bookbag from her and put his arm around her shoulder. "What happened?"

"He's been calling me names everyday. And this time I hit him...You think I did wrong?" She had never touched a white person before, even a little one, even to say hello, and the thought of what might happen was so frightening, she couldn't begin to imagine what the punishment would be. There were all kinds of stories.

"Sure. Don't worry. Those white boys are dirty. I was too far away to do anything, but looks like you hit him before he had half finished, like you knew what he was going to say before he said a thing. Fast on the draw." He was carrying on like she had hit just any-ole-body and won the fight. But it was a white boy! Wasn't he scared? Carrie was trying not to cry, but tears started down her face. M.T. stopped her where she stood and turned her face up to him.

"Naw. Don't you cry. I'd of never had the nerve to do what you did. Now, don't you dare cry."

"But I hit a white boy and yesterday I got in trouble calling names and fighting Beanie. What's Daddy gonna say about this. And Momma. They're gonna kill me if the sheriff doesn't. You know, the sheriff may come..." Her mouth suddenly felt dry. Just thinking about it was bad enough, but saying such a thing out loud made it so real. So close.

They turned back to walking down the side of the road. Lots of traffic suddenly began passing. The BAY Ferry at Kiptopeake must have put in a half-hour before. They kept their heads down and walked quickly. M.T. was afraid of somebody coming to get Carrie, too, but it wouldn't do to scare her worse.

"Ain't no pecking peckerwood gonna mess with us," he said under his breath. "You just stop worrying and listen to me!"

They walked on, picking up pace until the walking bordered on a run. Carrie could feel M.T.'s uneasiness in the way he nudged her along with his arm over her shoulder. He kept looking back toward the bus stop.

"What you think Daddy's gonna say?"

"Nothing. He won't say nothing." M.T. kept looking back over his shoulder.

Her throat seemed so dry, enough so she couldn't seem to swallow, and she didn't want to look back. Her brother tensed and she knew without a word that it wasn't over.

"Run, Carrie!" M.T. pushed her ahead of himself and yelled at her. "Run home and get Daddy. Shorty King's coming back with the bus. Run as fast as you can, girl."

She turned and looked back and hesitated. She could almost see the detailed shape of Shorty King hanging over the steering wheel of that big yellow "white" bus, a pale blur behind the windshield, barreling down the road toward them.

"Go on!" he shouted.

"Aren't you coming, M.T.?"

"Do what I say, Carrie." M.T. looked back at the approaching bus and turned and screamed at her. "Run home and tell Daddy. I'll be right behind you."

M.T. started running, pushing Carrie ahead of him, shouting at her between breaths and struggling against his own panic. The long stretch of woods to their left seemed endless. They had over a half-mile before their driveway.

The heat from the sun and the highway began to thicken the air in their lungs as they ran, frightened.

"If Shorty cuts us off, you jump the ditch and cut through the woods. Keep on running!"

Carrie's lungs ached. Normally, she could have run full out without feeling the effort, but she was afraid now and her breathing was out of control.

Carrie turned on her heels, looked back at the bus, and again was running as hard as she could toward home. The bookbag banged against M.T.'s hip off the shoulder strap. He lifted the strap over his head and threw the bag on the ground, his legs churning only at partial speed in order not to overrun his sister. There was a bad place in the shank of the road, right ahead, and there were too many cars to run on the asphalt. They slowed and picked their way over the gullied place, Carrie almost falling. They could hear the bus bearing down on them, its tires singing on the road.

"Keep on running, Carrie. Don't stop."

She put on more speed, and then the bus passed her by. The two of them stopped and watched, heaving for breath as Shorty pulled over to the shoulder a hundred feet or so ahead of them on the other side of the highway. Shorty exited the bus, rounded the front and stood waiting for the traffic to clear so he could cross. He wore a baseball cap pushed back on his head and glared at them with his hands on his hips while he chewed meanly on a chaw of tobacco, spitting as he waited. His clothes were unkempt jeans and a striped shirt open at the collar. It was obvious that he couldn't wait to get across the road.

M.T. grabbed Carrie by the shoulders and made her look at him.

"The woods is too tough, Carrie. You've got to run like hell 'cause Shorty's gonna try to stop us. Now you run and don't you stop for nothing. Not anything. Do you hear me? Now go on. Just keep running!" His voice was trembling. She had never heard him sound so scared. "Run straight down the road."

"But..."

"Go fast. Get Daddy. I won't let Shorty go after you. Go on before he crosses and catches you!"

Carrie hesitated, looking first at Shorty and then back at her brother. Cars and trucks were zooming by, throwing hot wind and grit and noise as they passed, but it wouldn't be long before the road would be clear of traffic. Every second counted and Carrie knew that; she was scared to leave M.T. alone and scared to remain. Shorty was kicking the dirt, impatient to cross the road.

"Carrie," M.T. screamed. "Get the hell outta here." He shoved her. She swiveled, jumped another eroded span of ground just ahead, and ran for her life. She was almost past Shorty's intercept point when

Shorty started across the highway, his entire body pitched forward with his fast walking efforts to cross and to cut Carrie off before she got past him along the shoulder.

"Come here, you little nigger," he yelled at her and shot into a run.

It was going to be close, and for a moment, time seemed to stand still, moreso for M.T. than for Carrie, who was running full out. Shorty would have closed the gap, and in fact, got an anger ridden grip on Carrie's blouse as she ran past him, except for M.T. Using everything he had learned about tackling in football, M.T. launched himself at Shorty, catching him hard around the waist, and knocked him violently to the ground.

Carrie looked back no longer. She was driven by a deathly fear and a subsequent speed faster than her best had ever been. She knew that her brother's survival might depend on her getting help, so she poured it on, pumping her legs so hard that everything in front of her was a blur.

Shorty and the boy went down in a tangle of arms and legs amidst Shorty's curses. M.T. landed on top of Shorty's outstretched legs, sprang to his feet and almost got past the angry man, when at the last moment, Shorty caught him by the ankle.

"You damn nigger sonovabitch," Shorty cursed at M.T. as he held onto his leg, dragged him to the ground and regaining his own footing, sent a powerful kick to the boy's abdomen. M.T. screamed and doubled up with pain. Shorty trembled with rage and paid little or no attention to anything except his anger and revenge upon the boy. Every child on the school bus was at the windows, screaming. They watched and gradually grew silent as they saw the punishment which Shorty dealt out to M.T. Shorty picked him up several times, punching him, slapping him about and kicking him, alternately. Several of the children left their seats and began crying.

It seemed like it took forever, but Carrie finally cleared the last of the woods, passed Mr. Wilson's yard and entered her own driveway. Her face and chest felt like they were on fire, and she couldn't hear her own voice as she called out of breath to her mother who was working on her flower beds near the front entrance steps. Carrie fell down halfway across the front lawn. Stella saw instantly that Carrie was in some terrible trouble and caught Carrie in her arms as she made hysterical efforts to get to her feet, screaming all the while for her father.

"What's wrong?" Turner came running out of his office, dressed in suit trousers and one of his finest dress shirts. He cleared the stoop and front steps in four strides, and once he understood what had happened, he ran to his car, drove straight out, and headed up the highway. Carrie and Stella followed on foot as fast as they could.

Turner drove onto the shoulder just short of Shorty and his son, and was instantly out of the car, shouting as he drew close. Shorty had M.T. by the shirt and had his arm drawn back to slap the boy once more when he heard Turner's shout and jumped away like a man who had just realized he was someplace where he shouldn't, for his life's sake, be. M.T. stumbled away from Shorty and moved bent over, more stumbling than walking, toward his father. Turner took a gentle hold on his son, bracing his weight with one hand while he pulled the boy's hand away from his bleeding mouth; at least one tooth was gone, both eyes were discolored and M.T. was holding on painfully to the rib area along his right side. Shorty was almost back across the road, and since Turner knew Stella was on her way toward them, he gently sat his son down and headed at a run for Shorty. There was practically no local traffic on the highway, and it would be another ninety minutes before the northbound ferry traffic would fill the road again, so the way was clear. Turner closed the distance, and using his right arm, blocked Shorty's efforts to swing the front bus doors shut. He pressed the doors open, got his shoulders and torso in amid screams of terror from the children on board, and in two strides had Shorty, who was screaming louder than the children, by the collar on both sides of his neck. Shorty's face was badly scratched. M.T. had dug his fingernails in deep.

"You've got business with me, Shorty," Turner's voice came out of breath but was intense with a rage just barely under control. With one hand Turner opened the bus door wide, and with the other, he pulled the struggling man out of the driver's seat, down the steps and off of the bus onto the ground. Turner dragged him kicking and cursing to the front of the bus where he leaned him back against the grill. By now, Stella and Carrie had reached M.T. who lay in a stupor on the grass of the ditch bank. He was moaning in terrific pain, both eyes were bruised shut and blood was oozing freely from the side of his mouth.

Stella bent fearfully over her son, and sitting down beside him on the ground, wiped carefully at his wounds to see if she could tell how badly he was hurt. She spoke to him softly, praising him for his courage and assuring him that he would be all right. Carrie, who had been watching her mother and brother, looked over at her father and Shorty King. She had to shield her eyes from the late afternoon sun, which glared directly into them.

"Oh, Momma. What's Daddy gonna do to Shorty?" Stella looked over at her husband as well, and her mouth trembled as she noted the way Turner was standing over Shorty King. She couldn't hear a word they were saying, but there was a fierceness in her husband and a fearful cowering in King which told her that Turner was at the very edge of destroying both their lives. Turner's six-foot-two-inch height made Shorty's five-foot-nine look minuscule. King had a reputation for hating Negroes and had been in a number of fights with some of the poorer whites. It was only his distant relationship to a member of the school board that had allowed him to keep his job. It was rumored that when off duty, he drank heavily. Without his one connection to respectability and power, there was no way he could have held a job as a school bus driver. Many of the white parents had complained about him, and it had been in the paper only a few weeks before that Shorty had been officially warned that if any direct evidence of his drinking should come to light, he would be fired.

Turner let go of Shorty's collar once he got him to stand still.

"You know better'n touch a white man, Turner," Shorty said, brushing at his clothes in an effort to restore some of his dignity.

Up to now, Turner had said very little. He had let the power in his arms talk for him. Up to now he had been careful not to hit Shorty, but he wanted to, and he knew he was angry enough to go beyond just putting the fear of God in the man.

"I don't know any such thing. You touch my children and you touch me, and no man, crazy white or black puts a hand on me."

Stella sent Carrie back toward home to call Dr. Reynolds to come. The bleeding from M.T.'s mouth had stopped, but she was afraid he might have at least one broken rib. Her greater fear was that he might be bleeding internally. She gently rocked M.T., wanting Turner to leave Shorty alone and to help her to get the boy home, but she dared not take his attention away from Shorty.

Carrie ran back down the side of the road as quickly as her tired body would let her. Having done with her crying, though still afraid, she was determined to do whatever she had to to help. For reasons that Carrie didn't fully understand, her mother had told her to make sure that neither she nor the housekeeper, Miz Rosie, called the sheriff.

Shorty took a deep breath and half hitched up his pants. "Now, I'm gonna git on my bus, Turner, and you ain't gonna touch me!"

"I'm waiting for you to try," Turner said. Shorty looked up and down the empty highway like he was searching for somebody in particular. He took a step, stopped and looked at his watch. The bus and the children were long overdue.

"I didn't mean no harm. That girl of your'n hit Eric Green and I just got mad, that's all."

"I'm more than a little mad myself," Turner said, his voice low and menacing. It had been less than a minute or so since he had crossed the road to the bus, but he had the oddest feeling that everything had slowed down to nothing, like he and Shorty and the whole world within his sight were suspended. Never in his adult life had he struggled with himself so hard over an issue that could, in the blow of one fist, change his destiny and that of his family forever. His impulse to grind Shorty into the dust went against all of his beliefs about how a civilized man should conduct himself. In this long moment of suspension, he experienced the microcosmic war of conflicting emotions that had been part of his life since he was a boy. He abhorred violence. Something about it tainted a man, no matter how righteous his cause. Yet he knew that a show of power sometimes demanded physical demonstration and reinforcement; that there were situations which other men only respected when power was leveraged. Turner knew in his moment of hesitancy that he could very easily kill Shorty King. The realization terrified him much more than the thought of his own death. Turner's fingers eased their grip. He let his hands fall to his sides, his eyes all but devouring Shorty's as he stared, still a bit undecided about what he might do next.

The look on Turner Allen's face would have struck terror and desperation into any intelligent man's heart, and this was mostly so with Shorty, whose intelligence to many was in doubt. Shorty was a strange breed of man, both a coward and one prone to be foolishly and inappropriately daring. He took Turner's letting him go as a sign that he could ease back onto the bus. He was mistaken. As he tried a second step, Turner grabbed him at the throat again and leaning close, breathed his words into Shorty's face.

"You stand right there, or something bad might just happen to you!" Turner shook Shorty and then let his shirt go again, still leaning close. He purposely lowered his hands again, knotted as they were into angry fists at his sides. He had managed up to now to just barely cross the line, which every Negro man had to toe whenever dealing with whites. He had conducted the funerals of any number of Negro men who had crossed that line in violently justified anger; most of them good men who had been sorely wronged. He had also buried many more who had done nothing wrong; they had simply been born black. His natural impulse was to smash Shorty into pieces. It was taking every ounce of his courage to contain himself. Yet he knew that whatever happened, it was absolutely necessary that he make the decision and not Shorty. He forced out of his mind images of his wounded son, his dear little boy; a boy he could not have dreamed into a finer reality, lying hurt across the road because of this stupid, racist fool. A fool who was the pawn of so many "respectable" whites and did openly to innocent Negroes what they didn't have the courage themselves to do. Turner forced himself to remember that his family and the boy's immediate welfare were more important than his reaping the revenge he was so tempted to take. Turner's jaws were clamped together so tightly that he was in pain.

Shorty sensed Turner's hesitation. He looked around again; into the faces of the waiting white children; over his left shoulder toward Pat's Place, where Pat, a tall fat dark Black stood in his soiled white apron watching the developments with half the neighborhood's black children standing around him; and across the road at Stella and M.T. Little Carrie, the cause of all of his troubles, was running down the road toward her yard. There was no doubt in his mind that he would find a way to hurt that little girl for what she'd done. A look of renewed hatred unmistakably entered his eyes, and with it, a sense of bravado.

"Shit," he said. "You lay a hand on me and they'll plant you in one of your own boxes in the morning. I'm nota scart ayou, undertaker man. All you good for is putting dead niggers in holes in the ground." He sneered, and stepped toward his right in an effort to round the front of the bus. Turner let him pass, grabbed his shoulder with one hand, the seat of his pants with the other, picked him up and held him bodily over the deep ditch that paralleled the highway. For years, Turner had been lifting caskets, some empty, some loaded with the leaden weight of newly dead grown men. His physical strength was something he knew he possessed, but had never measured. Shorty dangled, poised, and would have landed with an injurious thud and screams of both horror and delight from among the children on his bus had Turner thrown him. But instead, Turner set him on his feet at the very edge of the ditch as he leaned down into Shorty's face, his sardonic smile so riveting that Shorty was held from backing away only by his fear of falling.

"You tell any living white soul you know in Northampton County and the next that I'd rather die than let any man like you even breathe close on me! You tell 'em that and you stay the hell away from my family or I'll bury you myself."

It had only been three minutes or so since Turner had left M.T.'s side, but it seemed like an eternity. He rubbed his damp palms against his pants and trotted back across the road. Reaching for M.T., he caught Stella's eye, and for a moment, cupped her worried face in his hand. "I'll carry Morgan." Stella smiled, gratefully. She saw forgiveness where she had expected none. No, not forgiveness exactly. The look was more one of a deep understanding and appreciation in the midst of something which he knew was very complicated, and not so easily condemned. All during the last minutes she had watched him defending them all against a rabid disease, the likes of which she had so long denied as bearing any real direct danger for her immediate family. However light of color and straight of hair, and upstanding and accomplished, they were truly under attack now as full fledged members of the Negro race. There was no denying it, and even now, she saw no traces of "I told you so" in his eyes; nor heard one word of it on his lips.

If the situation hadn't been so frightening, she might have cried, both because she now understood and because understanding, they were no longer divided as they had been on the night before. She had prayed before sleeping that there would be a satisfactory answer, not realizing that the lesson learned would be at such a terrible price. She might have cried, but there was no time for that now. She helped her son into his father's arms and walked attentively beside them as Turner carried M.T. to the car. And she mistakenly thought that her own prejudices were overcome. Turner looked down tenderly at M.T., part of him still feeling that odd feeling of suspension, that this was not real. That this couldn't have happened. He had always been so careful not to cross that line. He had built his life on working hard and achieving and using friendships within both the Negro and white communities to forward his life.

He had never turned to violence to solve his problems, until today. He had crossed the line, no matter how gentle his discretion with Shorty, under the circumstances, and there was no stepping back over it as though he hadn't. And he would have done it again. Probably should have done more damage to Shorty while he was over on that alien side. This was such a fine boy, his boy, bright and eager, a good student; respectful and mischievous, tall for his age, a good athlete; everything he could ever want in a son, treated like some worthless thing, and he hadn't done much of anything to the man that did it. Turner closed his eyes in anguish as he walked, forced himself to breathe deeply, and then looked over at Stella walking beside him. They turned and opened the back door of the new black Buick sedan that served as the main funeral car for bereaved families—now his own family. It was so ironic that Stella should come face-to-face today with the very values he had challenged the night before. He knew she must be terrified. He was close to terror himself.

"Well, the stuff's hit the fan now," he said. His voice was a bit hoarse and breathy from anxiety and a heightened sense of alert. "I don't care about the whites. Somehow I know we can survive whatever reaction they send at us. I think most of the whites who know us will be appalled at what Shorty did."

He looked down at M.T. who lay inert now, his bruises well on their way to turning a dark red and purple. "It's Morgan. We've got to get help for him."

"I had Carrie call the doctor."

"I should have thought of that and called out to you when I first reached him," Turner said. "But I knew you were coming, I knew you'd do whatever had to be done, and I couldn't let Shorty get on that bus. I just couldn't!"

"You did fine, Turner. I thought you did just fine."

M.T. moaned, tried to sit up in his father's arms, and finding that he couldn't, relaxed again as he realized he was being placed on the back seat, his father placing his head and shoulders in his mother's lap.

"Few more minutes and we'll have you safe at home," Turner said.

M.T. smiled as best he could, feeling strangely lightheaded. He couldn't remember the last time he'd been carried in his father's arms. His pride gleamed from the one eye still partially open. His father had told him when he first came how proud of him he was, how well he had protected his sister. M.T. rested his head in his mother's arms and let his fears ebb away.

Carrie came running back up the road toward the car. Putting his arms out, Turner gathered Carrie to him. "Doc's coming. He said he's be here right away." Carrie looked into her father's face, searching for some sign of reproach for what she had done, but all she saw was the loving look of a concerned father. Yet behind that, there was a hardness in his eyes, like steel, that she recognized but had never seen before.

"Daddy, I didn't mean to . . ."

"Shheee," Turner said softly. "It's all right. It's done. For now, we've got to get your brother home." He kissed her, helped her onto the front seat, and as she moved across, he got in and started the engine.

Across the road from them, the yellow school bus was still standing in the same place, a frightened cluster of white children pulling at Shorty King who had mis-stepped and had fallen into the ditch after Morgan left him. He was moving, climbing back up onto the road, but slowly. Carrie knew now. Her brother was badly hurt and he was going to die. He was surely going to leave her, now, when they had just begun to find each other, and it was her doing. It was all her doing. Along with this fear was something of which she was becoming increasingly aware: the unjustified and ever pervasive meanness of white people; all of them; all of them.

Chapter VI

They worried. Walking home with their backs toward a closing white veil—a thing as strong to the senses as an asphyxiating gas—cloying, overwhelming their self determination, an invisible and certain thing. Climbing the back porch stairs, they worried. The steps creaked louder than they could remember, sounding like a crazed ghostly mourner whose voice was caught only for a moment on its doomed passage to that hellish place reserved for black people poised to meet white supremacist justice. They climbed the back porch steps in anxiety toward the cover of the back porch door.

Stella was somebody else now; or perhaps she was for now the person she really was. She moved to minister to her injured son with the precision and devotion of every loving mother since the beginning. Her awareness of what really was the truth of being coloured or Negro or Black in this world had never been quite clear to her, not only because it was such an unnatural assault upon her senses, but because she had managed to avoid it, both by accident and design like some nightmare she'd been expecting to awaken from all the days of her life, never letting herself believe for one moment that she was awake, and a life unoppressed was really the dream. To have allowed such a reality to penetrate would have killed something vital in her . . . Some guardian sentinel inside of herself had long ago come to that conclusion: miss the truth and spare the pain—the insanity of permanent irrationality from dawn to dawn forevermore.

Stella was a strong woman, a sensitive and determined woman, not made for the reality of her condition. She had never adjusted to being less, by nature of her racial attributes, than she really knew herself to be. For the time being, however, every nerve in her had caught up with the times, forced by love and fear and anger and an understanding of some thing much older than herself, which said she could survive the real world of being a Negro among a dominant people who hated black people with what seemed an absolute determination. Especially if, as now, it was to minister to the needs of someone she dearly loved. In an immediate emergency, she would and could do anything. In the back of her mind, however, it was deadly puzzling and something that seemed the anathema of all of mankind, this racism that Europe had brought against the coloured people of the earth. She wondered if the truth was that those whites who hated and those who were afraid to do anything about the hate were truly and simply insecure, and really, instead, hated themselves, perhaps because they were pale, couldn't stand the pain of such a reality, and thus projected their greatest hatred onto that group of people who were most visibly different from themselves: namely, the Negro, the African, the dark-skinned among them. It was a puzzle.

She put such thoughts away and made M.T. as comfortable as she knew how (he had fainted halfway home and had regained consciousness within a few minutes of being placed in bed) and managed to comfort Carrie and even Turner, inconsolable as they were.

Dr. Reynolds arrived, examined M.T., and finding him preliminarily in better condition than they had dared to hope, he had them bring him ten miles north to his office. By then, one of Turner's employees, a tall, lanky twenty-year-old named Chug Harris, and two neighbor men, Lonnie White and Benjamen Lewis, had arrived, complete with shotguns to guard the house. The word had passed quickly, and every member of the Negro community who had heard of the trouble expected more. Turner felt a lot better leaving the house guarded as he drove his family in their Buick sedan along Route 13 behind Dr. Reynolds's Cadillac. There were no Negro people on the streets, and the whites visible in the town stared as the cars passed through Cheriton before entering the open countryside of U.S. Highway Route 13.

They waited for what seemed forever for Dr. Reynolds to complete his examination. He was a thorough man, second in his class at MeHarry Medical School, and the only Negro doctor in all of Northampton and Accomack Counties. He had a soft, yet direct manner about him. Turner, Stella, and Carrie got to their feet as they heard his footsteps coming down the hall toward his office.

"Looks worse than it is," he said, standing in the doorway, his thin dark face very calm, as it always was unless he was watching or describing a good baseball game. "No broken bones, a very mild concussion, but no contusions or internal bleeding of any kind. I examined him quite thoroughly."

"But he fainted," Stella spoke with urgency, uncertain. "He passed out. Are you sure?" Stella didn't want to be soothed at a time like this when her boy might well be hurt worse than appearances.

"Don't misunderstand me, Stella." Doc walked toward his chair. "Shorty King laid some mean licks on that boy. I get the feeling that Shorty practically knocked him out and M.T. held onto him anyway until he saw help coming. He's got courage aplenty."

Turner spoke from the doorway on the opposite side of the room where he had walked absently as he heard the diagnosis. "Are you absolutely sure?"

"Well, you saw the x-rays yourself, Turner, and he had no difficulty responding normally to the tests I gave him." He reached into his pocket for cigarettes and matches. "I know you're worried. I'll come have another look at him first thing tomorrow morning. We can take some more pictures in a couple of days, barring any unusual symptoms, to make sure there's no change. And I want you two to take turns waking him up every hour on the hour until nine or ten tomorrow morning. If you can't wake him, you call me and then rush him back up here to me."

Alarm instantly showed in their eyes. Doc smiled. "Just a precaution. I don't expect anything except an annoyed M.T. every time you wake him up." He exhaled a deep draw of smoke, walked to his desk and settled himself into his chair, discarding a used match into an ashtray. "Why don't y'all sit down for a minute. Would you like some coffee or anything. You look beat and I bet you haven't eaten anything. I can phone Grace over at the house to bring some sandwiches or something. She would have been over here herself, but the baby's sick."

"No. No," Turner said. "Thank you." He walked over to Stella and put his arm around her. "We'd best be getting back home."

"Yeah." Doc ground out his cigarette and got to his feet. "Thank God he didn't need surgery. They still haven't approved me to operate at the County hospital and it would have been a mighty long drive to Richmond where I have privileges. It'll be a miracle if we ever see this county come into the twentieth century."

"Well, Doc," Turner said. "Maybe this is all that the twentieth century has to offer." They nodded, all of them unsure and yet understanding and said their good-byes. Gathering up their son, the Allens made their way back home in the dark with Carrie very silent on the big front seat with her father. M.T. slept and neither Turner beside her, nor Stella on the back seat with M.T.'s head cradled on her lap, noticed the solemn and disquieting look on her face.

"We've all got to eat," Stella said in the midst of a constantly ringing telephone and questions from Miz Rosie and Chug and Lonnie and Ben. She said it after putting M.T. to bed with a look that reassured everybody that doing a normal daily thing like making dinner would somehow restore things to an old easiness. Fresh green beans, candied yams, hot biscuits, and baked chicken, a Sunday menu cooked slowly while she kept an eye on M.T., and kept her mind off of all of the implications of the day. Dinner was served late.

Nobody ate anything.

The telephone had commenced its ringing before they had gotten M.T. home the first time. Then, as now, the bell echoed sharply through the house like a fire bell just after midnight on a cold winter morning, lonesome and shrill and so full of negative promise that it made them loathe to answer. Black folk had heard about the trouble, now, as far north as Exmore, and as far south as Cape Charles and Capeville. Pat Collins, at Pat's Place, and nearly a dozen children had seen the whole thing. They had told all that they knew and then some.

"You all right? You need any help now, Turner, just use the phone. Don't know what I kin do, but I'll come if you calls."

"Don't mean no harm, Mr. Allen, but you betta stay in the house outta sight 'til white folks cools a bit. I'se heard some bad talk up Cheriton way. No needayou axing for more trouble."

There were only a few whites who had anything supportive to volunteer. The Cheriton Postmaster and Lawyer Holcomb called and said about the same thing. "Turner. I'm so sorry to hear about what happened today. I'm quite familiar with Shorty King, and no decent white person would take his side over yours, no matter your race. But you stay close to home, just in case some hothead gets it in mind to do you further harm."

Others had heard. Their voices cracked and twanged over the line in splintered whispers, "Gonna kill you, nigger!" . . ."Turner, I certainly thought you niggers knew better than mess with a white man!" . . ."You need a lesson, Allen, you sonovabitch!" . . ."Gonna kill you, niggah!"

Turner slammed the phone down in rage many a time in the short space of early to mid-evening. And then there was the call from the local banker at Eastville. Thomas Lauderton had been a good friend over the years. If things had been different, Turner was certain that they would have been the closest of buddies. His voice was full of pain when he called.

"Turner, I feel so impotent. We grew up trying to overcome all of this hate and here we are, you threatened and me scared to risk helping you. I know that makes me a damn sight small in your eyes. I wouldn't blame you if you never thought a good thought about me again, but I don't know what else to do."

Turner listened, wondering if he would be saying the same words if their situations were reversed.

"I can loan you money anytime you need it, but I can't speak out right now; not the way things are. I'd lose everything I've worked for and my family would be threatened as surely as yours. It won't do any good for me to be no better off than you. I hope to God you understand. If it was just me, I'd be over there standing with you this minute, but I've got a family . . ." He stopped talking, waited as though he expected, at least hoped, that Turner would say that he understood and forgave him.

"Turner?"

"I'm here," Turner said. "Every man has to do what he has to do. I do understand that, Tom. I appreciate your calling."

There was another awkward holding of breath and then both men said good night and each one returned his phone to its cradle with a kind of softened gesture of regret.

Several other crank calls came in. After settling his nerves by sitting with his eyes closed beside the telephone, which he had taken off the hook, Turner finally called Luke Haskins, the County Sheriff. He had purposely put it off. He and Luke had grown up together and had never gotten along, so he had wanted some time to think. He had been pretty sure that Luke would not be the one calling him, unless he called with some taunting message, his voice disguised. His message to Luke had been short and precise.

"Luke, this is Turner Allen. As you probably know by now, Shorty King assaulted my son this afternoon. I want him arrested and charged. If you don't want to do it, I'll go to the governor if I have to."

There had been a silence, then a curse word hissed clearly into the phone, then the sound of Luke's receiver being slammed down onto its cradle.

Turner sat and stared, unseeing at first, at the white complexioned antique porcelain doll that sat routinely in the center of the antique bed which dominated his bedroom, his hand still gripping the telephone. He slammed the phone down, took a stride toward the bed and grabbed the doll in a rage, snapping off its head like it was a squab lying unattended in a nest. It landed grotesquely in the trash can near the bed stand. He'd buy Stella a new one, a black one. He shook his head in anguish. He sure hoped this incident would show her once and for all where her identity should lie. When he had left her last night after their argument, he had thought for awhile that their ways would have to part eventually if she was set on thinking the way she was. But then, he had realized that his victory in life would have been gone forever—replaced by the shadow of the white man in his bedroom, in his wife's head, in his own, in his children, in everything he touched and breathed. It had to stop and it wouldn't stop without being made to stop. He and Stella were going to work on the problem until it no longer existed, until they were united in an understanding of the beauty of coloured folk which would make them closer than they had ever been. He didn't want to hate whites. It was unbecoming, unnecessary, wrong overall, but he did want them to stop the white world from overshadowing the beauty and the worth of being black.

He picked up the beheaded doll, its eyes of blue wide open and riveted on him. He was tempted to walk to the back porch and leave it for burning. It was high time Negroes stopped raising idols to the ones who had enslaved them! But he knew that such an act was too extreme. He didn't want to destroy white people. He wanted black people to live as freely as whites. That was everything and all that he wanted. He placed the doll, head and body, into a drawer, his mind once more determined to find a balance between self-defense and aggression against those who would force black people into a place of inferiority.

It was ten o'clock p.m. Turner unlocked the gun rack in his den and loaded a .22 caliber repeater rifle and a 12 gauge shotgun. He placed the correct caliber and gauge of ammunition within quick reach. A .45 caliber revolver, loaded and on safety, was placed in the night table drawer of his bedroom, another .45 in the glove compartment of the Buick sedan, and he planned to walk outside of the house with a police model .38 in his jacket pocket. He would not be caught unprepared should the expected unexpectedly show itself.

There was no active Ku Klux Klan on the Shore so men in white sheets were not what he had to worry about. Most of the bondage was enforced through financial and economic controls. The Eastern Shore of Virginia, Maryland, and Delaware (fondly called the DelMarVa Peninsula by people of the region) was an agricultural belt, silently and viciously racist, the land mostly owned by whites and labored on by Negroes and a small collection of Spanish speaking migrant workers during the warmer months. The Negro population was larger than the white by several thousand, but as was the case in many southern counties, there were very few professionals, merchants, landowning farmers, and regular factory workers among the coloured. Negro people worked hard, dreaming of the success of their children, urging them to complete their studies so they might find a better life elsewhere. Most earned meager livings, comparatively, by working for whites in some capacity, much of that work menial and on the land.

Yet there was a wholesomeness and decency among Negro families despite hardship and reasons for bitterness. It never ceased to amaze Turner how strong and determined and balanced Negro people managed to be. To him they were a living miracle, his own parents highest on the list of those admired.

Even in the summers, especially in the summers, black people were frozen to the land on the Shore. If one wished to be more than the system allowed, the odds were so greatly against continued achievement at home beyond high school, that one had to leave for far off places. Philadelphia, Newark, and New York were often chosen, and even there, good paying work was often hard to find. Despite the good will of many whites that he knew and saw regularly as he plied his trade, he didn't trust them to be moral at a time like this. Based on what he had seen all of his life, he knew that his life and the lives of all

Negroes were held in the white mind as nowhere near important enough to be upheld when any white life was at stake. The very thought of that rankled a sore place in his stomach; made it growl and hurt and finally feel a wide deep emptiness.

He mulled over his conversation with Tom Lauderton. Tom was a good man and one of the few white men he knew with whom he was on a first name basis. For the most part, he was Turner to them and he was expected to call each one Mr. Whatever. Tom had always been a friend, but even Tom felt that he couldn't stand beside a black friend under these circumstances. Turner understood and didn't blame Tom, but it was this very wall of white cohesion, where no individual felt compelled to break through to help Negro people that made the system of segregation and discrimination work.

Turner figured that in fifty years all of this would probably seem bizarre to anyone looking back on it. In the next century, he figured, even whites would wonder at how it was possible that their ancestors treated black people so badly. They would probably want to deny that such a way of life had ever existed. They surely would say it had nothing to do with them. He was determined to do his part to rid the world of this way of life. He couldn't imagine things continuing the way they were for much longer. Too many Negro people were ready to explode and to say "No More!" And maybe they could convince a few white people like Tom Lauderton to join in the fight. Turner had to believe such a thing was possible. He knew that he had to if he was to find the strength to survive.

So what would he do now? Would he sit in his house and not live as he felt inclined to live? Turner shrugged, put the .38 into his pocket and headed for the back porch. Stella followed him to the back door. Even when she stopped washing the dishes and leaned close to the door in the kitchen, Carrie couldn't hear what they were saying. Their voices were muffled, keeping some dreadful secret about what was going to happen to them now that she had gone and beaten on a white boy. A guilt heavier than her own weight pressed down on her, standing at the sink, her mother's hands and voice saying still, clearly in her ears, "Why in heaven's name did you have to go and hit that boy. What on earth possessed you?" Carrie held onto the sink for support and strained to hear.

"Can't you do this in the morning?" Stella asked quietly.

"I could," he said, "but my life has to go on, Stella." His chin had a stubborn set to it.

"Turner, just for tonight, 'til things ease." She was determined to hold him if she could.

"White men after us never ease. If I waited for white folks' easiness, I'd grow old right here, just as scared as now. I've got my work to do. Three funerals coming up. We need those forms in shape for more vaults. Chug says they're bent everywhichaway."

He paused and ran his hand across her shoulder in the dim light from Carrie's bedroom window, which shone onto the porch, and then spoke so softly she could barely hear. "I want to go. I need to get out of the house."

"Turner, you know good and well you could wait 'til morning. My lands, do you want that fool man to kill you?"

"I need to know that what I own is mine—that this place is mine. Not Shorty King's. I won't let this house be a jail to me—a place to hide in." He glared out off of the porch into the leaves of the oak he had pruned in the fall. It had spread its new growth nicely, majestically. He said no more, but tensed his jaw so the muscles worked in his temples.

Stella knew the look and the meaning of it. She said, "Please be careful. Lock the vault house doors behind you. . . . I wish you had a phone back there."

Turner squeezed her shoulder gently as he turned to go, oddly like a little boy who had been given permission to play some daring game. His straight black hair was neatly combed back except for one curl that turned down toward his left temple. Stella kissed two fingers and reached up to place a love-pat against the curl. Turner smiled and hugged her. With her warm blessing, he would have gone immediately, but he caught sight of Carrie standing at the end of the porch in the light of the kitchen door. She looked so forlorn that the sight of her nearly broke his heart. He had been so busy with the phone and his anger, and checking the house to make sure it was secure, and giving directions to Chug and Lonnie and Ben, and worrying about M.T. that he hadn't given her any attention. It suddenly dawned upon him that she probably needed consolation more than anyone else.

"Before I go, I'm gonna put Carrie to bed." He nodded toward her and Stella turned to look at her as well. It was at that moment that she heard her own accusatory words, words said in an uncontrolled anger, and realized how cruel she had been. She led the way back to Carrie and before turning her over to her father, she whispered, "Please, Carrie, please forgive me for what I said today. Please forgive me. It's no excuse, but I was upset and shouldn't have blamed you. I know how awful it is to be called names by people." She kissed Carrie's cheek. "Can we talk about it?"

Carrie smiled, and then her lovely mouth trembled and turned down as she began to cry. "I'm so sorry, Momma. I'm so sorry."

"It's all right." Stella looked up at Turner for him to take her and wiped at her own tears with her apron hem. It had been such a painful day. . . .

Turner carried his daughter to the bathroom and washed her face and hands. "I don't care what's wrong, cool water on the face always makes a body feel better," he said. "Now, go put on your pajamas. You don't have to get a bath tonight." He grinned. "I'll look in on M.T. and then I'll come tuck you in."

He found his son sleeping soundly, apparently well. It had been twenty minutes since Stella last woke him. Turner returned to Carrie with a grateful heart. She was destined to be a spectacular beauty, what with her grit and flare for adventure in the midst of a stunning physical beauty that was already far too evident.

"Do I have to go to bed so early, Daddy? There's no school tomorrow." She suddenly remembered Earl. Earl was supposed to be coming. She couldn't see him or let him see her in pajamas. "Please, Daddy."

Turner shook his head and laughed. "Oh, I'm not worth much these days at saying no. Ok. You can stay up, maybe look at TV, but don't you even stick your nose out the door, do you hear?"

"Yes, sir."

"And you listen to me. About today—You know how I feel about fighting and violence. Fighting with Beanie was wrong and hitting that boy didn't exactly help matters. . . ."

"But, Daddy . . ."

"I know. What I was going to say was this. Sometimes we react to what other people do to us and can't quite help ourselves. He began the violence with his words. I can understand how you felt, and I might have done what you did."

"Really?"

"Yes. But promise me that in the future, you'll stop to think before you act. All through your life, people will say things or do things that make you angry or infringe on your rights. When you choose to lash out without thinking, you take the law into your own hands, and that is not only wrong 99 percent of the time, but it's also usually dangerous. Promise me you'll think before you attack somebody next time."

Carrie sighed and took another deep breath besides. "I promise, but I don't know if I'll do it right."

"I know. Don't worry about that. Just remember that your mother and I love you and we're with you, even when you make mistakes or get into trouble. Ok? It's hard to take abuse and not defend yourself, Sweetheart. Maybe if more of us found a way to strike back, we'd be free now."

They hugged and he left a kiss on her cheek as he walked from the room. Carrie wiped away the last of her tears, and feeling better, began to dress for her first meeting with Earl Lionel Togan since last summer.

Stella tried one more time as Turner passed through the kitchen to change his mind about going out. He was in a much better frame of mind and told her that Carrie had his permission to stay up a little longer. "Is that ok with you?"

She nodded yes. "Turner, can't Chug or one of the other men keep you company? Or me? I can handle a gun as well as you."

Turner shook his head no in answer. "I'll be ok. Chug is down in the office until I get back. Let him take care of the phone and the door if anyone comes by. Ben and Lonnie had to get on home, so Chug's all by himself. Yell for him if you hear anything suspicious." He took her by the shoulders and hugged her.

"I know you're worried. I just called Earl Togan. He wrote me from New York that he would be coming home about now, and he got home last night. Anyway, he and his father have been trying to get us ever since they heard about our troubles. He'll be coming over as soon as Jesse gets home with their truck. And Jesse and Tim have offered to take turns helping us keep an eye on the place. Does that make you feel better?"

He looked down at her and smiled, though he didn't feel like it. The day weighed so heavily that his very eyes hurt thinking about it.

"That helps. But can't you wait for Earl to get here?"

"He won't be long, and I've got to get started. I'll be fine. You lock the door after me, and keep the shades down and stay away from the windows."

"Oh, boy, this makes me feel really safe." She said sarcastically. They were so serious that it was almost funny. They both shook their heads and laughed so briefly that it brought on a renewed sadness and anger as the scarce sound of it seemed to remain in the air. Watching him disappear as he descended the stairs in the darkness, there seemed a million miles in between them. He was stubborn and bull headed, and a crazy man to be so set on getting shot by somebody full of hate. And there must be something greatly wrong with her for not being able to understand him and to make him feel that she could fathom his need to go out on such a night and take such a risk. Shorty King was no decent regular fellow with whom he had had a small disagreement. This man was a ruffian and a racist in the worst sense, and might be expected to prowl around looking for an opportunity for revenge. It didn't make sense to her that Turner should walk out into that darkness beyond the safety of his house to make himself a target for a madman. Tonight, the way things had been going, the way she had been thinking, there seemed never to have been any sense to the way of life as her people—she paused in her thinking and pondered her choosing that reference in her mind—her people, yes, but her people included Negroes, Indians and whites if one was to be accurate; truly there seemed never to have been any sense to the way of life as her people were forced to live it. No "rhyme or reason." Every defense she'd ever conjured up was falling to pieces. At least part of what Turner had said was true. There was no guarantee of safety in being light of skin. There wasn't any safety anywhere. How could she live; how could she live now that the last facade was down and this particular truth was so plain? Surely every day would be a nightmare from here on out, with no hollow to hide in.

Discouraged, Stella leaned against the door sill where the porch joined the kitchen and closed her eyes until she had stilled a rush of panic, which for a moment had threatened to overcome her. Then she went to care for Carrie, whom she felt she had greatly neglected, and to face the remainder of the night.

Chapter VII

Under the circumstances, Carrie didn't really feel like changing for bed. She wouldn't have taken a bath except that her mother offered to give her one, and since she was mostly in charge of her own baths these days and missed the times when her mother administered them, she stepped eagerly into the tub. The water was just right, hot without burning, and her mother's hands were soothing and comforting as they lathered her arms, legs, chest, and back.

They talked of many things: how well Carrie had done in school, a trip to Atlantic City planned for later in the summer, swimming lessons and maybe a trip to see the horse she had been begging for for so long. Granddaddy Lawrence had promised her a horse when she turned twelve. She would be eleven in August and it just so happened that one of his mare's had dropped a foal the year before that seemed perfect for her, so he had written that all was on schedule to deliver the filly early next summer. By then the young horse would be ready for riding. Stella said his letter had arrived in today's mail, inviting them to bring Carrie and M.T. for a visit, and she'd forgotten it until now. Grandaddy said that the children should stay for at least a week, or for as long as they wanted, to do all of the things they loved and to get acquainted with the horse.

Carrie was very excited. Having a horse of her own was a dream come true. Actually, she was expected to share with M.T., but there was no way she would mind that, especially after today. M.T. had never been very keen on horses. He loved baseball. Was nuts about pitching.

Eventually the conversation turned back to the day's tragic events, and much of the lightheartedness passed from both of them.

Stella told Carrie she could stay up a little longer if she remained quiet in her room. Carrie just assumed that Earl wouldn't be coming over now because of the trouble, so she didn't think to mention him and her mother didn't think to tell her that he was due to arrive at any minute.

Carrie lay on her bed, reading. Ever so often she peered through her bedroom window, hoping to catch a glimpse of her father returning to the house. He'd been gone a long time, now. If she could just see him, she knew he would be all right.

She heard her mother's footsteps coming toward her room down the hall. There was a soft knocking.

"Carrie, it's bedtime."

"Momma, please, can I stay dressed until Daddy gets back."

Stella entered and sat on the edge of the bed. She reached out to arrange Carrie's pigtails and fingered them as she talked.

"Your daddy's going to be fine. In fact, you'll be glad to know that your buddy, Earl Togan, is downstairs. He's come to help keep us safe."

"Oh, wow, Mom," Carrie sat up, exhibiting a burst of happiness which Stella hadn't seen in ages.

"Can I go down to see him? Please?"

"Now listen, honey. Earl and Chug are talking and making sure that everything is secure downstairs. Tonight's not the best time. He'll be back tomorrow."

"Ah, Mom, please. I just want to say hi."

"I know, but not tonight. Now, get ready for bed and pull up the covers. You've had one heck of a day, and you need rest almost as much as M.T."

"Yeah, he sure is sleeping like a log."

"Dr. Reynolds gave him a non-sedative painkiller so he would feel less discomfort from his bruises. Even with us waking him up every hour, I suspect he'll sleep well into the morning. Now, to bed with you."

Carrie knew it was no use, but once her mother had closed her door, she crawled into bed wearing a shirt and jeans, just in case there was the need to get up and going. There was no reason to have to waste time with getting dressed.

Turner had walked through the backyard toward the vault house in long, powerful strides. He turned to face every crackle of the bushes to the wind as he almost ploughed along, head down, hands in his pockets, his right hand fingering the gun.

The night was dark and clear so that every star in heaven seemed visible. Every new leaf was blowing from a warm intermittent breeze from the bay. The Chesapeake was just a half mile or so west of the house across a wide expanse of field and pine forest. He could smell the brine mixed with pine and newly cut grass. It was an aroma as much a part of summers in his memory, and as dear as his early childhood days of romping freely for hours on end. It seemed out of place on this particular night when his very life might come to an end.

He picked up his pace. It was a pretty good walk from the back of the house to the end of the lot where he made vaults. Despite a feeling of introspection about his life, he was alert to everything around him as he passed a tool shed and the garage complex where he kept two hearses, a station wagon and a flatbed truck.

He felt more helpless having to carry the gun—having to put men on guard in his house. Having to walk so scared that rattling leaves made him expect to find himself going down, dead from some white bullet. He turned a few steps and walked backwards, looking back at the massive rise of his house standing high above the ground. He knew practically every board and nail in it. His first professional training had been in the carpenter and brick mason trades. They were his love. He had also studied design and had done most of the planning and layout of the buildings at this location as well as completing the actual building. A few miles north he was just beginning to lay the foundations of what would be the first apartment complex on the Shore, which was owned, operated, and occupied by Negroes. Teachers who came to Northampton County to teach for the nine month school year had to find housing by living in with the families who would take them. This was not always the best arrangement. He figured that if he built several small apartments, he would have no trouble renting them. He had done a feasibility survey among the teachers and had found that there were more than enough of them who expressed an interest in renting a place year round. If he lived through these next few weeks until things simmered down, he had all kinds of enterprising plans.

Right now he didn't feel that he could really protect all that he loved and owned. Never in his life had he felt more like the nigger that whites had intended him to be. He felt a resurgence of anger move higher up into his chest as he forced himself to walk on.

The vault yard seemed to stretch out broader than he had ever seen it. He slipped into a run and entered the side door of the vault house, turning the lights on and quickly looking around. Everything seemed fine. He locked himself in and placed the handgun on the worktable near the cement mixer. He removed an old shotgun from a cabinet and sat it with several shells against the wall near where he would work.

The air inside was still close and sour from the recently removed body of an unidentified man who had burned to death. The authorities never found out who he was, so Turner had buried him in Potter's Field after keeping him for over three weeks, waiting for some word on who he was. Man, he sure had stunk up the place. Since Turner couldn't afford a freezer storage system for bodies, and seldom needed one, the only recourse in such a rare instance as this one had been was to cover the body with lime. It had helped, but not enough.

Turner climbed the wall ladder at the end of the room and opened a window near the rafters. He did the same at the other end of the building so fresh air would draw.

Getting the forms bent back into shape was important, but even if it hadn't been, Turner knew that building up a sweat would help to clear his mind. There was something about free physical sweat-popping labor that was necessary when he was really frustrated by an obstacle. As a boy he had worked out many a problem while chopping wood or hauling fish nets or hauling heavy potato sacks from loading docks onto wagons, and later, trucks. Never mind the task so long as sweat came pouring out of him and he could feel his own power clearing his head.

Turner moved to his work, his mind only partially on the repair job ahead of him as his eyes roamed over each section of vault form. He immediately found an end piece, which was out of shape, and he grunted as he pulled the heavy iron away from the rack and dropped it with an angry noise across two huge saw horses. He pulled a large steel block into place under the damaged section of form and raised it with a foot pedal until it was flush with the underside of the form. Carefully aiming each blow, he began pounding away at the dented portions of the iron, changing the position of the block from time-to-time so that the metal regained its original shape. If he could curve it back down he could make it fit into the slot of the adjoining side. He hoped he wouldn't have to fire the thing to shape it right. If so, he'd have to get Jesse Togan to help with his forge. He sure wasn't going to junk it. A new set of forms was expensive. Jesse would do the work and charge a fair price, but every penny spent was a penny gone. Turner cleared his throat and grunted and pounded and pumped and pulled, building up to a rhythm and a sweat that should have been satisfying.

The scenes of the day passed like a motion picture before his eyes as he worked, so that instead of feeling better as he went along, his anger drew deeper. It was the craziest thing. A no good white man could beat on his son, threaten his life and family, and here he was, Turner Morgan Allen of the well bred seventh generation American Allens—educated, money in the bank and property worth thousands more, the epitome of Negro American enterprise and decent respectability, complete with light brown to high yellow skin and blow hair that would carpet the ocean highway smooth from Maine to Florida, and he could do nothing about it.

Sure, he would bring a formal complaint against Shorty in the morning. That was the first thing, and the whites would mess around. They wouldn't arrest Shorty, that was for sure. They'd put him on his honor, and they'd stall and maybe set the proceedings, whatever they were, for six months down the road a piece. Turner would be stuck with the local prosecuting attorney, who would suddenly discover that he didn't know his rear end from a hole in the ground and in the end, they wouldn't have a case. But despite the prospects, Turner was determined to take the thing as far as he could make it go.

Power. Where was the secret of Negro people getting power; the power to make the sheriff and the school board and the average white citizen responsible in their conduct toward Negroes? Obviously it couldn't be left to their sense of what was right and decent.

He already knew the most important answer: Economics, finances, money! Until Negroes developed a strong economic base with strong, well-backed institutions, and until they were able to get certain laws changed and others upheld, nothing was going to move from blocking the door.

The neighbors calling like they did to encourage and to offer help was a good sign. Maybe the time was coming when the Negroes in Northampton County were going to be willing to organize and get themselves together.

Turner stopped hammering the form, opened his shirt and wiped at the sweat trickling down his chest. His shirt was soaked. He rubbed his lower back, rubbed the back of his neck and ran his hand through his hair. His thoughts were working him like he was pulling a plow across dried rain-packed clay.

For the first time in years, despite himself, he tasted the very essence of an anger which seemed to stretch as far back in his soul as the taking of the first African slaves by the Portuguese, the Spanish, and then the English. Turner loved history and had done considerable research during his college years. Under the auspices of papal bulls issued by the Vatican from 1443 onward, until the disguised motives of the Catholic church's supposed saving of Negro souls fell to the true effort to make money by selling slaves to the highest bidders, millions of African people had been destroyed and misused. So many scars, so many episodes of humiliation had scored his own life since he was a tiny child, and he had never found a way to adequately release the pain which had mounted in his heart over the years. And he was successful, compared to practically all of his fellows. How in heaven's name did Chug and Lonnie and Benjamin and so many other Negro men stay sane, when at every turn the white man, and many a white woman, had set traps and obstacles and dug pits and had just plain said no to every effort they made toward their dreams.

Turner leaned his head back and closed his eyes, aware of his awareness like a man standing naked and surrounded by giants with knives. Even a pair of drawers would make a difference. Everything hanging out and vulnerable and moving out of unison with any struggles he might make was the most insecure position in which a man could find himself; to have his manhood and his sense of manhood entirely exposed to his enemies. And this was essentially the position of every Negro man he had ever known or heard of for as far back as "the new world" had existed.

The answer wasn't in brooding alone. Every Negro in the world was, and up to now each had remained, for all it was worth, inside of a closed shell where defense and aggression were concerned. And each was being oppressed by the same white criminality and hypocrisy, all in the name of white supremacy.

So, he must do something and encourage others to do something. Dr. Reynolds and the Togan men would be an excellent start. He could trust them. It was time Negro men in Northampton County built a means, a power base of some kind. They would have to talk about their options and then carefully select other men to join. The more Turner thought about calling a meeting, the more his heart calmed and he could feel the tension leaving his shoulders. It was high time he stepped out and did more than simply live. Tonight he would sit at his desk and formulate some ideas to present to the others, the risk be damned. They needed to form an economic base, pool their resources and begin building some enterprise that could channel money back into the community. This was a farming district. Perhaps some kind of farmers cooperative might be the way.

There was darkness peeking in at Turner through a small window directly in front of him, behind and to the side of the cement mixer and just above waist high. It seemed like nothing existed beyond the glass but darkness. From the doorway where he had entered, that window had looked tightly closed, and when shut, the vertical slats across it made it impossible for anyone to see inside. As he stared at it, he realized, Lord, the window. Standing most of the time he had been there with his back to that window like he was begging Shorty King to come kill him dead.

Turner started for the window to close it when he saw the barrel of a shotgun aimed directly at his chest. A blast exploded the silence. He slammed into the floor as two more rounds went off, echoing across the Negro neighborhood like a volley from hell and gone.

Chapter VIII

Carrie sat straight up on the rug like a sapling bent back and let go. A second shotgun round went off. By the third, she was out of bed and trying desperately to see something through her back window.

Her mother was downstairs somewhere, shouting something to somebody. Carrie rushed to M.T.'s room where there was a better view of the back yard. M.T. moved in his sleep but showed no sign of waking.

Carrie was afraid of her own thoughts, afraid to attempt to say or to ask what the gunshots meant, even of herself. The shots had come from the back yard and her father was back there. She was frozen at that point in her thinking, her mind struggling against the most obvious conclusion.

The room was large and dark and empty despite her sleeping brother's presence, like a room with nothing but walls: an attic somewhere at the top of a stranger's house. Or like a well. She had fallen into her grandfather's well once; way down into the hollow dark water. No . . . She had dreamed it; dreamed she had fallen. And this was like that, waking to shotgun blasts out of the emptiness of a night threatened and threatening to end her father's life.

Her father was dead. He was gone, like all of those people he picked up and funeralized and buried. Shorty King and Carrie Marie Allen had killed him. She shouldn't have struck that boy. It was the law not to fight white people, no matter what they did to you. It was the law.

She sat back on the edge of M.T.'s bed, a terror creeping over her, dwarfing her into a speck of something, lost and falling down a well infinitely deep. Sometimes in her dreams, the water came up racing to engulf her face, and she could feel somebody holding her upside down and saying they were trying to pull her up for air, but only holding her steady so she couldn't breathe at all again. She couldn't cry, couldn't speak, couldn't move. The pitch blackness of the room moved in on her.

How long she sat there she didn't know. But a thought came and moved her away from the bed. Her father was in trouble and she was just sitting. He was in trouble. Not dead. He couldn't be dead!

Carrie looked around to see what she could do, and she remembered the gun: M.T.'s pellet rifle. It was more than strong enough to kill a man if it was aimed expertly, and Carrie knew she was a pretty good shot.

Finding it in the dark took a couple of minutes. M.T. had stored it against the back wall of his closet. The pellets were in a drawer under three old dirty socks, which M.T. had stuffed there. Carrie loaded quickly. She'd shot it many times, and felt confident that she could most assuredly shoot at Shorty King. She ran lightly on her feet down the hall, through the kitchen and porch and down the back steps. She crept to the other side of the house through the breezeway which separated the rear of the main building from the morgue, and was about to step clear of the building when she heard someone running in her direction up toward the back of the morgue. She pulled back into the shadows and raised the gun, ready.

He studied his hands. At a time so critical, he couldn't take his eyes off of them for what seemed a long time. The grainy cement and sand on the floor of the vault house put abrasions on the heels of his palms as he scuffed across it, diving from the explosions. Now he looked at his open, empty hands, little pieces of skin sticking up, little hair-fine trickles of blood rising up, and rising with them, a hot cool pain. It reminded him of trees rubbed of bark in places, when he was a child riding through the woods with his father, James Randolph, where the horse drawn wagon scraped them; little trickles of colorless sap, tree blood, oozing from the hurt. A minor small expanse of hurt; so small, yet the uppermost branches must have known.

An anger rose in his hands as well now. The window frame was blown out where a shotgun blast had ripped it to smithereens. He had just seen the barrel poking through toward the interior of the vault house in time to launch himself off to the side as the barrel emptied. Then there had been two other blasts from up toward the house, and then another close by, and whoever had shot at him had pulled the shotgun away. There was no way of knowing if the culprit was still just outside the window. Turner rolled over and inched toward his revolver, all on his side, sliding knee and hip and elbow forward while his eyes watched the window for harm. He reached the worktable and inched the handle of the gun into his hand, all the while keeping his eyes on the window. Staying down and away from the window, he crawled across the floor and turned off the lights. He started when a flurry of heavy pounding landed on the vault house door a short distance from his head.

"Mr. Allen. Mr. Allen. You in there? You all right?"

"Chug?"

"Yes, sir. You all right?"

"Yeah. That you shooting?"

"Them las' three, yes, suh. Let me in!"

Turner hurriedly unbolted the door. Chug slipped into the darkened room quietly and helped Turner secure the door. They both sat on the dirt floor, quiet for a moment, listening, before Turner spoke.

"What about Stella and the kids?"

"Hold on. No problem. Earl Togan up there wit' 'em." Chug took a deep breath and cleared his throat.

"Earl jest come by and set hisself down good when John Wilson called on the phone from next do'. Said he seen what looked like a white man prowling in the vault yard from where he was on his back porch. I grabbed up the gun and come runnin'. Lef' Earl wit' his gun to guard the house. When I cleared the go-rage, I seen somebody all right. He crossed near the light pole out front of the vault house, then disappeared around back. Couldn't see who it was, but he sho looked white to me. He was totin' a long gun and slinking yo' way, so I raised my gun to shoot in the air when I heared him shoot. Lord, I thought you was a gonner. I shot off two rounds in the air to scare 'im, come a runnin' and shot one mo' time in case he was waiting. I inched around the back there with my flashlight and jest seen somebody disappearing into the corn over yonder. Thank the Lord you ain't hurt."

"You saved my life, Chug." Turner felt for Chug's hand in the darkness and shook it, thumbs up.

Chug's voice filled with emotion. "Lord, I sure hopes so. There wasn't nothin' much else to do."

"Well, after that first round went off, whoever had that shotgun could have gotten off a clean shot at me on the floor here. The lights were on and I just did sidestep the barrel. He might have gotten me in his sights if you hadn't shot the way you did. I don't know why I didn't notice that window."

"Seems like its always them little things we don't see that gits us," Chug said. "We gone have to double check everything until we gets pass this here time. I was glad I didn't get a clean sight of whoever it was prowlin'. God knows I don't want to have to shoot nobody."

"I know."

"I kep' thinkin' that if'n I shot me a white man, I'd spen' the res' of my life in jail if'n they didn't hang me. Lord knows part of me wanted to shoot 'im."

Turner thought about the fact that he should have punished Shorty more this afternoon when he had the chance, instead of just holding him over that ditch. But he had faced the same problem as now: This is a white man and if you kill him or hurt him badly, you're as good as dead and your family is as good as dead. More importantly, he had always held human life as precious. What bothered him most were the injustices allowed within the system of justice. A Negro man killing a Negro man had a chance of pulling a lighter sentence than a white man killing a white man. A white man killing a Negro would serve little or no time at all. A Negro killing a white man would be sure to pay with his life. So Negro men were set up to prey on one another or to be preyed upon. Turner shook his head, anger rising in him for the umpteenth time.

"You did right, Chug," Turner reassured him. "Neither of us are killers. This whole situation is downright absurd. Let's not worry about that now. What happened next?"

"Man," Chug chuckled. "That dude haul ass th'ough Wilson's corn patch. Must a cut a hundid holes in hisself running th'ough the briars and shit behind that corn."

Relief of a kind came over Turner's mind as he listened. The war was on, but thank the Lord, Stella and the kids weren't alone. Even so, he wanted to get back to the house. By now, with the shooting, the prowler was probably long gone and Stella and the kids would be worried sick.

"Did the man look like Shorty?"

"'bout his size, but I kain't say for sure."

94

"You did fine, Chug. If you hadn't been on your toes, there's no telling what he might have..." Turner put his hand on Chug's shoulder in the dark. "I'm really grateful to you, Chug."

Chug grunted a satisfied tone in the darkness and got to his feet. There was nothing he could think to say in reply to something like that, especially coming from a man like Turner Allen. He would remember it all of his days.

"Well, we'd best get back to the house."

"I'm wit' you. You go furst and I'll cover yo' tail."

"Ok. Let's use the window on the other side. Take it slow and careful and use the vaults for cover, then the out buildings and the trees until we can run clear to the house."

They paused just long enough to look around outside the vault house window, and then Turner led the way, moving slowly in a bee line through the darkness.

In the dark semi-light, where things were shadows and strangers, she saw her father's familiar form, crouched slightly and moving at a run just ahead of Chug. Carrie lowered the pellet gun and let them pass without calling attention to herself. She heard them enter the house, and then Stella and a man's voice mixed with emotion to welcome them. She leaned back against the morgue door and took several deep breaths. Her father was all right. He was all right.

The wind stirred a sound in the bushes of Mrs. Lukus's back yard lot. Carrie turned in alarm. Nothing was there, but the night was ominous again, just in that small crackle of weeds. She jumped into a run, past the breezeway, under the oak, up the stairway and behind the porch door, which she locked. She calmed down after awhile, thinking M.T. would be bugged with himself like crazy that he had slept through all of this.

A shadow moved from the tangle of young trees and honey suckle vines at the place from where the sound had come. The man had watched Carrie run away. He stood now, a little amused at how frightened a run Carrie had made, but was more regretful that he hadn't seen her sooner. He might have made Turner the truly sorry one. And he would. He would take his time and enjoy the fun of it.

95

He hadn't always hated niggers. Hadn't always thought of them that way. He would never forget the shaming he took from his father when he was eight years old. He had brought a black boy home with him from school to go fishing and his father had whipped him in front of the boy, telling him that he was worse than a low down dirty nigger to bring such trash home with him. His father called him a nigger for more than a year afterwards, until he was not only convinced that Shorty no longer had the slightest inclination to like Negroes, but that he actively hated them.

His father was dead, now, but Shorty wanted him to know that he still believed the way he had been taught. Overall, his father had been good to him, had taught him to drink and smoke and helped him to get his first woman for sex—one of his father's old girlfriends who was still young and pretty. He never wanted to let his father down and imagined that the old man was always there, passing judgment on whatever he did.

Shorty moved back into the shadows and finally walked away. Another chance would come. He was a patient man, and on occasions like tonight, he was a drinking man, and between the two, he would hold out fine until the right opportunity presented itself.

There were quiet voices talking behind the closed doors of the office: Stella, Turner, Chug, and somebody else. They'd been in there a long time now. The phone had been ringing a lot. Carrie walked on tiptoe into the chapel. She almost entered the office, but felt suddenly shy. Her father was safe. She knew that and that was the only important thing on her mind. She didn't want to just walk in and stare with everybody else there. She could also hear another man's voice in there. She knew it must be Earl Togan. They'd just tell her to go back to bed, anyway, if she intruded. She'd wait for Earl and her father to come out. She wanted to hug them both. The soft presence of their voices was assurance enough for the moment.

The chapel was dimly lit by one funeral lamp. It stood on a long, decorated stem with a round and pretty glass globe at the top which shed a soft, shell pink light.

Carrie wandered back and forth between rows of empty caskets set out for display. Each one sat on a special carrier truck. They rolled easily when pushed to give the caskets mobility. The slightest touch of a finger and they would move when the wheels weren't locked.

Her fingers glided over the lace trimming along the lid of one rather expensive casket. The price tag on the pillow read $950, she knew, even though she couldn't see it in the dim light. The lowest priced funeral was $250 and the highest $2,500. The price included everything; removal of the body, embalming, general arrangements, the casket, and in the higher priced funerals, the vault came along, too. Her father did a lot of business, but most of the funerals were low priced. Her daddy said coloured folk didn't have a whole lot of money to spend on burying, though a whole lot of folk seemed in his judgment to spend too much. He said it was as if a coloured person's funeral was often the one thing, no matter how poorly the person had lived, which had to be done with style and show. He said that half the time, families went into serious debt because they felt they had to make one last effort to do right by their loved one, and he wished to holy heaven that they showed the same unity about caring for the living. Sometimes they felt guilty and were trying to make up for mistreating the dead relatives while they lived. Sometimes they were showing off to their friends and neighbors. He also said that it wasn't unusual for white folks to act the same way; at least that was what he had heard from a white undertaker friend of his.

Most times, though, he talked people into a lower price because he knew they couldn't pay without it being a hardship, and he would end up feeling badly that the family had spent too much of their small supply of money. And quite often, folks would end up owing him money that he needed for a month of Sundays and then some.

Carrie swiveled in a circle, letting her hand drag along the plush fabric of the next casket. She was still a little dazed and confused about all that had happened in the last two days. There was a mild odor of glue and cedar in the room. She liked the way caskets smelled; the sharp sweet odor of new lumber. The room was strangely comforting. She had played many games here, and she could hear the rise and fall of her parents' voices, speaking calmly. She wondered what Beanie would say when she heard about all the trouble.

A twinge of shame came over Carrie. She hadn't meant to call Beanie a nigger. Yet, she knew she had meant it at the time. It was just that now she was beginning to understand that everybody was a nigger to white folks, and that made the whole thing seem different. She wondered if there were any white people in Cheriton and Cape Charles, in the whole county, who were really decent. If there were, it seemed to her that they were doing a good job of keeping it a secret. She was inclined to believe her father, because of the way things had been going. It was dangerous to assume that nice white people were really nice, and straight hair on a coloured person's head that made you look closer to white didn't make you better. You had to take each white person one by one to find out whether that person was a racist or not.

Maybe her mother was wrong and just didn't understand. Her father had seemed upset the other day, even though he tried not to show it. It was when she told him that she had gotten the idea that niggers were dark-skinned coloured people from her mother. And that night, he and her mother had screamed at each other and she hadn't slept all night, mostly scared. She wondered if there wasn't something wrong deep within herself to cause her parents to fight. It seemed she was always causing trouble for somebody or other.

Carrie stepped toward the organ alcove, intent on sitting quietly on the bench. She was going to wait for her father and Earl as long as it took; for one thing because she didn't want to go upstairs into her room alone. The light from the funeral lamp just barely crossed the tips of her sneakers. She looked down, idly, drowsiness moving like a hand over her eyes.

The back door of the storage room opened and then slowly whined shut until it clicked softly. Soft footsteps touched down against the floor, coming from the storage room toward her. The heavy draperies at the end of the chapel in front of her swayed just a little with the draft caused by the opening and closing of the door. There was a door behind the drapes, which allowed entrance into the storage room. The section of drapes covering the entrance was up and the door open, but the room was dark, so Carrie couldn't see anything as she looked up out of her sleepiness in alarm. She could just hear the soft footfalls coming closer. The back door wasn't locked! In the excitement, somehow it had been left unlocked and somebody was creeping into the house!

Carrie stood away from the bench and bumped into a casket as she moved through the chapel toward the office. She almost lost her balance and grabbed one of the decorative handles to stop its casket from banging into another. She didn't want to make any noise. Being quiet seemed the better thing to do. Maybe she could reach the office and alert the family before the intruder dared enter the chapel. Her father would know what to do. She chastised herself for leaving the pellet gun upstairs.

Carrie took step after step backward, her eyes straining to see through the dark doorway.

A shadowy figure passed across the threshold. She saw the man clearly as he stepped into the light. He was tall, but nowhere near as tall as her daddy. His shoulders were broad and his dark brown face looked so smooth in the soft light behind him that it seemed he couldn't possibly shave. But being twenty-three years old, he had been shaving awhile. He was dressed in grey slacks and a tan shirt, real pretty, with nice dark brown leather shoes, and like always, his black tightly curled hair was neatly trimmed and a little longer than most coloured men wore it. He looked good. He looked better than she could remember.

When he saw her, her back pressed against the side of a casket, he laid his shotgun carefully on the floor, beckoned her with his hands and smiled the way he smiled when he was really pleased. "Come here, Carrie," Earl said softly. "My, you're almost grown."

She had thought he was in the office with her parents and Chug. She smiled and stood hesitantly, shyness back again, ready to stay. His smile broadened into a grin, which beamed into his eyes. She walked and then ran into his arms, hugging him and leaving a peck of a kiss on his cheek. He lifted her up off of the floor and swung her around.

"Lordy, girl, you're tall, and you weigh a ton. But you kiss something terrible. Do that again." Carrie giggled and kissed him full on his cheek this time. He returned her to her feet, walked her to the bench and gave her a good looking over in the lamplight.

"Still wearing blue jeans, I see. And still got a smile fit for hallelujah morning! But looka there." He moved a finger along her cheek, under each eye and then tweaked her nose. "That nose is a might red, and pale pink eyeballs. Tear streaks on your face and look at the little smudges you've got here. Girl, you've got a hucky face.

99

Hucky, I said." Carrie burst out laughing, shamefaced. Earl shook his head and laughed to beat the band. He hugged her and sat down on the bench, nodding his head with enjoyment.

"It's all right, Rabbit. Things are going to be fine. Don't worry about Shorty King hurting anybody. Sit down here and tell me what you've been doing since I left." Carrie sighed happily and shook her head. It was the hardest thing to figure. He always seemed to know what she was thinking about, long before she said one single solitary word.

"How'd you get in the back?" Carrie looked down at the gun.

"I just got here before the shooting started. I called your Dad as soon as I heard about Shorty King beating up your brother. So when your Dad and Chug came back in, I decided to take a look around outside. And just in case, I checked the rest of the doors and then let myself out of the storage room. I just stood in the alcove back there awhile and listened and looked, like you do on a good hunting stand. Figured if anything was moving, I'd hear it. Then I came back in and found you."

Earl paused. His face grew serious and he made a sucking sound against his teeth before he spoke. "Your father told me what happened to you today. I'm sorry you had to endure what that boy said to you, not to mention Shorty King."

Carrie looked down at the light across her shoes. "I did wrong, hitting him like I did."

"Who said so?"

"Nobody, exactly. Mostly me. Momma said it and took it back, but she was right. And I know Daddy wished I'd kept on walking."

Earl was quiet for a moment. He sucked his teeth again and took her by the hand. "Carrie, did you ever hear of World War II?"

"Yeah."

"What was it?"

"It was a big war. We fought the Nazi's and the Japanese. Did you know we just studied that at school?"

"No, I didn't, but that's the answer. Why did we fight?"

"Because they were bad. . . They were against us."

"That's right." Earl crossed his hands over his knees and leaned forward. "The United States went to war against Germany and Japan, with a segregated army, no less, because our citizens and leaders were sure that this country was threatened by the actions and the attitudes of the Germans and Japanese. America exercised her right of aggressive self-defense."

He was always using such big words, and listening to him made his words make sense. She could understand the gist of them and then, remembering a few, she often found herself using them when she talked.

"Are you listening?"

"Yes. You bet."

He smiled and winked. "Ok. Now, this country was willing to lose thousands of men in battle in order to protect itself against other countries and other people who wanted to rule and destroy it. And among other people, your father and my father were in the American Army.

"This afternoon, a white boy threatened you. Name calling isn't the same as shooting or hitting, but in this country and in most places, when one person keeps on insulting another, somebody is bound to get hurt. Now, white people have done many terrible things to black people."

Carrie wasn't used to hearing the word "black." In fact, lots of people took it as an insult. She was used to hearing coloured or Negro. Her mouth opened in surprise and she wanted to ask him about it, but as he often had told her, he was on a roll with his idea. So seeing that he had raised his hand just a little for her not to interrupt, she put the question away for awhile.

"That boy calling you names, insulting you the way he did, was an act of violence against you. In a small but important way, he carried out an act of aggression, which fits into a larger pattern and often leads to black people being mistreated, cheated, and killed. Whites think they can curse us and cheat us of our labor and money and then kill us without ever paying for it. Today, you did the same thing that the U.S. government did against our national enemies. You fought back. And if more of us were like you, we'd be a free nation of people within this country. Don't you let me hear you scorn yourself for having courage."

"Huh?"

101

"You done good! Or to be proper, you did well, my child. Maybe instead of Rabbit, I should call you Lioness or something." He laughed and drew his finger lightly in a straight line down over her forehead, ending with a light tap of his fingertip against her nose.

"Oh, please don't. I like Rabbit better."

"Ok, it's Rabbit forevermore."

Carrie cleared her throat. "I was scared, but, I don't know, I guess that boy made me so mad, I couldn't help myself." Carrie burst into animated conversation as though a dike had been opened.

"I just knew ole Shorty King was gonna get us." She thought about M.T. and the shooting and sobered again. "But Earl, it doesn't do any good. We don't have a army like America. What if they come and get Daddy?"

Earl leaned closer. Carrie was a sister/daughter to him. He remembered how his father had teased Turner on the morning she was born for running down the main highway past his neighbors' houses telling everybody that he had himself a baby girl. And he remembered the look of awe and happiness on Turner's face whenever he picked her tiny self up and showed her off. Then Turner had let him hold her and it seemed he'd been involved in bringing her up ever since. She was such a beautiful bright little kid. Always asking questions, full of spunk; what his mother called "bright eyed and bushy tailed."

"Carrie, you're a little girl right now. And things may seem much bigger and much more difficult than they are. Even when you grow up, things will be hard to understand, but you will have learned a lot more to help you. Your daddy and mother are strong, and so am I. We're grown and we know enough to protect you, so don't you worry. Not even a little bit."

He hugged her and hoped that he was right as he stood, picked up his gun, and walked toward the office holding her hand. "Everything will be fine. You just have faith in your men folk."

Chug was half asleep on the couch where he planned to spend the night. Turner was talking to some neighbor men who were standing, about to leave, at the front door, and Stella was on the phone. The men left and Earl handed Carrie over to her father. She kissed everybody in the office goodnight, and as Turner carried her up the steps and down the hall toward her room in his great strong arms, she wasn't afraid anymore. At least she didn't think she was.

Chapter IX

She awoke very early the next morning and the next and the next. Days passed all the same, beginning early when the light was unconfirmed. There was a certain calmness about those mornings, on things, when bird calls were shrill staccatos above the deafness of the sunrise and people gazed past curtains and blinds, window shades and faded rags hung against glass and cardboard panes to make sure the light of day had really come.

Carrie peeked through her window at dawn, wondering if Shorty King would bother them on this day. She was very tired, since she was one prone to sleep in. Since the day of the incident, she had been having trouble sleeping; lying wakeful in her bed at night and holding sleep off for as long as possible, while finding herself wide awake at the first sign of the new day. It had been almost a week now.

Earl and Chug had been around the house every day now since the trouble, watching with their guns ready. She was hoping a chance to talk with Earl would present itself. Today was Earl's last time to guard them for the next few days. He was going to work with his brother, Tim, tomorrow, on his diesel truck. Tim hauled produce for Curtis Brewer and on long trips he needed help with the driving and loading. His regular helper was off sick.

Every summer for several years, Earl had alternately helped his father on the farm and worked for Turner. He only drove for Tim once in awhile, but he always seemed to look forward to those trips with Tim, and of course, he made good money.

Earl was well known in the county for being one of the finest students to ever graduate from the Northampton County school system. His aptitude scores were not only the highest recorded among students at the Negro high school, but also exceeded those of whites as well. He had maintained a straight "A" average while earning letters in basketball, football, and track. He also played piano well and soloed on the saxophone in the school band. Upon graduating from college, he had been awarded the Bryce/Shepherd Fellowship, which paid for all of his graduate work. Mr. James Bryce, who lived in another part of Virginia now, across the Bay, but who had grown up in Bridgetown, a few miles north, and whose family was the richest Negro family in the state of Virginia, and his wife, the former Miss Jennifer Shepherd, also from a well-to-do Negro family in Bridgetown, had established the Fellowship in memory of James' parents and in honor of Jennifer's parents who were both still living. Earl Lionel Togan was their first recipient. It was a very generous award, devised to allow the chosen student to be free to study without financial worries. Still, Earl worked for money to help his family.

Carrie had seen some of Earl's law books. He had brought quite a few home with him each summer, and he had explained to her that from here on out, in the midst of working for her father and on his own part-time, he would be spending a lot of his time studying. And next summer he would be working all summer for the law firm where he was an intern during the school year. So this was her last summer to ask Earl if there was any chance that he could wait for her until she was grown enough for them to get married, yet the more she thought about asking him, the more difficult the task became. Time was always a fast moving thing in the summer time. Broaching the subject was beginning to worry her.

She wasn't aware of any more trouble with Shorty up to now. The Sheriff had come by, and she had hidden because she thought he had come to arrest her, but shortly after she hid up in the huge maple tree in the front yard—she had a good view from there—the sheriff drove away. She never did find out what he came for.

Weeks passed. Weeks flew by. The summer moved through June and simmered into July. The calmness in the county was an anxious thing. No sign of action from Shorty or the sheriff or from any of the whites who either warned or threatened or who promised to make things right. Not one word. Not one shoo fly.

Some of the men folk at the Baptist Church held a meeting on the Sunday after school closed. Reverend Brady was concerned about the danger hanging over the Allen family, and he had joined Turner and Dr. Reynolds and the Togans in a secret effort to plan ways for the community to organize. He had suggested four others, and quickly sent word to those men as soon as the last hymn was sung and the benediction given. It was understood that everyone would meet in a half-hour at Jesse Togan's barn.

Those who lived near Turner would keep a vigilant watch on his property. Turner had set up a few more outdoor lights; particularly around the doors and windows at ground level, as well as in the back lot where there were great patches of darkness.

Those men who lived near Shorty would keep an eye on him. One in particular knew his habits and his hangouts. Willie Johnson said, "Shorty always sees Captain Harris at the sto'e on Saturday morning. Never fails. An' if he got anything on his mind, he talks about it right on like I ain't there."

Charley Stuart volunteered, "I sees him at the creek every day from about five-thirty 'til sunset. He come wit' his fishing pole, gits his scow and sets out for jest near the channel marker buoy. Sets right-chere 'til dark, and then we walks home together. I thinks I'm about the onliest coloured man Shorty will even speak to, and he's tole me what a honor he's paying me. Well, I'se gonna honor him and tell you all everything he does that I sees."

Al Gordon added what he knew. "Shorty works for Mr. Oliver Branch in the summer months. That's who I works for. I got dead wood eyes on him while he's there abouts." The word would be passed to brothers all over the county who might hear or see anything pertaining to Turner and the general trouble.

As for Sheriff Luke Haskins, the Negro trusty at the jail could be counted on to know pretty much what he and his two deputies were up to. They talked around trusty ole Uncle Lee like he was a piece of planking in the floor; and he heard and remembered every word. Al Gordon said he would pass the word to Uncle Lee who was always serving time for something or other.

But nothing out of the way occurred, and though the community slowly relaxed, Turner felt the tension becoming a part of his back and something which ached in his head. At least worry over M.T. had ceased. The boy had made a quick and complete recovery. But Turner had expected a stronger reaction from the whites, yet up to now, no pressure had been put on him at all—not economic nor through threats of outright violence or whatever, except for the one shotgun blast. They had even arrested Shorty long enough to have him released immediately on bail, and Turner hadn't expected the sheriff to do that much. Usually, when a Negro man brought charges against a white, the sheriff never shadowed the white person's door. Bail, if it got that far, was arranged without the white man ever leaving his yard. Shorty's bail was set at the unheard of low amount of $25.00.

Arrangements were made through the new organization to meet foreseeable problems with the whites, but the real danger was in the unforeseeable, so that each man in his own way felt helpless.

Expecting trouble and finding unusual courtesy and even expressed concern on the part of certain white citizens made Turner all the more suspicious. Maybe there was a conspiracy to make him think everything was forgotten so that when he relaxed, somebody could pick him off.

Some nights he didn't sleep at all, wondering if he'd used good judgment in even touching Shorty the little bit that he had. He knew the answer to that, but sometimes it seemed a stupid move. He had had the time to think his way out of touching Shorty, yet his anger and his understanding that nothing would be done to punish him if he didn't had dominated his actions. He wasn't sorry for what he had done, but he also didn't want to pay any more dearly for the stand he had taken. M.T. and the entire family had already paid enough.

He discussed this with Earl over and over again as they drove together daily in Turner's car as he conducted business. Everywhere they went, the whites were courteously silent. Earl's point of view was exactly what Turner's was: "There are times when a man has to do what a man has to do. I would have done the same, if not more. But we keep helping them to reinforce their beliefs that a white man's life is worth more."

They were sitting in Turner's white Chevy station wagon in the yard of a family who had just lost their wife and mother to cancer. Even though Turner was running late, he wasn't ready to end the conversation.

"Earl, if you look at it in terms of who has the power, a white life *is* worth more. And that's what we've got to change. The power and the worth. Every life is precious. But whites have the power to come down on us anytime they want. The fact that we haven't had more trouble from them over this school bus mess with Shorty can only be attributed to their using their power to pull strings as they want them pulled. Even the white boy's parents didn't raise any fuss over Carrie hitting him. I know they're up to something."

"Seems to me," Earl said, "they're playing a game. The whites here get at folks through jobs and wages and the way they look through you like you're not there. They put you off guard with their show of respectability and decency, like they'd be the last people in the world to treat you badly while they ignore you at the same time. So when somebody hurts a Negro, you can't prove who's behind it, or if you can, he gets off through the courts.

"I love my folks and the farm and all, but I downright hate this place, the way it is. I hate the way white people slip around the law." Earl hung his head to stretch the muscles in the back of his neck and then moved his head way back as far as he could. "Man, my neck hurts."

Turner chuckled. "Yours, too?"

Earl laughed and went into an exaggerated 'Neeegrooow' mode. "Yeah. This here white man sho' is a pain in the neck, and my rear end ain't feeling too good, neither." The two of them shook their heads and laughed, the release of tension bringing a twinkle to their eyes.

Several days later, the word came. Between Uncle Lee and Willie Johnson, enough pieces had been put together to make a pretty sensible story about why it was that the whites of Northampton County had been so congenial and low key.

Politics was behind it, as Turner figured he should have known. Elections would be coming up in the fall for Sheriff and Mayor and County Attorney and so on. And it seemed that black folk in various parts of the north and south had been raising a whole lot of fuss lately, boycotting here and marching there, and sitting in and such. The whites of the county, considering their close proximity to Washington, D.C. and the eye of what seemed to them a nigger happy federal government (considering the school desegregation goof and all) didn't particularly want any demonstrations or notoriety. Of course, any sheriff or town mayor or whatnot who happened to be in charge when trouble was allowed to demonstrate itself against the white and peaceful community, would be sure to lose any election he dared enter, especially considering that a large portion of the county's Negro people who were eligible to vote were also registered.

What made things worse was the fact that Turner Allen was the biggest (richest, most successful, powerful and pleasant) nigger in the county since the Bryces and Shepherds had moved to the western shore. Messing with him because some po white trash had messed with his little girl and his son just wasn't worth all the trouble. So there it was. Uncle Lee had done his work well.

There was still Shorty King to contend with, so Turner kept a steady eye on things. Even if Luke and the other officials had turned off the heat, it was known through several sources that King had said on at least four occasions, "That rich nigger's gonna turn his back one day, and I'm telling you, I'm just the man to stick a knife between that SOB's ribs—right straight through to the other side!"

The burning heat of mid-summer increased the tension. Carrie played through it all, somewhat detached from her parents' fear. They thought she was childishly unaware of how dangerous things were, but Carrie was numb. She could taste the danger in the looks cast at her by whites when she walked their way. The people behind the counters in the stores didn't act the same, were no longer friendly and smiling, and now, she and her mother never shopped unless one of the neighborhood men was with them.

Since she was confined to the yard most of the time, Carrie played as best she could. She longed to roam the neighborhood, free like the summers before. M.T. couldn't leave the yard to play either, but he had a job in the vault house for the summer and was too busy to play with her. He even had Susie come by to visit him and to watch his face heal. Once he found out that the scars were going away, he was proud of every sign of the fight left to linger before Susie's eyes. Beanie's mother wouldn't let her visit Carrie.

So Carrie played with dolls and made mud pies and sang to herself. She mostly sat among the weeds and trees of Mrs. Lukus's lot and stared at the sky, thinking how much she wanted to see Beanie or to talk to Earl.

A couple of times she sneaked away for short runs in the woods, or back to the housing settlement where Beanie lived. Thus far, her parents were ignorant of her trips, and she always remained beyond the sight of any grownups who might squeal on her. Beanie, of course, was sworn to secrecy.

Then there were Earl's visits, like today, sitting under a tree with her, talking up a breeze. She wished he could come every day. She wanted so much to ask him to wait for her. It wouldn't take her very many years to grow up, but she was still afraid.

"Earl, what should I be when I grow up?"

"You never will."

"Huh?"

"Grow up."

"Yes I will. Don't play. What should I be?"

"No. Your body will grow. You'll cover more ground, but like me and a few others, you'll always be a child at heart in your head."

"Earl, you kid all the time. Grown ups are grown up, aren't they? They're smarter and all?"

"Yes and no. Some grown ups just get older. But you my dear will mature. I can see that clearly. You'll be young all of your life because your attitudes are so full of energy and a love of life. You'll grow wise. Too many adults merely accumulate reasons to hesitate and to be afraid. Some are downright senile at middle age."

"That's when you're eighty, isn't it?"

Earl laughed. "No baby. That's the state of most adult minds." He chuckled to himself.

"You're playing word games again."

"Yes, I am, but everybody plays word games at one time or another. Quite often, people don't say what they mean. There's so much fear in people. But not in me, today. At least for today I'm not afraid, so listen to me." He paused and brought his knees up near his chest, putting his arms around them.

"Not what should you be, but who. Not how, but why. Not where, but when. To be grown up is to understand that one is responsible for everything, everyone, Carrie, even when you can't take responsibility." He looked straight at her, his eyes bright and intent.

111

"To be grown up is to accept through the will, to embrace, to hold willingly, the payment, taking responsibility within an unlimited account, and to face making all payments due on or before time. Such a thing is impossible for most black people most of the time in this country under the present system. That's because practices are corrupt despite the law and our ideals. Maybe for you there'll be the right mix of time and history and place for you to be truly grown in your adult life."

"What?"

"Grown up should be a kind of perfection combining a youthful heart and a fierce striving, but people still haven't learned how to treat one another fairly without making exceptions for race and state of wealth and other areas of prejudice. It takes real sacrifice to learn how, and most people aren't willing. Perfection demands sacrifice. White Americans, for the most part, merely demand that people of colour sacrifice for them; that we be perfect citizens perfectly denied."

Carrie thought it through for a minute. It was hard to fit his words together. "So nobody can be grown up? Is that it?"

"I didn't say that, did I?" He laughed.

"I don't know." Carrie laughed, too.

"Well, if I did, I didn't mean to. I think the black people of the U.S. have the best chance of growing up, if they'll only let go of ole massa. We've been 'puttin' on ole massa' for some time now, though he's killed the hell out of us along the way. We need to let him go completely. That's what King and Rosa Parks started to do down in Montgomery. We've been sacrificing left and right, but we've got to learn all over this country to channel all of that glorious righteousness so we can teach massa how to grow up, too."

"So who should I be when I grow up?" Not understanding much of what Earl meant, Carrie thought she would get back to the question she started with.

"Thatta girl. Who? Well, let's see." Earl frowned and popped his mouth from the side of his cheek with his finger. "Can you do that? Let me see. Do it." He popped his mouth again. Carrie tried, failed and fell over on her side, giggling. She always giggled at least a little halfway through a conversation with Earl.

He reached over and sat her back up again. "Be a student of Carrie Marie Allen, and as you check her out, respect her and love her and let her look around at things with her mind and eyes open to what she sees so her heart can know what it wants. Go places. Make sure she goes places. Make her see the world; Carry Carrie everywhere, and let her find out what's good and lovely in the world, who her friends are, who her enemies are, and then help her to find a way to uphold what brings her life and to defeat what promises death.

"Take Carrie wherever there's knowledge, and when she has some idea of who she is, make sure she meets a fine black man and let her fall in love. Let her at least consider marriage. And if she and her husband have more love to give, let her give the world beautiful black babies who, with her help and her strong husband's help, will grow into adults as she may never quite be."

"Huh?"

Earl laughed and pulled at the end of one of her braids.

"Earl." She had heard the words marriage and husband. Now was the time. Now or maybe never.

"Will you be my husband? Will you marry me?" Her breath suddenly hung in the air, escaped from her lungs forever. Her young face, full of light and hope, hung poised and waiting, suspended before the dark brown of the tree's bark and the shady green of low-hanging maple limbs and plush grass. Earl was deeply touched, and for a moment, couldn't speak. He knew she meant it as best as a ten year old girl could; and this one was exceptional in her sensitivity to him and to the world around her. This he knew and cherished.

"Carrie . . . Sweetheart, I'm . . . I'm not good enough for you . . ."

"Oh, yes you are. You're . . ."

"No. Listen. I'm past your time. You'll need a young man of your age, your time. See, I'm a forerunner of the man who'll be right to marry you. The next ten to twenty years ahead of you will make you a different kind of special adult from me, and you'll need a young man who has been through the fire with you."

"What fire?" Carrie looked down, crestfallen and suddenly very sad. Earl lifted her face back toward him with the tip of his finger delicately under her chin.

113

"The fire between you and the kind of freedom for black people that Martin Luther King and so many like me dream of. It'll be you who gets through the burning and the fear to reap what we're sowing. You'll have opportunities to fly like none we've ever known, and you'll need a young man who has helped lead the way beside you.

"Most white people are going to change and won't remember themselves as now and you two will be ready to enjoy a life as equals in every respect that I can only dream about. All of us have to make things better for everybody, Rabbit, or what will come will be worse than what we have now. It seems to me that if black people aren't able to reap the American Dream, some of us will go mad. If the white supremacists win, and the strong young ones among us go mad, America will become a most dangerous place and the Dream will be doomed. You'll need a strong young man to make the changes happen with you and to keep the dream alive.

"I'll always love you. I'll always dream the best dreams for you. I'll always be your friend, Rabbit. That's the best I can do. I was born too early to do any more."

Carrie sighed. Maybe one day he would change his mind. She could hope for that. "You promise to always be my friend."

"Oh, yes. Always." He laughed and got to his feet, pulling her up briskly from the grass.

"Gotta run, little sugar, and gather in some bread. Be back to see you soon." And he was gone. He would only be able to come once in a while to talk to her, but time with him was golden. It seemed so strange to her how things could change so when one special person was there or when he was suddenly gone. It was so strange. The summer would have been a horror, a living massacre of all joy, if Earl Lionel Togan hadn't found the time to come see her when he came.

She had another visitor as well. He came unseen, unannounced, unnoticed for some reason. Perhaps because he watched the watchers and knew when their eyes weren't on him. Even with his liquor drinking.

Shorty often knew when Earl visited Carrie. He often knew when Turner was at home and when he was not. He knew that Carrie had visited Beanie one afternoon, and in watching, he waited for that next time when she would be alone and vulnerable.

Luke and all the others were crazy. Out of their minds telling him to back off. Nobody, especially a nigger, had the right to humiliate him the way Turner Allen had. No man could lay hands on him and get away with it, and with nigger Allen, the payment would be taken with pleasure from his little girl. Yes, Lord.

Chapter X

When he was a boy
He dreamed he was a truck
Without a driver,
When he was a boy.
Blasting down that road
On eighteen wheels,
Gears in his belly
And exhaust pipes for ears.
When he was a boy
He dreamed he was a truck
Without a driver.

The August heat came in deadly earnest. It was a sweltering heat full of humidity and a clinging salty residue from the Atlantic and the Chesapeake. Yet there was no hint of the coming of rain. The earth was dry, the days clear and muggy. It seemed to Earl that much more than a week had passed since that last day in July when he had sat with Carrie and listened to her proposal of marriage. July had been cool, compared to the fierce and unrelenting furnace brought by the first week of August.

With help from his parents and his new wife's savings, Earl's brother, Tim, had finally saved enough money for the down payment on a truck, and Earl was mighty proud of him. Coming up with that kind of money had taken a lot of hard work and planning. It had taken several years of working out of doors night and day in heat like this and in freezing cold.

The truck was a Mack diesel, all grunt, rumble and power. Tim called her Sweet Georgia Brown because of her disposition. Not only was she the prettiest, finest tractor-trailer rig in all of creation, but Tim said she held the road the way his woman was supposed to hold onto him; strong and never tiring 'til he turned her off and set her down.

The big Mack cab was a metallic blue,
And the trailer was a shiny silver.
A long square pipe of brass tinged hue,
Coughed and spat and blew black smoke,

Daring the white clouds to move over.

Earl had accompanied Tim on two trips to New York and one to Chicago thus far this summer, hauling crated tomatoes. But Tim, of course, had been on the road practically every day since early June. Curtis Brewer usually sent his drivers out day in and day out, with just enough time to catch absolutely necessary sleep, for the entire summer without giving them a breather, but the primary conveyor belt at his grader had given out and everybody had gotten a day to rest.

Tim and Earl arrived at Tim's house about four a.m. on Wednesday, dead beat and ready to snooze awhile. Word had been left for Tim that repairs on the conveyor weren't expected to be complete for at least another day, so both he and Earl went to sleep with the serious intent of staying in that state for quite awhile. Turner Allen had also told Earl before he left to take a couple of days rest because things were so quiet, so Earl had fallen into bed with a feeling of peace and freedom for the first time all summer.

Earl only occasionally spent the night at Tim's instead of with Jesse and Eliza, particularly if it was late at night when he arrived. His father slept light-feathered, he called it, and always woke up and broke his rest when Earl's foot touched the porch. There was no need of putting him through those kinds of changes since Tim had a place now, nearby.

Tim had fixed up an old piece of a house so that it was pretty comfortable. He'd only been married a couple of weeks, so Earl was careful to tiptoe around. Alice was mighty particular about being invaded by her brother-in-law before the honeymoon had even started. They couldn't afford a trip anywhere, so they were staying close to home whenever Tim wasn't on the road. Most folk didn't even know they were living way back in the woods because Alice thought they'd be more private that way, and she had insisted that Tim not tell any of his friends at work. She had his old phone number transferred secretly to the new house to leave messages about work. Lord bless that woman, she had made such a secret of their place of residence that Earl swore she didn't even know she lived back there herself. Yet and still, Earl tried not to be noticeable on the few occasions when he had found it necessary to spend the night.

He climbed out of bed around noon, a very late hour for him to sleep no matter how late he had gotten to bed. His body was stiff, achy, and sluggish from all of the riding and loading and toting. He dressed in blue jeans, a paint stained shirt, and a pair of new black and white sneakers. He had been forced to throw away his favorite pair, so old and full of holes that Alice said, "They belongs rightly in Mr. Turner Allen's morgue, except he couldn't get close enough to the funk to bury 'em." Alice definitely had a way with words.

The outhouse needed painting and it had long ago been tipped a little sideways, but Earl took a leak anyhow, figuring no concerned part of him was that particular.

Next, he walked outside brushing his teeth with a glass of water in his hand since he didn't like the idea of brushing his teeth at the kitchen sink. His lathery spit struck a passing chicken as he paused from brushing. He said, by way of consolation, "Don't pay to get up some days, do it bird?" and chuckling, washed out his mouth and headed for the ice box. It was literally an ice box, as old as the hills.

The last verse of his poem about Tim and Sweet Georgia Brown coasted through his mind.

When he was a boy,
A truck was just a toy.
Now he was grown.
He had a Mack truck of his own.
Funny now how that truck
Didn't really matter.
It was work, fit to bust;
Work right straight hard and tough
And the earning of the truck
That made the clatter.

He hadn't quite figured out the rest. That last verse bothered him. The whole thing wouldn't have started a halfway decent fire. He'd have to rewrite it and there wasn't a thing in the refrigerator that he knew how to cook. He'd have to go out to Pat's Place.

Earl returned to his room, opened a small tote bag and rummaged through the contents. Yeah. There it was, the gift for Carrie. It was gaily wrapped with a tiny little red and white bow. He placed it into a small, paper gift shop bag and bounded down the stairs. Carrie had been so lonely all summer, it was high time he gave her something special to cheer her little bones.

It was hot outside, especially when the tree cover around his path grew thin. The ground was as hot as a stove lid just right for a pan of chicken to fry and greens to boil, with heat rising, making the distance shimmer. There was a faint breeze, as hot as the ground but refreshing just the same, simply because it was there.

One of the mirrors on the diesel cab caught a flicker of sunlight as Earl walked past. They had disconnected Sweet Georgia's trailer early this morning on their way home and had left it parked at the end of one of the loading platforms at Brewer's grader. As soon as the belt was repaired, it would be loaded and Tim would reconnect and begin another trip north or west. Earl was looking forward to finishing school so he could help Tim to make the payments. Keeping them up was going to be a strain, and Earl envisioned his earning large fees as a lawyer. Yes, Lord.

He cut through the woods. It was a two-mile walk to the asphalt road that ran past his father's farm.

Earl's thoughts moved quickly from one thing to another, like a scanner looking for something substantial. It occurred to him that Turner Allen was talking some mighty interesting stuff these days. All of the trouble had triggered something profound in the man. Whenever Earl was with him now and they were alone to talk, Turner worked on developing his theories aloud. Earl was honored at Turner's trust, but more than that, he was excited about the man's ideas as they applied to Northampton County.

Turner had already arranged for two black lawyer friends of his, one from Norfolk and one from Philadelphia, to come down in about two weeks to do a survey. They were specialists in economics and planned to analyze the nature of black folks' spending power on the Shore. Turner said he already knew that the major power was in retail buying, that was obvious, but he didn't know how much black folks were spending and where their trade was the heaviest. If boycotting was to be effective, it had to be targeted properly.

Earl broke his trend of thought for a moment. When he had first arrived and used the word "black" out loud to describe Negroes, like people were doing in New York City, Turner had been noticeably uncomfortable, but now Turner had begun to use that term himself, at least occasionally. Earl had explained that the term was obviously less accurate than African or Afro American, but the idea was to take the stigma and the association of something negative and ugly from the word black, since whites had been using the word against black people for so long. It was exciting to see the changes coming. It really turned him on.

Turner was also talking about building several key businesses, which could allow black people to channel their spending back into the community. Of course, financing would be the biggest problem. Perhaps a co-op would work. Using existing organizations like the Church, the Masons, the Tent Ladies and such would allow for a quicker start. It was a matter of helping those organizations to change or to shift their emphasis enough to encompass economic self-determination.

"Then there's Bryce Canning," he had said with a gleam in his eye. "The Bryce's have a multi-million dollar operation up at Bridgetown. Charles Shepherd, who manages the factory for James Bryce, is semi-retired now and traveling abroad. James is also away on travel, but I've left word for both of them to call me. I think they will be most helpful on the financial end. . . . We need to do all of this very quietly."

"What about Abrams," Earl asked, "and Sister Clark at the Baptist Church who blocked the union effort two years ago by snitching to the whites?"

"That can be handled. We can find a way. I haven't figured it all out yet." They had been talking on this particular day while facing each other on two lawn chairs on Turner's patio. Turner reached over and tapped Earl's knee, as he might have a man his own age. It was a small gesture and yet it meant a lot to Earl to be accepted into Turner's confidence as though he was in every way, a peer.

"Listen," Turner had said, leaning forward. "There'll be a meeting next Tuesday. About seven of us. It'll take months to get things thought through, but I'd welcome your input. Maybe after you get back to New York, you can send us books and other resource materials we might need."

"Sure, Mr. Allen. I'd be honored."

"You still calling me that?"

Earl started to explain.

"No. I understand and I appreciate the edification. We need more of that, but please, call me Turner."

"Ok, Turner." Earl smiled. "I'll be sure to explain real quick when I call you Turner in front of my father." They both chuckled.

Yes, it was an honor and a privilege to be privy to Turner Allen's thoughts and to his respect. Earl was determined not to miss that meeting and to help the county of Northampton in the State of Virginia to build a better age. It was a bold thing Turner was planning. This kind of thing was still mostly unheard of, and it was a pity that this was so. It was a pity.

Earl's thoughts came back to his surroundings as he wiped his shirt tail across his sweaty face. The corn in his father's field was almost shoulder high. He crossed the asphalt road and looked straight down Jesse's sand road up to the barn. That road was five hundred yards long, straight and true—his father's masterpiece. He didn't see any activity up near the barn; the doors were closed. His father was probably up at the house having lunch.

Earl decided he would stop on the way back. Right now, his mother would be busy washing clothes and ironing. She would gladly stop what she was doing to cook his breakfast, but he didn't want to bother her.

He had written a song about her the summer before. "Sing, Eliza, Sing. Love young, Eliza, love. Be Eliza, whatever you can be. So you can sing, Eliza, sing." The tune he had chosen possessed the disquieting sweetness of a Negro spiritual. He often found himself humming it, as now, and each time his rich tenor voice created the sounds, he thought of one day in particular when the sight of his mother had inspired the song.

He saw her standing in the yard one day; saw something about her he hadn't seen before. It had taken him so many years of living to recognize that look in her eyes, in the angle of her shoulders and back. She let her feelings slip from behind her mind occasionally when she thought no one was watching; a longing wishful look. Earl was certain she had never let it emerge in his father's presence.

She was kneeling in her grassless, chicken-doo splattered yard among her chicken scratched flowers. He almost spoke to her, but the look of her stopped him, the way she was stooping in the dirt like sitting on the edge of an unsatisfactory wedding bed, all hunched over and sorrowful and empty.

At first he thought she was sick. Her hands were much darker than her face and seasons of work had left them parched dry from years of washing white folks' clothes outdoors in the wintertime.

She pulled a drooping petunia from the ground by its roots and curled the petals between her fingers. From one patch of beaten flowers to the next, up and down the front of the porch, not a leaf had been spared.

"I cain't seem to grow nothin' pretty nohow. Everytime I plants something, them chickens come along. Put a basket around them beds and they scratches jest the same. Chickens like white folks. Always digging and scratching 'til the roots is gone . . . Well, I'm gonna get Jesse to fix up that chicken house and the wire in the yard these next few days, or by God he's gonna sleep alone. I'm tired of him saying he's gonna fix things with them chickens and then off to the track to shoe horses." She took a deep breath and threw the wilted flower angrily at a chicken whose curiosity had brought it too close, and when it jumped high, squawking and fluttering stupidly in mid-air, Eliza shook her head and laughed half-heartedly.

She leaned her weight against the steps to help herself to her feet. Forty-five years old, and at that moment, she looked closer to seventy. Earl felt a pang of anguish. He saw her face clearly as she shaded her eyes and looked across the field toward the barn where the faint, but metallically sharp and persistent pounding of Jesse's hammer upon anvil and shoe gave evidence of his presence there. Earl turned away quickly and moved out of her line of sight so she wouldn't know he had seen and heard her outpouring of grief. He was almost past the washstand, having passed behind the detached garage, when he turned to look again, and Lordy, there she was, as fast as that, walking tall with a bucket of water in one hand and a tablespoon in the other. She was going to plant every flower again and put up a stronger barrier against the chickens. He watched as she rolled out a thickly coiled roll of new chicken wire from the small storage room beside the house. He had no doubt that Jesse would soon be busy making repairs, and she looked at least ten years younger to him, then. He was so pleased with her spirit that he made himself late for his own job by running to help her.

A crow swooped down low over Earl's head toward the corn, flew close over the tassel tops, climbed high and cawed three notes as clear as the shine on its wings. Then it floated toward the woods, flipped to its side and disappeared into the thick cover of a tree.

The sky was a pale blue with no clouds showing, bordered on all sides by the tops of tall evergreen trees. Birds were everywhere, noisy and busy. The ditch was full of green weeds and little clumps of purple vetch. Honeybees were busy scooting and doing. Every living thing was taking care of business. Earl was sorry he had missed the morning. It must have been a good one to leave the afternoon so fine.

He thought of Carrie again, and her proposal. What a sweet, innocent little girl. He had come to love her more than he could express.

He wet his lips, now a bit dry from the heat. It was another mile to the main highway, and then another mile to Pat's Place. He probably should have taken the truck, but the walking was good for his legs and he'd been riding around with Turner and Tim so much this summer that he had put on a few pounds. He would be more than ready to eat, and his conscience would be good and clear after a vigorous walk.

He wiped at the sweat on his face and down his neck. His armpits were soaked already. He hoped his deodorant from the day before would hold. Should have taken a shower before confronting the world. Naw. He hadn't felt like it. The world would have to keep its nose away or take him in as he was. He'd feel like cleaning up when he got back. He gave each armpit a sniff and was relieved that he still smelled just like the deodorant.

His mother had installed a bathtub. Lord, she'd wanted an indoor toilet all of her life, and Jesse finally told her they had the money. Tim only had a shower. It was odd to look at, but it worked. Since it was on the end of his back porch, it wouldn't be worth much in cold weather, but with a little preparation it was just right in the summer's heat. Right now, all of his money was going to Sweet Georgia Brown.

Smart dude, that Tim. He was so thrilled over being married to Alice; he was breaking his behind trying to please her. Earl had to admit she was a fox. Stacked up some stuff, and sweet. Lord bless her disposition. Of course, Alice wasn't like Peggy. Now Peggy was a different kinda sweet. Long, tall, fine woman. Full of fire and hard to keep straight. She had such a mind of her own it was frightening sometimes.

Peggy. There she was in his head again. He couldn't really explain Peggy being on his mind, and for some reason, he required an explanation. He was always fighting her. Always trying not to get serious about her. It wasn't that she was beating him over the head for attention. She hadn't ever said anything about marriage or anything permanent. Her eyes always got to him though. Those eyes could read more than words on paper. They were soft, silent, intent, fiery. Her face would break into a smile and lay it on him and he'd end up feeling she knew something about his feelings which he hadn't yet realized, but would one day. That kinda woman was damn dangerous. She was wonderful. Earl burst into a smile.

He shifted Carrie's gift package from one arm to the other, and with it he changed his thoughts. He hoped Carrie would like the gift. It was the beginning of her extracurricular education on black folk. She might have trouble reading it alone, but he would help, and he was sure her parents would. It was almost impossible to find children's books about black people. The main thing was to get her started so she would know that there were black writers who had written significantly about her people and her country and the world.

Earl passed three houses rented by black families. For the most part they were run down with a dozen and a half young children running around among the chickens and ducks, playing. Earl waved at Mrs. Shortnin' Bread, an old lady known for her baking skills. She waved and spoke from her porch. "How do, Earl? Good to see you home."

"Yes, 'um. I've been home since early June."

"My lans. Do tell. Funny I h'ain't seen you befo' now."

"Yes, 'um." Sweet old lady. Kept half the kids in the neighborhood alive with her sweet breads. She had filled his stomach many a time. She waved again and watched Earl as he paused close to

125

a two-year-old boy seated in a ton of dusty powder in the middle of the rude series of ruts which served as her driveway. Heavy yellow blobs of mucus bubbled from the boy's nostrils. His grimy little skinny hands were grey with dust and ashen. He was busy driving a homemade car in what was left of a dry mud hole and what would surely be a swamp if it rained the least bit.

"Hey, son," Earl said.

The boy, Shelton, looked up blankly; said "hey," and sat his car down in the dust. Earl placed Carrie's package carefully on a patch of grass, knelt beside the boy, tore away a piece of his own shirttail and held it to the boy's nose.

"Let's clear some of that cold away. Blow, son. Give it a steady honk."

Shelton's chest was heavily congested. He did his best to clear his nose, but more mucus replaced the gross amount that he discharged. The child's belly was distended and his limbs were small, skin over bone.

"Bet you haven't eaten right in days, huh, boy?" Shelton lifted the car and said, "hey, hey, hey" as he jiggled it in the air above his head.

"Come on." Earl lifted him and carried him onto Mrs. Shortnin's porch, where he placed him in her lap.

"He needs some care, m'am. I'll leave him with you." Earl tossed the rag in his hand into a trash can.

She shook her head. "What these here chilluns needs to live ain't noways comin' from me, Earl. I doesn't have noways enough these days."

"Yes, 'um. I know you'll do what you can." She nodded. "His baby suster died a month ago come Friday; four months old, she was. I 'spect he'll follow soon. His momma died birthin' and his Daddy stay drunk all the live long day. He ain't no account. I went to the Welfare peoples las' week and they say they's gonna send somebody outchere to look about 'im. But I 'spect it's Shelton and me or he gonna waste away to nothin'. If them folks doesn't give me a check soon to he'p out, we'se both gonna starve."

Earl felt a sudden need to get away. His feelings were getting to be too tender. Tears of helplessness and rage were already on the brink of wetting his face. He'd seen this same thing enough times to be hard about it by now. He couldn't stand to go on much further feeling every lick of what he saw. It got so a person had to feel shallow to protect himself from grieving all the time. Black folks had to always feel that way since most of the conditions seemed too overwhelming to change. The more aware and helpless, the more shallow. Built-in personality stunter of oppression; see it and hear it but never feel it or your guts will turn to living fire and you'll never have even a second's peace.

He wiped at his eyes and was back on the road again, walking fast, and when he finally reached Pat's, he wasn't quite hungry. Pat fixed him a fine spread: eggs, sausage, biscuits, and fried apples. Earl sat at the counter staring and dabbing with his fork.

"Pat."

"Yeah." Pat moved toward him from the grill. He was an extremely tall man, very fat with a round expressionless face. He almost never smiled.

"Pick out some groceries for me, if you don't mind. You know. Grits, bacon, eggs, bread, milk, flour. Make it ten dollars worth. And some strawberry jam."

Earl immediately concentrated on his food. Just saying those words had perked up his appetite. He could do with just a couple of bucks until pay day.

"Oh, hey, I've got a run to make down to the Allen's. You mind having that stuff for me when I get back? No rush."

"No problem." Pat moved slowly, as was his manner, toward the storage shelves with a large paper sack.

"You hand toting these here?"

"Yeah."

"Where you want 'em to go?"

"Mrs. Shortenin' Bread's . . . Mrs. Williams's house just short of Dad's farm."

"Oh, well, that's a piece a walkin' with all these groceries. You come on back here and Jimmy'll take you by there."

"Hey, that's good of you, Pat. Thanks. I'll be back this way in an hour or so."

"Fine. You takes your time."

Pat returned to his stove, removed a lid from a steaming pot and stirred its contents. The bell on the door jingled and both men turned to see who was coming in. As soon as Earl saw her, he turned his attention back fully to eating, suddenly very interested in his food. Pat flashed his eyes at the ceiling and pressed a split hot dog against the grill with a spatula. The girl walked past Earl and sat next to him on one of the stools.

"How about a Coke, Pat?"

Showing a dread which any black person would have spied immediately, Pat turned slowly toward the young woman, wiping his face with the back of his hand, his hand immediately wiping nervously against his soiled white apron.

"Miss Brewer," he said. "I don't mind selling you no Coke, but you knows white people ain't supposed to sit down to eat here. It's against ...."

"Now, Pat," the girl said. "I can sit wheresoever I please. Just get the Coke, huh."

"But Miss Brewer, you knows ..."

The girl brought her hands together on the counter and rotated her thumbs around each other impatiently. Pat glanced at Earl with irritation and shrugged helplessly. "Yes, 'um. All right. But please don't drink it in here. Your daddy been afta me about this...."

"Ah, my daddy won't know. Unless you run and tell him. Just get the Coke."

Pat moved to the cooler, took out a bottle, and placed it unopened on the counter before her. Earl took a few more mouthfuls of sausage and apples and then dug into his pockets for some change.

"What's the bill, Pat?"

"Huh. Coming man. Coming." Pat was flustered. Curtis Brewer had given him a hard time, had downright chewed him out with curses and threats, the last time Lynn had come in and sat down—as if it was Pat's fault that the girl caused trouble.

Nor had Earl managed to escape encounters with her since his return home. She was dangerously flirtatious. Forever up in the face of some black man, causing all kinds of sweat. And since Tim worked for her father, a man known to be nasty about anybody, white or black, looking even sideways at his "little girl," things were all the more ticklish. He sure didn't want to say something to her that would lose

Tim his job. Sweet Georgia Brown would be long gone if that happened, and that truck had quickly become Tim's soul.

It seemed like Pat was taking all year to tell him what he owed. Earl wanted to get away now. He'd make a quick stop by the Allens and give the gift to Carrie, and then he'd return for the groceries. The more he thought of it, the more he realized that Mrs. Shortnin' needed him to hurry. He felt sorry for Lynn and was afraid of her at the same time. She was a wildly loose cannon. Curtis Brewer was a lousy father and Earl had seen the evidence of this first hand; when they were younger, Earl and Lynn had been friends. That was long before puberty set it. It appalled him how she had changed, but Earl knew from gossip that she had had at least one abortion and was considered a slut by whites. She had been such a fine little girl, excited about her life and wanting to be a hair designer like she saw in a popular magazine. By the time they were ten, her father had put an end to their being friends and Earl's own parents had warned him to be very careful not to continue the friendship in any way. He looked at her now and wished things had been different.

Lynn used the counter to pop the top off of the Coke. Pat, who had been watching, threw his hands up and turned back to the grill. He worked so hard to keep the counter from being scarred up by patrons. Lynn leaned her head back, her lovely blonde hair cascading long in the air behind her. As she wiped her mouth and sat up straight, her hair fell luxuriously across her shoulders.

"How you, Earl?" Lynn leaned sideways on her elbow toward Earl, her palm under her chin and a big smile on her face. She was pretty—beautiful actually, but Earl had no interest in recognizing it. He struggled to ignore her and slapped three quarters down on the counter.

"Hey, Pat. Seventy-five cents should do it, and here's a ten spot for the groceries. I'll see you when I get back."

"Yeah, man. Tha's Ok." Pat put the hot dog into a bun, reached for a jar of mustard, fumbling nervously, took a bite, and chewed like mad.

"You running away from me, Earl, boy?" Lynn continued to lean and to look directly at Earl. She had a fairly nice body. Her blouse was low cut and showing cleavage from the way she was leaning. Earl was standing now. He looked back into her face.

"No, Lynn. No need to run from you."

"No need. Oh, yes there is, because I'm a white woman and you're a nigger and you're flirting with me." She sat back up straight, a look of anticipation on her smiling face. Pat turned around, startled, and then looked off through the front window, praying silently for a good ending to what he knew could be deadly serious and mean beyond any reckoning.

Any number of responses went through Earl's mind. He almost called her Lynnette, a name she treasured when they were kids, but he didn't want to prolong the agony, and the training of a lifetime was hard to break. He knew she wouldn't let them be friends again. He had tried the summer before. She looked like she could cause trouble all the way to hell and back. The barest trace of a smile came across Earl's face, and as he looked at Lynn, he said what he really wanted to say, all things considered. "You have yourself a nice day, Lynnette. See you, Pat."

Lynn held back her surprise. His response seemed paradoxical—a kind of friendly disdain. She read Earl's remarks as mocking beneath pretended warmth, and she detested anyone laughing at her. Surely no nigger had the right. They might have a few friends in the Supreme Court, but it seemed to her that niggers were carrying the whole thing too far.

"You run real good, black boy," she said, forcing a laugh. "You got a whole lot of muscle to be so short on balls."

Earl was almost at the door, and a look of relief had just begun to show on Pat's face. Earl turned, his eyes narrowing, then growing soft. "Look, why don't we call a truce. I'm the same guy who used to race you across the grass down at King's Creek. The same one who liked to go fishing and crabbing with you all summer long. There's no fight between us." He eased through the door behind him, never looking back. She was Pat's problem now. Let him handle her from behind the counter. Still, he felt a twinge of regret. They should have been life-long friends. He wished he could get through to her. Her life was obviously hurting her to death.

130

Earl admitted as he walked down the side of the highway that he didn't have what it took to bridge the gap between them. Reflex sure was a strong thing. All of his life he'd been trained to stay away from white girls, to stay away from white people, in general, for that matter. But their women were the ones. With all the power, all the guns and the meanness, it was just plain suicide to spend time even thinking about a white girl in any way, no matter how innocent the thoughts. It was the funniest thing, but the white man's myths about his women reminded Earl of "...me thinks thou dust protest too much...." He'd dated a few fine young white women, here and there in New York, beautiful girls, some middle class and some from rich families. He had dated them at first because they were forbidden and eager; but then he had discovered them as people and he gained a real sense of their being human beings in his arms, in bed loving one another. There had been lust and fun, but since they hadn't been in love, there had also been an emptiness, which gave him a chill when he thought of it. He had ultimately felt that way with all of the young women with whom he had been intimate since he was sixteen, whatever their race, until Peggy. He was so concerned with his dilemma over Lynn that his realization about Peggy's uniqueness didn't register. All he could think of was what a shame it was that he didn't know how to restore his friendship with Lynn. It was such a waste.

Earl sighed, lowered his head and walked on down the road, all of the energy gone from his stride.

Chapter XI

Lynn Brewer stood at the door of Pat's Place, watching Earl's receding figure. My, he sure was a fine hunk of brown. She'd have to go easier on him the next time. A little honey instead of salt. She smiled and then frowned. Earl was rather likable. She really liked him. He wasn't like most niggers. He was in college and all. And she was fond of those days years ago when they had truly been friends. For a moment she let herself remember what good friends they had been. Earl's words had gotten to her despite her determination to keep black people always lower in her estimation than herself. Every summer for years they had raced and played tag and spent hours in a little skiff looking for crabs or wetting their fishing lines.

But like everybody else, like her father and mother and even her brother, Chuck, people didn't respond to her the way she wanted. They were always going the other way. Earl couldn't be a friend, no matter how hard he tried. His being a nigger made friendship impossible and she hated him for that. He was the one person she could remember in her whole life who truly had been her friend—who truly had seemed to understand her. Why couldn't he have been white? Why did he have to be a nigger? She was better than he would ever be and she had to keep it that way or else there was no bottom to hit that wasn't too deep.

And then there was her father. Curtis had been worse since he started making all that money with the trucking and the grader. He never should have won that money at the race track. Now he was a big businessman, all full of himself. But he was still ignorant and mean and had no time for his only daughter. He wasn't much of a father, but somehow, the money was supposed to make it better. It hadn't. He was worse, now. Everybody was worse off because he didn't even have the time to curse her or her mother out of his way these days.

So why shouldn't she tease around with the coloured? They didn't matter anyway. Of all the people in the world, they had no right to do anything but tolerate her. That Earl. Thinking himself something special for going to college. She could see it in the way he walked; the way he talked like white people instead of dumb bad English like most niggers. He was just another nigger, really. She was going to trade school next year, anyway. That would make her able to hold down a job, which was something the average college student wasn't prepared to do.

Earl shouldn't have run off like that. He was a highfalooting uppity nigger. Shit. Trying to act superior to her, condescending as he was. Damn his black sassy nerve.

Lynn turned away and slowly walked back to the counter. She put the half drunk bottle of Coke down and left without paying. Then she walked slowly back toward her house, struggling as she went against crying. Everything was so boring and useless. She had never had anything nice until the money came out of nowhere, and now she still couldn't get her hands on enough to leave the shitty Eastern Shore and go where people did things differently. Curtis wouldn't even buy a new dress for her mother because it cost more than forty dollars and he said that was indecent. He spent his money on liquor and guns and stud poker and fixing a game room in the pretty basement he'd built. At least he'd had the kitchen redone for her momma. But that was only because he liked to show it off and he liked to eat. Hell! Her momma looked more down in the mouth than the po white trash down at Oyster. Hell! Plus his basement was a joke anyhow. Because of the ground water level, it was above ground, mostly; it was not really a basement.

Pat watched Lynn go and hung over his counter for a full five minutes, trying to recover. The Coke wasn't even a sacrifice. He would have given a whole case to see that she never returned. He would have given more than a gross.

Two tall silver maples spread their shade beneath the breeze which passed across the Allen's front lawn. And under the lowest limbs sat two white wrought-iron chairs. Earl walked into the yard and sat down, the gift across his knees. His twenty-three years seemed older to him now and leaden with the terrible weight of inadequacy. He sat questioning his own judgment, his own common sense, his own courage. It had left a sinking feeling in the pit of his stomach.

It was strange how weirdly vulnerable he felt to the Lynn Brewers of the world. They came like yellow jackets and stung strong places into a bewildering numbness. He'd never really dealt with the threat of lost white women. He would have to think through what he knew of Lynn, now, and find out just what he could do in the future should he find himself facing Lynn again. There were facts of life to be faced, but there was also his dignity and hers. Perhaps such a situation could be handled, if he trained himself well enough, so that he came out feeling less a failure. He believed that every person mattered and that there would be no ultimate success until the vast majority of humans treated one another with respect. Even Christ hadn't managed to get that to happen yet. Who was he to think he could figure out such an enigma?

Peggy would be preaching to him now if she were here, reminding him that he didn't have to react simply because Lynn Brewer demanded it. It was a funny thing about Peggy. He wasn't in love with her, but she sure was on his mind.

They had met early one February during his first year at Columbia. She was the bright student in a Spanish Lit class. Tall and willowy girl, a dark golden brown with almost black eyes. She had turned him on from the moment he first saw her, but he didn't seem to have much of an impact on her. Instead, she introduced him to Garvey and DuBois, Pushkin, David Walker, George Moses Horton and other writers and philosophers out of Black history. She took him to the Baron, in Harlem, and a few quiet places in the Village where the brothers blew love notes on horns and wrapped their fingers over bass strings and clarinet keys and wailed. Peggy. Gone to Detroit for the summer. Vital woman, almost as tall as he.

She fit fine in his arms. He owed her a letter now. Maybe he was in love with her. Hey! . . . Hey, maybe he was.

Earl sat forward on the chair and smiled to himself. "Yeah. Peggy. I'll be damned. What am I fighting you for?"

Great God, his heart was all of a sudden racing. What was wrong with him? Peggy. It was such a thing to find out, right now, in the middle of an afternoon. He would write to Peggy tonight! He'd even been dreaming about the woman, at night, in his sleep, waking and then thinking about her and saying he wasn't going to do anything about it. Why not, for God's sake?

But what would he say? What would he write to her? It was such a confounding thing. All of a sudden, out of the trees—where had

Peggy come from to swoop down on him like this? He laughed. Somebody in him had known the truth all the live long ding dong time and hadn't had the courtesy to tell him.

Earl leaned back against the chair, his head resting on the hard bark of the tree. In the midst of a wonderful excitement, relaxation was coming into him like spring rain spilling onto newly turned ground. Peggy. "Dear Peggy," he would write, wishing he could speak low into her ear, whispering the words and phrases with the grace of a poet.

"You are a fine dream to consider. All the while of three years of school and I'm just now aware of how much I've studied you. It has come to my mind like lightning on a summer evening, when the colors of sun and night touch just above the ground air of the day. Purples and soft reds, pale and deepening at once, to make a curtain on all that has passed. And then the lightning, too far away to make a sound, yet close to the eye and full of promise and power. That's how I see you now, Peggy, and I don't know why it has taken me so many long days and nights.

"You are a fine dream and a real dream. A dream necessary to me now. Don't make time with anybody else until you've seen me again. September isn't far. If I had the bread, I'd be with you by morning. Just read my words and get it into your head and your heart that I Love You.

"I know you think I've gone crazy, Peggy, writing to you like this. It's more than loneliness. I've been lonely most of my life. It's that I want urgently to see you again, to talk to you as soon as we can get together inside the Apple. Looking back on things you've said and things you've done, I can see now that you were telling me how much you loved me and I was deaf and blind and unfeeling; off in some zone of my own. I suddenly feel so lonely without you. Just six more weeks and we'll be together.

"Take care and write to me."

Earl dotted the last period. He read over his words, scribbled hurriedly on the front and back of a crumpled envelope he'd had in his pocket along with a nubbin pencil, which he always kept on himself.

Glory. He had just covered a few million miles in a handful of minutes. Unless something way beyond his understanding happened, he had found himself a wife. His every instinct told him she would say yes.

Turner's car turned into the driveway. The new Cadillac was all over the place, it was so long and full of gleam. Turner got out and walked to the other side, opened the door and reached in to help Mr. Acre to his feet. Earl moved out of what had almost become a trance to help him.

"Hi, Earl. I'll get him. How about you hold the door for us?"

Earl moved quickly to the front door and waited, ready to open it and to assist in any way he was needed. He watched the painful look on Mr. Acre's face as he eased from the seat. The old man had lived bent over from way before the time Earl was born. His eyes were dark. The darkest Earl had ever seen, and his clothes were homespun, clean, and always frayed. His teeth were even, unstained, and store bought. He was such an old man with the laughter and the eyes of someone living in a timeless time. They seemed to know everything, his eyes. His face was black-brown and his long gray hair looked like unraveled steel wool with soft white soap powder brushed in for shading. He would have been six feet tall or near it.

Mr. Acre said one time he could just remember being that tall. He said one time, "When I were a boy growing onto a man, I was tall as a half grow'd pine tree."

He turned his head slowly to the side whenever he remembered something pleasant about his life, eyes twinkling. "Them pains in my back turned me right straight into a humpbacked fool. I ain't been able to stand straight up from the waist since I was twenty. Doctor said I had tuberculosis of the spine. Damn shame. I was a real handsome fella, I was."

The old man finally eased his feet to the ground and put his weight on them. Turner offered him an arm, but Mr. Acre waved it away.

"Doctor say I got to move these here bones my own self. Don't want no help."

Earl held the door wide open as Mr. Acre moved across the office threshold. He looked down briefly into the ancient upturned face and saw tears set around his eyes, not quite ready to fall. The sight struck

Earl like a blow. The eyes were dull now and unsheathed. A lifetime of sorrow veiled behind tears.

It was Peter, Mr. Acre's grandson. He was dead. Sickle Cell Anemia. All the old man had left of kin in the world was gone.

Earl moved to go. He didn't want to intrude. Carrie was out shopping so he would bring the gift another time; like he told Turner, maybe on Sunday.

"Meetings been postponed," Turner said. "For about a week."

Earl nodded. "Chug almost caught Shorty last night. He was prowling near the house, but he got away. Shorty should be sporting a bruised left eye for it though." Turner shook his head and nodded toward a handgun near the telephone. "That thing's becoming as much a part of me as my hand."

"You let me know if you need me," Earl said. Turner shook his hand, grasping Earl's elbow firmly with his other hand so that there was the sense of some vast and eternal connection between them, which extended far beyond the moment.

"You're quite a man, Earl Togan. I'll never forget you for your commitment to us this summer. And don't you ever forget that. I'll always be your friend." The two men looked squarely at one another, both of them pleased at what they saw.

Earl started back for Pat's Place, hoping Lynn was definitely long gone, but her significance had been dwarfed in his mind now by the other events of the day. He had the feeling that this day marked a departure from the person he had been over the last few years. He could still feel Turner's firm grip upon his arm. To be held in high esteem by such a man, in such a way, meant that one was truly a man himself. To discover that one was ready to take on a wife meant that one was a man. To feel such a burning responsibility to care for an old woman and a lost child seemed similarly significant. To be certain of the uncertainty of life so keenly etched into the back of an old man's grieving eyes with so much impact that it tore a pain in his heart . . . like he had never quite felt before. . . surely he was now, perhaps for the first time in his life, truly a full grown man.

A joy rose steeply in his heart as he walked back along the side of the road. He would type up, no, he would carefully hand write the letter to Peggy, and he would add that he would be calling her on

Sunday evening; that he wanted her to think about what he had written and not to call him first.

Part of him was exhausted and felt a weariness—the part which recognized the struggles which people, including himself, had to face. He thought again of Lynn Brewer and wondered what it was within her that made her want to harm him, for surely, under the circumstances, she knew the meaning of her flirtations. It was potentially a deadly game she had played, was playing, even with Pat, who, innocent as he was, could be badly hurt by her regular presence in his store.

At least Mrs. Shortnin' would eat decently for a few days, she and Shelton. Knowing that perked him up a little; that part of him which, striding side-by-side with his joy, seemed determined to be sad. But what of ten days from now when the flour and other supplies were gone? What really was the promise of Welfare beyond subsistence, and when that dear old lady closed her eyes to dream, what of joy in this life, save her day of Salvation, could she see?

In the back of his mind he kept seeing Mr. Acre's eyes, the sadness in them. Life was such a crazy, cruel, gloriously outrageous thing. It made no sense at all.

Chapter XII

For as long as Carrie could remember, summer days were days for meandering; days for following brooks and streams and branches of water to where they went or where they came from. Hot days playing hide and go seek under Mrs. Lukus's grapevines and fig trees where chickens had made the ground a soft powder. Hot days in cool woods, rugged hills, and so thick with green, it was dark and shadowy inside. Days at Picket's Harbor beach with her skin tanned brown and coated with the sweetish salt of the Bay waves which rolled forever over swimmers near the shore where she most enjoyed playing. It was so strange to her not to be able to leave the yard, and troubling, too. Every day was finally sitting someplace and day dreaming into a blank stare or watching TV when there was nothing on the screen that looked like her. They only had three black and white channels full of white folks shootin' at each other, except for "Amos 'N Andy" who, according to Ms. Lukus, "made every Negro look like a fool and a jackass in one."

She had played every game she could imagine by now. There was no one with whom to play. Most of her friends had fieldwork to do and some were afraid of the funeral home and wouldn't enter her yard. She surely wished she could jump on her bike and ride over to Earl's. She hadn't had her bike out of the yard all summer, and the ride to his place would be better than just riding to the store. The trip was about four miles. It was a long way, but she was strong. She was certain she could make the trip easily.

Carrie turned over under the covers and continued along a trail of water in her daydreams. The stream led over sticks and leaves, down the side of a hill in the woods. The sun was peeking through treetops here and there, and swimming and crawling to safety over sticks which formed bridges above the trickling stream was a sweet water bug. She loved to pick them up, sniffing in wonder that such sweetness could come from something so strange looking. Birds walked and hopscotched in the bushes and the trees.

Carrie sat up in bed and looked around, staring wide eyed. Her face was wet, but she couldn't recall crying in her sleep. She did have a vague memory of her mother coming into her room in the middle of the night. Her mother woke her and asked if she was all right. "You were having a nightmare, baby. You were moaning real loud like you were in pain."

Stella had brought a warm wet washcloth and had gently wiped Carrie's face with it. It was soft and smelled good, like her mother's face cream. She felt a mild ache of tears, which welled into her eyes and caused her to hug her mother, grateful, and suddenly filled with a soft joy which came from no place she should measure.

"Feel better?"

"Uh huh."

"What were you dreaming about. Do you remember?"

"Not much. I felt sad about being cooped up all summer. Momma, why do people die?"

Stella eased Carrie over and moved into bed beside her, her arm around her shoulders.

"It's God's way of bringing us to another place. Life is a kind of test, I think, Carrie. The Lord gives us life and it's up to us to use it well before we pass on to another stage of existence. . . Why do you ask?"

"I didn't dream about him, but Mr. Acre's been on my mind ever since the funeral yesterday. He didn't know me and he thought I was Peter."

"I know, baby." Stella rested her cheek against the topside of Carrie's head, putting the cloth on the dresser. "People do strange things at funerals. It's very hard to accept the death of someone you love very much. Life is very hard where dying and living on are concerned. It takes courage and determination and time to get over the shock. Mr. Acre will be fine. He has so many friends. Did you notice how many people came to the funeral? The church was packed with so many of his friends, and the Togans don't live far from him. I know they'll be keeping an eye on him. He was just grieving and wishing out loud when he called you Peter."

"You sure?"

"Uh huh."

"May I go see him to make him feel better. He asked me. Think I can?"

"Yes-sir-ree-bob," Stella hugged Carrie harder to her for a second, and getting out of bed, planted a kiss on her forehead. She rolled Carrie over fast onto her side, all with Carrie's help, and pulled up the covers.

"Sleep tight. Don't let the bedbugs bite." Carrie curled up into a comfortable knot.

"When can I go see him, Momma?"

"Oh, one day soon." Stella paused. "Maybe Monday afternoon. We'll see. Now close your eyes and think of happiness and teddy bears and sunshine and dumplin's."

Carrie laughed, "Oh, Momma, you're so nutty." She reached up to kiss Stella.

"I know. Try putting the dumplin's at the ends of a rainbow. By the time you get the dumplin's in place, you'll be asleep."

"Oh, Momma." Earl's definition of a rainbow crossed her mind. He said they came from the coloured peoples of the world and were bridges of peace across the sky.

"Momma, do you like Earl?"

"Uh huh. I sure do."

"Why won't he wait for me? I'm almost eleven. I asked him to wait for me so we can get married when I grow up, and he said I would need somebody my own age."

Stella sat back down on the edge of the bed, a frown barely creasing her forehead. This was the last question in the world she might have expected to hear in the middle of the night, so she stalled for time, not wanting to let it go, but not quite ready to answer.

"Why do you want Earl to wait for you?"

"I love him, Momma. He's fantastic. He's fun and he's good looking. I love him very much, Momma." Carrie rolled over onto her back and waited for her mother's response. In a matter of such importance concerning love and marriage, her mother was the one who would know the best thing to think and to do.

Stella smoothed Carrie's hair, feeling grave rather than amused at Carrie's little girl view of marriage and loving a man.

"Yes, he's nice and lots of fun, and in his own way, he's handsome .....," and she was thinking, *but not handsome enough for my little girl*. Then there was Turner's way of looking at Earl. From his point of view, Earl was quite satisfactory as a model for Carrie's future husband. What Stella really wanted out of habit to say to Carrie, she was unsure of now. It seemed a natural thing to speak to Carrie seriously about marriage, since the opportunity had presented itself, even though Carrie's feelings for Earl were puppy love.

Conflicting words hung in Stella's throat, stemming from the uneasiness that she had been struggling to understand all of her life. Particularly since she and Turner had argued, and M.T. had been attacked. Stella closed her eyes and plunged into her thoughts, saying in her mind what she would have said to Carrie without hesitation a short six weeks before.

. . .some folk might not understand what i feel and think. or better yet, they might understand all too well, agreeing with me somewhere in their most secret hearts, and feel repulsed by hearing me say such things out loud. time will show you, carrie, what i mean . . .earl's a fine person, but he's not like us; not like your daddy and brother and aunt claire and you and me.

Stella wiped her brow. She was sweating. Carrie was still lying on her pillow, waiting for her to say something, but she could have sworn that Carrie had shouted a questioning "What!" of indignation at her.

Stella struggled with herself. It was difficult to put her feelings into audible thoughts within her brain so she could hear them above confusion. The world was changing, but not that much. She had to teach Carrie certain things for her own good; like she had been taught by her mother and father. It would be better in the long run. Black people had never welcomed her into their hearts. She had never felt comfortable. They inevitably called her yellow or shit colored and kept her outside their circle; or they just looked at her with no warmth. At least it had happened to her enough in her life to make her feel unwanted, and from them, her darker brothers and sisters, a combination of hatred and envy. She had told Turner that, but he hadn't understood.

carrie, our family for years back has been very careful about marrying black negroes, particularly those with kinky hair. you already have some idea of what i mean. kinky hair is unruly. they have to straighten it with heat and even then it looks bad when they

144

sweat. but more important, the darker you are, the worse your hair, the harder it is for you to make a good life. the whites take full advantage when you look that way.

now, when you grow up and decide to marry, i want you to choose a young man who looks more like us, more like your family. then your children will have a better chance in this country not to be picked on. it's a shame to bring helpless little black babies into the world.

earl is nice and lots of fun, but not only is he too old for you, you'll get over your crush in time, but more important, he just doesn't look like anybody i'd want you to marry. i swear you'll understand better one day.

stella could swear that carrie was sitting up on her elbow, her mouth dropped open in shock, closing and then beginning to fight against what she was thinking with a distinct, "no! that's not what daddy said," fighting tears. "daddy said i should be proud to be black. that i am black, a light shade of black. that earl is fine and nice and handsome and good. That i shouldn't ever talk or think badly about beanie or joe joe because i'll be thinking badly about myself because we're all the same. momma. . .?"

i know this sounds terrible. . . .

and again, carrie's voice, shouting, "but it's not fair. it's not right,"her voice trailing off and her small body turning away, tucking her face down into the pillow, crying softly.

honey, please don't worry about this now. you're too young to worry about all this. you'll see what i mean in time.

stella leaned over to kiss carrie, but her daughter pulled away. oh, lord, she thought. it's so hard to know what's right sometimes. what turner said made good sense, maybe, but i just can't feel it in my heart. this place is so mean for the coloured. i want my children to make a good life. not be victims, and things won't change that much for them. it'll be the same.

Stella sat drenched in the sweat of silence, looking at her baby girl who was looking expectantly up at her in the dim light shed by the lamp on the night table.

"Momma, are you Ok?"

Carrie sat up for the first time since her mother had gotten out of her bed. Stella was so quiet. She hadn't said a word for over five minutes, now.

"Yes, darling. Momma's all right. I'm just thinking. I was thinking of me when I was almost your age. I fell in love with the young man who lived across the cornfield from Poppa's farm. He wasn't very tall; he was short and fine-boned and thin. Oh, but he was handsome. I think he was the handsomest man I've ever seen. His face was a fine, even smooth dark brown, his hair was black and softly knit on his head. It felt like cotton to the touch and not one hair ever seemed out of place. His teeth were white and even and shone beautifully when he smiled. His eyes sparkled and his voice was dark and rich, a joy to hear. I loved him so much, even though he was eleven years older than I."

Carrie sat up on her elbow, her mouth dropping open . . . She had never stopped to think that anybody else her age could fall in love with an older man.

"There was some trouble. A white girl who lived down the road liked him, too. In fact, from all I could tell, she genuinely fell head over heels in love with him. Her father let it be known to his father that he didn't appreciate the situation; that things might get out of hand if George stayed around. So George packed up and left and I cried for months, probably for years, off and on."

Even now, sometimes when she thought of the meaning of George's plight, she still cried. That people had the power to chase away the dearest thing in another person's heart; that they could crush the important sweet things, had overwhelmed her ever since. What was the use in believing that you could get by in your life when what you wanted and had a perfect right to was forbidden to flower, to be itself, and to take its own natural course. Sometime after, years after, when she could no longer remember the process of half dreams which led her to conclusions, she discovered that what her father and mother had taught her was true, and she no longer trusted black people who were her own and forbidden to her like everything else by a white world which was God. And even now, it was difficult to grasp that it was George and the anguish and the lonely incomprehension of the power behind his banishment that had set the whole thing spinning.

146

Even now, trying to say something sound to her baby girl about loving black men, she didn't know what she knew quite well enough to explain it to herself or to Carrie. Things had happened to her. Processes had taken place, leaving in her, with her, around her, beneath her, a dread of recognizing some long dropped truth about daring to love that which was forbidden. It was still so dangerous to the heart to love a dark black man. Their lives were so much in the hands of those who hated their manhood . . .make out the best you can, STELLA, make out the best you can, some little persistent voice had whispered, whispered, whispered, but don't you dare love a dark brown-skinned Negro man, nor let your children love such a one. When he is punished, so will you be punished. Stay clear!

"Momma," Carrie shook Stella. "What happened to George?"

"He went to Philadelphia and eventually married a girl and they still live there. His children are almost through college now."

Carrie pressed her mother's arm. "Momma. Will Earl go away, too?" Stella could hear the fear and the heartache in Carrie's voice.

"Listen to me, Carrie," she hugged her daughter very close to her. "Life is not a regular thing. I used to think so, but it's a strange experience. We have hopes and dreams and it seems that there's sense to things, but then we get older and we begin to see that the sense is mostly in the nonsense of happenings."

"Huh? You sound like Earl."

"Darling, you're very young and Earl cannot wait. Nobody can wait very long. Even when they want to, they have to move on. And it's best that in this case Earl move on. He needs to marry someone his own age or he'll miss the best years of being grown up and young. And you have so many boys to meet."

Carrie hugged her mother closer, thinking hard and trying not to cry.

throw away your fear, carrie. i'm saying all of this as i learn it, and even now i'm not certain that i understand. it's not because i know this is the only way a mother can answer such a question from her ten year old daughter, but because it's positive. i once had another view to give you; a negative and hateful view. even a moment ago.

one born out of hurt and confusion. you don't deserve that and neither do i. your father has shaken me from that awful view, and if i hold fast to it out of habit or fear or convenience, i'll lose him and i'll lose you because you are your father's child. so listen to what i'm telling you about me and my life and don't recognize the fear and the dubious nature of my commitment to positive answers when i'm still searching.

Stella hugged her daughter close. "So Carrie, love Earl and enjoy him and ask him again if he'll wait and see what he says again and be prepared for whatever his answer is and don't be sad. It will go as it should go. He loves you and is our friend. You'll always remember that."

"Hey, that's what Earl said; that he'd always be my friend."

"Yes, even if he tells you tomorrow that he plans to marry some lovely young woman from New York. He's a man and you're a child, and there's a way things are supposed to be. Children grow up and grown men grow old ... And crying won't change it."

Carrie had been so brave up to now, but now the tears swamped her eyes and she held on hard to her mother for comfort. It was so hard to imagine Earl going away and never being in her life again. It was so hard to understand.

Stella held her until she fell asleep, wondering if her heart would ever feel a pure joy again. She had been so secure with the negative thoughts. They explained why things were as they were. To accept the pure worth of black lives, even her own, was to be vulnerable to something, which made her shudder with fear. Yet this coming of awareness, having been seen, could not be denied.

So, the night had ended. She had no memory of her mother having left her room, but just before waking there had been a feeling of sadness mixed with dreams about summer days the way they used to be.

There was a restlessness in Carrie now that she was fully awake. Her mother had made it sound like Earl was going to up and get married any minute. Even before she got a chance to ask him, at least one more time, if he'd wait for her.

Carrie jumped out of bed. She was going to find Earl, right now, and get it all straight once and for all. Naw ... She stopped before reaching the chair where clean clothes waited. She had already asked him once, and he'd seemed pretty sure that it was better for them both for her to grow up and to marry someone else. It made a lot of sense when he explained, and her mother's reasons had sounded right when she talked.

Heck, even if she didn't talk about his waiting for her, she just wanted to see him and she needed to go for a bike ride. Today was Friday and her parents had two funerals, so they'd be busy practically the whole day. Carrie was determined that she wasn't going to spend this day stuck in the yard. Shorty King wasn't a bother anymore. Her father hadn't said anything much about him for weeks.

By the time Carrie was dressed, she was convinced, and her intentions for the day were definite and confirmed.

Chapter XIII

Everything was going her way. Carrie had managed to fool Miz Rosie with no difficulty. Miz Rosie thought she was way back in the vault yard, playing. And since her parents had just left on the first funeral, it would be five or six hours before they returned home. Carrie checked her wristwatch. It was 11:00 a.m. She would make it a point to be back home no later than 4:00 this afternoon. She had packed a lunch in her knapsack, so Miz Rosie wouldn't suspect anything when she didn't come back to the house to eat. She had done this and stayed out playing in the back many a time. Everything should go well.

She rode quickly past Pat's Place, past the two "white" churches, and crossing the main street of Cheriton. She took a shortcut through a park-like area behind the only grocery store in town. This brought her out on Cherrystone Road past all but two of the shops, allowing her to miss most of the people who might notice her. Now she could relax and take in the day, all mixed with summer and a great sense of adventure.

There was a truck parked behind one of the stores. Shorty King was drinking good corn liquor and talking with friends. Carrie didn't see him, but he saw her.

Her long pigtails flew behind her in the wind and rose and fell in light taps against her back as the air blew by. She'd forgotten how good it was to ride a bicycle free.

As she passed several white children playing in their yards, she thought of Eric Green and the look on his face after she hit him. Carrie leaned with a new urgency into the peddling. All of a sudden she was uneasy. It wouldn't hurt to get to Earl's as soon as she could.

She passed one house, which was gigantic; old and well kept with a lawn so green and big you could play a whole football game on it. This place was nothing like the Line, where Beanie lived. All of the Line houses were dead looking rental houses, no paint and broken down everything was everywhere. Folks didn't make much of a living and whenever she went over to play with Beanie, Beanie never let her go inside. Beanie was ashamed of how her house looked inside.

Folks who lived there didn't make much money. She wondered why it was that folks who didn't make much money all seemed to end up living next to each other.

Out of the corner of her eye, Carrie caught a glimpse of a white girl seated on a fine white pony as the two of them cantered onto the lawn. Carrie watched as long as she could until she had to turn her eyes back in the direction she was going. It wouldn't be long before Granddaddy Lawrence would bring her filly, a beautiful red bay. She could barely wait until her birthday on August 17. Then, if she stayed very busy, another year would go by, a long year that she could make shorter by thinking about a million zillion things, and her filly would be hers. Golly!

Carrie passed the last of the nice houses, all of them, just like the poor houses, clustered next to one another, and glided around a slow curve. She thought that it would be better if the poor houses and the rich ones were side-by-side while she pumped hard whenever the bike slowed. When she reached her best speed, she coasted free from the surge of power. Sweat was all over her by now, pouring in heavy beads into her white T-shirt and red shorts.

The rest of the road ahead of her struck out between fields on both sides with no houses in sight. There was an old tomato field, going rotten-dry now. Next came a cornfield directly on her right, and to the left, white potato plants, yet unharvested, waved close to the ground in the breeze. The flowering time had come and gone, but the potato market had been poor and many acres had been left unharvested in the ground to die.

She heard a car coming behind her and moved off of the asphalt. The going was rough on the side of the road, but the car quickly whooshed by, giving her a wide berth and lots of hot breeze, and soon disappeared around the next curve.

Carrie pumped hard and fast and stood balanced on the peddles to coast. She leaned forward against the handlebars and jerked back, making the front wheel hop over a small pothole she couldn't avoid in time. Sometimes when she peddled, she liked to let the bike slip to the left and then to the right of her body with each stroke. This took more balance and she had practiced for the longest time over the years, imitating M.T.

She eased into the middle of the asphalt road and began slalom motions back and forth from one edge to the other. She hadn't ridden this way all summer. The bicycle took wings and flew over the road. She was more than halfway to Earl's now. He sure would be surprised.

The heat and the exertion began getting to her, so she slowed and peddled with less effort, wiping at the sweat every so often. Ahead, not far off now, was Mr. Acre's turnoff road. He lived back behind the woods in a clearing to the right. The Togan farm could be reached by veering left at the same juncture. Carrie was considering turning off toward Mr. Acre's place, but she figured it would be better to do so on the way back. She surely didn't want Earl to pass on his way to her house and not see her. He said he was going to bring the present today, and if she missed him, he'd arrive and ask Miz Rosie where she was and they'd look for her and find her gone. Then Miz Rosie would tell her father, and mercy, she didn't want to think about that. Nothing in the world was worse than her Daddy getting mad. Seemed like he wasn't her father anymore. His face would lose its smile and out he would send her to find her own instrument of punishment, a cherry switch. Most of the time he didn't use it, but the thought of it stinging her legs was more than enough.

The first turnoff road was really the back way to Earl's anyhow. He usually used the road at the farm that came out onto the asphalt from the barn. That was another half mile the way she was going past the turnoff.

Carrie ran her tongue over her lips. Her mouth was scorching. She thought of stopping to get a drink from her thermos, which was packed in the saddlebags that hung over the back fender. It was turning out to be awfully hard work going to Earl's. Maybe she should stop and drink something and then turn back. Nobody had seen her as far as she knew. Her pace slowed a little more, showing just the slightest hint of reluctance to go on. The sun had gone crazy. Hot as Halifax—Mr. Acre's word for hell. Her father always laughed when Mr. Acre said that because Halifax was a city far north in Nova Scotia where it was cold.

A couple dozen more peddles and she would be beside the first turnoff. She decided against using it when she got there. Her primary goal was Earl's house and she wasn't a quitter, so since the most direct route was along the hard surfaced road, that was the way she would go. If Earl left before she got there, this was also her best chance at intercepting him.

Carrie heard another vehicle approaching from the rear. It sounded like a truck. She coasted back onto the dirt shank and stood on the peddles to cushion the bumps from scattered rocks and thick clumps of grass. As the truck came closer, it picked up speed, rattling and roaring louder each second. She threw a quick glance over her shoulder, the truck was so loud, and confirmed that it was a beat up old pickup truck. Returning her attention to the narrow path between the asphalt and the ditch, she marked time in difficult, jerky peddling, waiting for the truck to pass so she could return to the road. The truck drove up directly beside her, like it was going to pass at high speed, and then there was a screech of brakes, which screamed out so loud and sudden that it nearly startled Carrie into the ditch.

The bike careened near the edge. She pulled all of her weight back the other way to stop from plunging over and shot a look of alarm toward the truck, still beside her and now traveling at her speed. Her eyes focused after long seconds of squinting into the dark cab.

There was a man, a white man, grinning at her, laughing. His voice burst out at her, loud, mocking, and harsh. It was Shorty King.

For a time she was in shock, suspended, bumping along on the bike, looking into Shorty's evil face and his mouth full of brownish teeth gaped open in laughter. The bicycle hit something and Carrie's right foot slipped. Her chin slammed into the middle of the handlebars, causing her to bite her tongue as the other foot came to earth and the bike toppled sharply toward the ditch. She struggled valiantly to get the thing under control, but it was going too fast for her strength. The front wheel turned sideways and plummeted into the deep trench. As the bike slammed into the embankment, the handlebars were jerked from her hands and she was thrown ahead of them into a patch of weeds.

An immediate and sharp pain throbbed at her chin, and she tasted blood and a sharp burning from her tongue. The heels of her palms were scuffed, as well. Carrie struggled up the opposite side away from the bicycle and Shorty. He had stopped the truck just a little ahead and was staring back at her through the rear window of the cab. He revved the engine, shoved the shift lever into reverse and backed up. Carrie scrambled for the bike and tugged to get it up into the field before Shorty could leave the truck.

Shorty halted the pickup beside her and remained in the cab, watching and grinning. Carrie glanced nervously around. There was nobody in sight and open road and corn field everywhere. Next thing, she was running, frantically trying to put some distance between herself and Shorty. She ducked into the heavily leaved corn and spied on Shorty as she struggled to catch her breath. It was hot and a swarm of mosquitoes descended on her as she crouched low. It was obvious she wouldn't be able to stay still where she was. She swiped faintly at the insects as they bit and dived past her ears and face, and she moved as little as possible so she wouldn't attract Shorty's attention.

If she went home without the bike her father would know she'd been out of the yard, and if she went to Earl's without it, she'd have to explain why she left it in order to get Earl to help her retrieve it. Shorty would surely steal the bike if she didn't take it with her. Carrie crouched and moved from row to row for the longest time as she agonized over what to do and flailed with her hands and arms at the persistent mosquitoes. Shorty remained still, grinning.

He was chewing tobacco. That's what that brown stuff was on his teeth.

"You know I kin see you, don't you, little nigger gal?" Shorty pointed a finger at her. "There you are, little nigger gal."

Carrie pulled back and wiped the sweat from her upper lip and forehead. She accidentally smeared grit into her mouth. The grains irritated the hurt place on her tongue. But more than anything else, the mosquitoes were driving her crazy. She held on for another couple of minutes and then made a decision.

Carrie stood to her full height and walked slowly toward her bicycle and away from the protective cover of the corn. She had decided that if Shorty got out of the truck she would make a run for it back through the corn. She had to try to get the bike. Her Daddy would really give it to her and never let her out of the yard again if he found out she had left the yard, and she knew her mother would see it the same way. Even worse, her father might do what he had said he felt like doing when they had first had the trouble with Shorty. She overheard him talking to Earl and he said he came so close to jamming Shorty into that ditch that it scared him. This time he might kill Shorty and then the white people would kill her father for killing a white man.

Carrie crept closer, bending down a little like a cat ready to spring, while her eyes never left Shorty, and in the back of her mind there was a building terror and a building hatred for this man who was so mean, so white. For some reason, he didn't move, just sat there, grinning. As her hands closed around the handlebar grip, Shorty jerked forward.

"Boo." He said rearing back with laughter.

Carrie jumped backwards, startled, and lost her balance. Shorty laughed even harder. He howled with delight at his power.

Carrie eased close again, dug her feet into a firm position, braced her weight and heaved.

"You got all kinds a spunk, ain't you, little nigger gal? Where's your Daddy, now? Huh? You see him around here? I hear tell he's off burying him a nigger this afternoon. Hmp," he chuckled. "I'm gonna give him some mo'e work before this here day goes by much mo'e."

The bike's front tire came up. She wished for the lighter weight bike in the store window that she'd asked for for Christmas. Instead she had gotten her brother's repaired and refurbished heavy framed 26 incher. It was so heavy she was almost sure that it was about to be lost forever. She grabbed for the front wheel and put all of her strength into lifting its heaviness up the embankment. Next she held it in place with one hand and began tugging at the back wheel. Her eyes, sweat draining down into them, never moved from watching Shorty. He returned her stare, amused.

The bike was almost hers when Shorty eased across the seat, stuck his head out of the window and said, "You need any help with that, missy nigger gal?"

Her teeth clamped down tighter, hatred renewing itself as she glared back. The sweat on her hands made her grip on the metal a hard thing to keep. Her eyes were stuck to his, and a sickness was growing in her stomach. She hesitated, but Shorty didn't move any further. With one last jerky effort, Carrie pulled the bike out of the ditch.

"You one strong little nigger gal, huh? But it's so hot, sugar. Why don't you come over here in the shade a my truck. I got me a whole bottle of corn. Hot corn. You want some?" Shorty howled. He hung his head down, enjoying his laughter, bent over almost on top of the dashboard, rubbing himself where he was growing erect.

"Lord, that sure feels good, and it's agonna feel even better in a minute when I gets you where I wants you, little nigger gal."

Never in all of her born days had Carrie ridden a bicycle for her life, but she knew her life was at stake now. She hopped on and pumped as fast as she could down along the side of the ditch. It was terribly rough going. It was closer to Mr. Acre's from where she was than to anywhere else. She'd have to fly to beat Shorty back to the turnoff road, but luckily, a dirt road angled through the corn, connected with another just ahead which continued on straight in the same direction she was traveling. She took it, veering off to the right. She could hear the truck starting up behind. Maybe she could still hide in the corn if he got too close.

She was halfway to the woods when Shorty turned into the dirt road and followed, grinning. He knew she had to come out somewhere up ahead, and with all of the heat, he knew he could overtake her.

Carrie looked back over her shoulder. She was also on the main turnoff road now, well ahead of the truck. Shorty sure was coming slow to be chasing her. Even Carrie could see in the midst of her fear that he was moving deliberately slow.

"Right where I want you, little nigger gal. Right in the big old woods." Shorty laughed wickedly and swigged from his corn bottle and nodded his head. He was more than ready. It was time he put on some speed.

Carrie rounded a narrow curve as she entered the woods, so tired now that every pump on the peddles was like the last. Her head throbbed with the heat and her legs ached to the bone. Never in her memory had her chest hurt so much, all of her breath rasping out, close to impossible to reclaim. The truck was a constant and growling hum behind her, pushing her frantically forward.

There was not time to worry about the bicycle now. It was getting too late for that. Shorty was roaring down that road now. She could hear him getting dangerously closer. Her only chance was to hide herself. She shoved the bike and let it roll into some bushes and ran at her best speed into the thickness of the woods.

The more she pushed herself, the more her strength seemed to drag away, until she was all but falling at a wild run, terror the only emotion in her. It was just like that day with the school bus, except her brother wasn't with her and she was too far from home to get help. Maybe Mr. Acre could help her. Maybe. But he was so old and half out of his mind with grief. He might not even be able to understand what was wrong, and Shorty might hurt him; but he might be her only chance.

Carrie kept on, running at a bias to Mr. Acre's house in the long distance through the thick trees. If she could get to him or find a place to hide, maybe Shorty would go away. Part of her held on desperately to this thought while another voice told her that mean white people would never go away. They were everywhere. They stopped you from getting a drink of water except where they put the word "coloured;" they wouldn't let you go to the bathroom anywhere in town; they made you stand if you wanted to buy something to eat and wouldn't let you sit at the counter; they wouldn't let you go to church with them. She knew deep in her heart that Shorty King would never go away if she didn't find a way to make him. She ran harder, ran and ran and fell down and ran until she thought she couldn't run anymore. She leaned against a tree, panting so heavily that she gagged.

"Oh, Momma." The tears started down her hot face. "Somebody. Please somebody." She gripped the side of the tree trunk; dug her nails in and held on so she wouldn't fall down, then catching her breath for a moment, she stumbled away again, almost blind with fear.

There was a large tree root sticking up above the surface of the ground that she didn't see in time. She fell sprawling to the ground. She crawled and turned to look back in terror as she heard the heavy footfalls of a man approaching at a run. It had to be Shorty. She froze. Closed her eyes and almost waited. He was going to catch her and hurt her ... Something, perhaps a primordial reflex in her mind, urged her to move. From within the fatigue and the weakness, her drive to overcome drove her to move. She crawled toward a mass of overgrown logs all piled high by some woodsman, and wedged herself into a knot between the woodpile and the protruding roots and the base of a thick bush and laid as quietly as she could. She lay with her hands covering the top of her head, the sweat pouring off of her like tears and

158

her panting louder than shouting. Like a deer run half to death, she lay there, her breath hot, the loose dirt clinging to her mouth, too afraid to think, and listened to footfalls coming unerringly for her hiding place.

Chapter XIV

Shafts of turbid light curved and bent their way through the tangled leaves before her face. She raised her head just enough to get a clear view of a man's body from the waist down. Carrie immediately lowered her head again. Shorty King had followed her right up to the disheveled bushes and was looking about him now, searching her out. He scratched his head and wiped his face with a handkerchief.

"Where you hiding, little nigger gal?" He turned around several times. "Shit," he said, "I ain't never been worth a damn, tracking." He moved off a little and kicked at some of the underbrush a few feet away from her. Carrie cringed closer to the roots of the bush and struggled to keep her eyes open. She struggled out of a coma of panic to see. The woods was a quiet place, almost serene with distant bird sounds and the busy movements of small living things. Her breathing was quieter now, too, but her heart was so hard at work that she could feel tremors in her fingertips and along the entire length of her arms. A weak nervousness had a hold of her so that she felt lightheaded and the splintered glimpses of light hurt her eyes.

Shorty picked up a stick and began poking into the bushes. If she got away he'd be in a pickle. Turner sure wasn't scared of him, and he'd be coming after him bent on killing just as sure. Why'd he been so damn stupid to let her get so far ahead.

Shorty moved about in a panic, his fear and the corn liquor making his movements erratic and unproductive.

"Come on," he shouted. "Come on out with me. I won't hurt you, little nigger gal. I just want to play." He laughed a sound which made Carrie think of Halloween witches. "That's it. I just want to play." He turned in a drunken footed circle, the sound of his laughter trailing off.

"All right. So you ain't coming. You just stay hid, you hear! But I tell you, nigger gal, if you tell anybody about this, I'll kill 'em. You tell that Daddy a your'n or your brother or that Earl Togan, and I'll shoot 'em dead."

He stumbled toward her and Carrie ground her teeth so hard that a sharp pain shot through her jaws. The end of Shorty's stick entered her small hiding place and she covered her eyes as it thrust a few inches from her face. She suppressed an impulse to scream.

"Shit!" Shorty grunted and threw the stick away. He kicked angrily at a bush or two and turned back. The sound of his footsteps crackled against the woods floor and finally receded after a time. In the distance she heard the truck start up and drive back in the direction from where it had come.

The distance covered was a blur in her mind. She only knew that her arms and legs and lungs and heart had managed to continue to move because she found herself coming to a halt on the bicycle amidst a scattering of chickens and geese in the Togan yard. Tim was sitting on his parents' porch, his legs dangling off the edge to the ground. He looked up, surprised.

"Hey, Carrie," he said as he stood to his feet. "What you doing over here, girl?"

Carrie smiled weakly, amazed she had made it. Fatigue shrouded her eyes. "Just took a ride," she said, her voice sounding strange to herself. "Came to see Earl. He here?"

All of a sudden, the thought really registered. Earl might not be home. Maybe she had missed him and he was on his way to her house ... She had been so dumb to ride all the way over here alone. It took Tim the longest time to answer.

"Yeah. He's here. He's way over yonder down to the barn." Tim was nothing like Earl. He looked different, was shorter and a lighter shade of brown. He had only finished high school and spoke more slowly, walked more slowly. He seemed to do everything with a slower, quieter style than his younger brother. There was a bright gleam in his eyes, a look of keen intelligence. He walked over to Carrie, and studied her face and clothes. She was smattered with dirt, scratches and grass stains, and there was a good-sized bruise along the underside of her chin.

"What happened to you, Carrie? You run into something?"

Carrie lowered her head involuntarily. "Uh huh." She took a deep breath. A breeze was cooling the sweat off of her, but instead of being refreshing, it was making her feel ill. "I fell down a ways back." Lies of omission as well as commission. Lord, what would her momma say if she could see her and hear her. She was trembling, but Tim didn't seem to notice.

"Well, you let Alice take a look at you. Come on in the house. I'll call Earl up here whilst the women cleans you up some." Tim guided Carrie into the house. The cool of the sitting room gave Carrie a chill. She'd sure be in a worse mess if she got sick now. She wanted to lie down and close her eyes and sleep. A wave of nausea passed over her. She swallowed it back and forced herself to concentrate. She sure couldn't act sick. There would have to be too many explanations.

"Alice. Eliza. Come see who I got here. The cat done dragged in a mouse." He laughed an infectious laugh as Alice poked her head around the kitchen door.

"Well, I do declare. What you doing way over here, Carrie?" Eliza stepped into the room behind Alice. "Your momma outside?"

Carrie flinched. "No ma'am. I rode my bike over by myself." Tim explained what had happened to her, as best he knew, saving Carrie the burden of lying further. She was too tired to do much thinking, and she was afraid that any minute she was going to break down and cry. It seemed to her that crying was mostly what she had been doing since the day she fought with Beanie. She had gotten into more trouble this summer than in her entire life. She wondered what was wrong with her. Surely she was becoming somebody else.

Eliza, tying the bow of her apron, came toward Carrie, shaking her head.

"Child, you come all this way alone? Lord have mercy. I thought Earl say your Daddy was keeping you all in the yard because of the Shorty King trouble?" Eliza shared glances with Alice and Tim. "Carrie Allen, did you run away from home?"

"No ma'm. No. I just took a ride." Carrie backed up a few steps and looked helplessly into the faces of the three adults who loomed over her. She wanted to lie down. Her head was throbbing and hot, and the room suddenly seemed to be floating above the floor.

"And looka here. You'se all scarred up."

Carrie dropped her head to her chest. She'd forgotten to brush herself off. She should have stopped and made herself look better. Maybe she looked worse than she should if she had just fallen from her bike. But they couldn't know. Surely they couldn't know what had really happened. Carrie looked from face to face, wishing for Earl and a place to lie down. Her head was beating inside itself like crazy. Where was Earl? Maybe he'd left and Tim didn't know.

"Your folks know where you is?"

Carrie's heart seemed to desert her. "Please don't tell Daddy, Miz Eliza." She pleaded so softly they barely heard her. "Please don't tell." Carrie closed her eyes. Exhaustion forced tears up and out of her. "Please, I didn't mean any harm. I just wanted to get out of the yard. Please don't tell on me?"

Eliza pulled Carrie close and held her against her while her hand moved soothingly in strokes over her shoulder and back.

"Ah, chile. We don't mean you no harm." She looked down into Carrie's face. "Look at me, baby. Look at me. We's gonna fix things right straight and fine." She smiled. "Tim, you go get Earl right quick." She tapped Carrie playfully on her nose and led her over to the couch where she sat her down. Carrie sighed and leaned back. Eliza pressed against her shoulder, moving her to lie down fully on her side. The soft cushions seemed to envelop her.

Carrie's crying didn't fully stop until Eliza washed her face with a warm wet cloth. The cloth reminded Carrie of her mother coming to talk to her in the middle of the night. Next, Eliza placed a cold cloth under her chin to soothe the bruise.

Earl favored his mother. He had the same high cheekbones and deep brown skin. The same rounded nose and large, even white teeth and dark, shiny eyes, and they even smiled the same way. Carrie closed her eyes, a keen sadness coming over her. So many thoughts crowded her mind; so many feelings. What her mother had said was worrying her. Earl wouldn't go get married. She had to ask him to wait one more time. And what Shorty King had said about killing whoever she told frightened her, but she wasn't going to think about him. She wasn't going to mention his name again. She was just going to hate him and hate him and ask God to damn him to hell forever and ever more. Earl would fix things. He'd get her home before her parents returned from the funerals, and there was no need of telling him about Shorty. Shorty would kill him for sure; kill everybody she loved if she ever breathed a word to a soul.

But as sure as she was lying here, Shorty King would be better off if he up'd and died before she was grown. If he didn't, she was going to kill him for sure. One day she'd be big enough and she was going to kill him. The thought echoed through her mind like a calling.

Miz Eliza brought a bottle of alcohol. "This gonna sting, baby, but not very long." She touched the scratches with wetted cotton. Carrie gave no reaction to the sharp stings.

"And mosquito bites all over you. I counts at least a dozen. Such a pretty little face to mess up with falling down and bug bites and crying. Don't you worry, now. Earl was just saying he planned to go out to your house. You almost missed him. He'll take you home. And we ain't seen a thing, baby. We and the chickens can keep a secret. If them chickens don't tell, you knows Tim and Jesse and Alice and Earl and me won't breathe a word." She laughed a warm laugh and kissed Carrie on the cheek, throwing in a hug for extra reassurance. Carrie put her arms around Miz Eliza's neck and saying nothing, rested there as she tried not to think about the horror of Shorty King and the dizziness in her head.

"Now," Eliza said, smiling, "your Daddy is just crazy about my blueberry pie, and if you'se his baby, and I know you is, you gonna love a nice big piece a pie. How about that with some cold milk?"

Carrie shook her head, "No ma'm," and eased her head back to the couch. "I better just go home." Eliza frowned and dabbed at the tears that continued to flow silently.

"Hush up your crying now, baby. You jest lie there and Earl'll be here in a minute. And you promise me you won't leave home again like this. You promise me right now."

"I promise. I promise." Her voice was a tiny whisper, pitiful, tiny and hushed.

Carrie closed her eyes and curled into a tight knot. In the darkness she saw Shorty King's legs and the stick and him poking out at her. She opened her eyes and stared blankly, praying for Earl and frightened in a strange way that made her feel that any minute she was going to fall or tumble or scream and never see light again if she didn't grit her teeth and hold on tight.

Eliza moved away and into the kitchen, more than disturbed by Carrie's behavior. She shook her head and spoke in a low voice. "Alice, you think they's something happened to that child?"

"No, Ma. I think she's just dead tired from riding all that way and falling. It's mighty hot and it's some distance. Then too, she's been stuck in that yard all summer and she's scared we'll tell on her. I bet she didn't think about that until she got here."

"Yes," Eliza said with resignation. "I recken you're right, but still. She's such a lively child. You know it ain't no way like her to act so solemn." Eliza pressed a mess of turnip greens down into a steaming pot to boil. "I sure hopes she's all right. I'd never forgive myself if something was wrong and I didn't help her. She looks so sickly."

Alice was a small woman, a little shorter than Eliza, and tiny in her bones and features. She smiled reassuringly at her mother-in-law, who possessed one of the biggest hearts in all the world, and handed her the lid to the pot. "You just wait, Mom Eliza. Give her some sleep and she'll be bouncing again in the morning."

Eliza nodded and moved to the kitchen table to peel some sweet potatoes. "Suppose you're right. I sure hopes Earl can soothe what's wrong."

Chapter XV

Earl leaned down over Carrie. She was fast asleep. He touched her gently and spoke softly, "Hey, Rabbit," and kissed her on the cheek. "I hear you've got troubles."

The touch of his hand sent a shudder through her. She put her hand over her face as though to ward off danger and screamed, turning away. Then her eyes opened and Earl was saying, "Whoa, Rabbit, it's me," and she was hugging him, almost choking him with relief.

"Hey, you all right?"

Carrie caught her breath and nodded yes. Earl held her for several minutes, Eliza and Alice looking on with concern. When any apparent trembling was over, Earl pulled Carrie away. "Bad dream?"

Carrie nodded yes.

"That ole cat's got your tongue again, huh?"

She looked away, still visibly shaken by whatever was wrong.

"Ok, I can see you're pooped. Let's get you home." He glanced at his mother and shrugged his shoulders. "Be back shortly."

He placed Carrie on the seat of his father's pickup and loaded the bike behind the cab. Just before he climbed into the driver's seat, he spoke to Eliza.

"I don't think she's more than tired," he lied.

Eliza nodded and handed him the gift. He climbed aboard, started the engine and drove off. The family watched until the truck disappeared through the corn. Jesse and Tim were fiddling with an old tractor just outside the barn doors. Earl waved. Carrie was oblivious to everything going on around her, except for Earl's presence. He was with her and it was certain everything was going to be fine now. She fell toward an exhausted sleep with her head on Earl's lap. He looked down at her, worried. She wasn't herself; was strangely unlike herself.

"Carrie."

She opened her eyes and looked up as best she could without moving. Fear caught in her throat because of his tone. "Momma said you said you fell off your bike. You didn't have any other trouble getting to the house, did you?"

"No." She lied, not wanting to lie. The truck rumbled softly along the road away from the barn. It was a smooth ride on Jesse's sand road.

She would never tell anyone about Shorty; especially Earl and her father. They were grown men, but they were black men, and she was certain they were not only powerless, but vulnerable. It was best not to say a word. Black folks weren't any kind of a match for the whites. Whites had too much deceit and meanness in them, and all of the power. Still, forming only vaguely in her mind, she thought that there must be some secret way to stop white people from hurting black people. She still couldn't understand why they hated black people so much. They were so united. They wouldn't go to church with black people, even though black people were Christians just like white people. They wouldn't let you drink water at a fountain or go to the same bathroom. She had never been able to even sit at the counter at the drugstore to eat ice cream. They made you stand up over to the side until every new white person who came in had been waited on and then, if the white woman behind the counter had enough time to give you what you wanted before another white person came in, you could buy your cone or whatever you asked for. Sometimes that woman would have a black person's ice cream in the scoop, almost on the cone or in the carton, and if another white person came in, she would return the ice cream to the cooler and go immediately to help the new white person. It had taken Carrie forty minutes one Sunday to get one cone of ice cream. She mostly didn't go there anymore, but sometimes she wanted a cone and there was no other place to buy one. And even if she stopped going, there were other Negro people who wanted ice cream. It was the same if you needed a prescription. Everywhere she went, there were white people who enforced segregation. The movie theater, the beach, the bus, the schools— everywhere she went it was the same way. There had to be a secret way that nobody knew about yet to make things better.

"Carrie." Earl's voice was almost a whisper. "Is there something you aren't telling me?"

"No." She was determined to protect him. She yawned, showing a disinterest she hoped he would believe.

"You're sure, now. You know you can tell me." She shook her head, no.

"Ok." Earl wasn't really satisfied. "But you know you shouldn't have taken the chance, riding over here to the farm all by yourself."

"I know."

"Next time you get this restless, call me or Pop or Alice. Maybe we'll be able to help."

Earl turned the truck onto the asphalt road and headed south toward Cheriton. The engine droned a comforting hum, which returned her to the edge of sleep.

"Your folk haven't kept you home all summer to punish you, you know. Shorty King and all of the cranks who called on the phone are dangerous."

She sure knew that.

"They might hurt you if they see you off by yourself. All of this will pass in time. I know time seems like it crawls when you're your age, but Carrie, things will get better. White people may seem like a strange lot, but most of them are scared to do anything to help us. Moral courage is really rare. Most people aren't willing to risk their way of life to help somebody that they've been taught is inferior. Whites have become sick with a kind of brainwashing that has convinced them that we're a menace to them. It feeds on itself and we're the only one's who can demand our freedom. We have to take our freedom. We have to change the racist mind. Win it over on moral grounds. Somehow, I know we'll prevail ..." His voice trailed off. He looked down at Carrie. Her eyes were open. She seemed to be listening.

He wanted so much for her not to become bitter and hopeless. "The whites who don't mean us any harm are so naive. I've had them stand right in my face and tell me with the best of intentions that being "black" couldn't be as bad as I say it is. Whites either hate us or they don't want to believe what some of their own are doing to us. Between the two groups, we get squeezed in the middle and the one's who mean us no harm do us harm by default."

Carrie was trying hard to listen. She struggled against drifting off. Earl used such big words, even little words that she didn't understand.

169

"I don't want you to ever go off alone like this again, ok?"

"Ok," she said. "I promise." Her head nodded forward so she cuddled closer so her head would rest more steadily. Earl patted her shoulder and hoped he might one day be as close to his own children as he felt to Carrie.

"That's my Rabbit." He was certain she would eventually tell him what the trouble was. He sure wasn't going to try to pry it out of her. Carrie fell entirely into a heavy sleep and Earl drove along, thinking long thoughts, his brow furrowed.

They drove in silence from then on. It was comfortably warm in the truck, by the way Carrie looked, but Earl was sweating. He pulled off the highway at Pat's Place to get a soda. Carrie was fast asleep, but he knew she would enjoy a strawberry Nehi when she got home.

When Earl entered the store, he almost turned immediately around. Lord bless it if Lynn Brewer wasn't draped over the counter, looking at a rack of change purses hanging on the wall behind it. He had never known her to hang around Pat's so much, and Pat, obviously aggravated, was bending over a cookie jar, busy refilling it and spilling half of his new supply. He was disturbed to see Earl. Lynn swung around on the stool and looked Earl up and down.

"Hey, man," Pat said, replacing the lid. "I hope you ain't hungry. Ain't got nothin' much ready that you like to eat. You jest as well get on back home and wait on Miz Eliza." Pat waited, hope almost popping off his face, he wanted Earl to leave so badly. That last run-in between Earl and Lynn had scared him.

"Hi, Pat. That's Ok. All I want's a soda."

"Right." Pat was relieved and glancing at Lynn, shrugged his shoulders and walked around the counter. As he opened the cooler and dipped into the icy water for a bottle, Lynn stood down from the stool.

"Make it a Coke and a Nehi strawberry, Pat."

"Sure."

"Hey Earl," she said. "Ain't you gonna speak to me and offer me a drink?" She chuckled a half laugh.

Earl tried to ignore her. His usual patient attitude was a bit weary of itself right about now. Lynn was irritating, the way she was always messing over poor Pat. If Pat threw her out, Pat could easily lose everything he had worked for all of his life. He owed money and white people could call in their loans. Product and supply deliveries could be delayed, and his store would curl up and die the long quick death. If he let Lynn stay, he could be hauled in for serving whites in a segregated coloured shop. Damned every which way.

Lynn walked over toward Earl. Her stride was sensuous and slow. As she reached him, he could smell the stench of alcohol. She glided unsteadily past him, rubbing the front of her dress against his rear, *by accident*, as he moved toward the counter and laid down the correct change. The odor of her whiskey sour breath was all mixed with the heat and the sweetness of her perfume, which was paradoxically clean and fresh.

"Just open the Coke, huh, Pat?" Earl was determined, damn it, that he was going to take his time. She wasn't going to run him off. He wasn't going to lose his temper. He wasn't going to be hurtful or rude or cruel. He was going to be a well-mannered man who believed in not only his own dignity, but everybody's. He had decided that this would be his way after he read about Ms. Rosa Parks and the dignity she demonstrated in Montgomery and Lynn had surely been giving him ample opportunity to practice.

The top popped off and sodas in hand, Earl turned to leave. Lynn was all over the doorway, blocking his path.

"Excuse me," Earl spoke softly.

"What for, tar baby. You ain't done nothing yet. Where you always running off to? You scared a me?" She giggled drunkenly and leaned her full weight against Earl. Sweating with uneasiness, Earl backed away and side stepped. Lynn lost her balance and teetered headlong into the counter, knocking her leg a hard blow against one of the bottle racks. She landed with a thud, her legs and body sprawled across the doorway. Earl shifted the sodas to one hand and reached to help her to her feet. She refused the offer and slowly pulled herself up, her face flushed and distorted with anger.

"Damn you," she screamed. "You watch what you're doing, nigger!"

Pat wiped his hands nervously on his apron and started forward to give her a hand.

"You leave me alone, too." She shouted at Pat and he pulled up short. "You both a you no good. Every time I see you, you looking at me, looking at my legs and all like you could see through my dress or something."

"Naw. Naw Miss Lynn, it ain't nothing like that," Pat pleaded. But she ignored him, whirling about at Earl, talking danger worse than fire burning up a man's pants leg. "What you trip me for, nigger? What you touch me for?" Her hand clamped down on Earl's arm, making him spill Coke over his hand and shoes.

Earl was stunned at the sheer hate in her face and voice. Her nails were digging into his wrist. He simply stared at her, ignoring the pain, astounded at her behavior and determined that he would not lose control.

"Did you keep that puppy you found that last summer we fished together?"

"What? What did you say, nigger boy?" Lynn brought her hands to her hips and set her stance rigidly in front of the door.

"Lynn, what's happened to you? We were friends. Why are you . . .?"

"Don't you talk to me like that," she continued, "and don't you dare touch me, neither. Now you apologize to me or you're gonna meet up with my Daddy just as sure as you just laid hands on a white woman." She leaned forward, hands on her hips, waggling her head with her lips turned down at the corners all up in his face.

"You know something," Earl spit the words out, ready to let them go free like they wanted, but he caught himself. He couldn't break his promise to himself to not let any white person make him hateful. He eased firmly past her. The door, inadvertently released as he moved by, slammed back with the tension of its spring, a loud clap in Lynn's face.

Earl, no longer interested in the Coke, threw it into the trash can beside the truck. Despite his distress, he was careful not to wake Carrie as he climbed into the cab, buried his face in frustration against his arm and leaned against the steering wheel, the strawberry soda shining a bloody liquid red beside his face in the afternoon sun. He suppressed a sob and thought of all of the things he should have done and said. He should have picked her up and thrown her out of a window, to hell with the consequences. He was angry enough to strangle her lifeless. All of his self-control was to no avail if he came away angry at himself for being peaceful. Damn! She got next to him

172

every damn time like he was a complete fool, or worse yet, a little biddy boy-child, ignorant of white people and how to hold his own among them. "Damn! Damn! Damn! Shit!" The words hissed in an exasperated whisper out of him.

Lynn would have followed Earl, but doing what he knew might amount to taking his own life into his hands, Pat detained her, holding onto her with his hands while he coaxed her with soothing words to leave that no account alone. He was scared to death that she would carry out her threat against Earl, and for all it was worth, he was pretty sure she wouldn't take out her vengeance on him. But Earl was different. Earl was young and sexy and the best of what his people had in this world and there was no way he was going to let this pitiful, sad, vile girl of a woman go after Earl without at least trying to stop her. Pat coaxed her softly and talked about Earl as though he wasn't worth her bothering with in the slightest. And all the while he listened to hear the truck start up and drive away, and he prayed.

Yet and still, though Earl was out of ear shot, she said over and over again under her breath, "You dirty nigger bastard. You gonna be sorry you messed with me. You gonna be sorry, acting so superior. You better run from here to God and back. You better run and hide. You hear! You hear me!" Pat listened and coaxed and felt his blood run cold.

First gear, second, third; hard and fast in a sputtered, double-clutching, half-assed-roar, Earl drove away full of a grieving anger. If Carrie hadn't been with him, he'd have filled the cab with curses, with what felt like impotence, but she was with him and he'd wake her up if he let out his rage. She'd have plenty of time to curse at white people, as little as she was.

He looked down at her, tears of rage flooding his eyes, and as he wiped them away, all of the tenderness that he felt for Carrie and for black people eased its way into his consciousness. She was dead tired, flat out sleeping with her head propped up on her present, just as peaceful as good times. He smoothed out her pigtails and hung his head as he pulled into the center lane and waited on the oncoming traffic. There was no place to put his anger but down into his gut where it would ache awhile and come up and out when he least expected it. So many black men hurt and even killed one another because of a misdirected rage that really stemmed from their frustration with racism. He wondered if that would one day happen to him. That he would misdirect his anger at whites onto his own people, at his wife or his child or a co-worker. And here was this beautiful little girl in his care and he didn't know if he would ever be able to protect her or his own children, yet unborn, or his wife, yet unclaimed, or anything else that mattered to him. And now he'd have to go around worrying about that dumb woman's threats. She was just crazy enough to tell her father or somebody. Good God, he should have handled it differently, somehow, dammit! She could get Tim fired and then he might lose his new truck. Earl shook his head and heaved with anguish and helplessness.

The last of the oncoming traffic, a truck rig, passed, and then he turned into the Allen's driveway. The hearse garage, straight through to the back, was still empty. The folks hadn't gotten home yet, so Carrie could ease in without her secret being known. He parked in the back, and almost numb with the residue of his anger, put her bike away.

"Hey, little sister Rabbit. You're home."

Carrie turned over out of the heaviness of sleeping and struggled to focus on him standing in the truck doorway as she sat up.

"We here?"

"Yeah," he forced a smile. "We here. Let's get you into the house."

"Are the folks back?" There was suddenly fear in her voice.

"No. No problem. Relax."

She slipped across the seat to him, the present securely in her arms. Before he lifted her down, Earl tied her long pigtails together below her chin while he talked.

"Carrie, you study this present hard and you remember something for me. Until this world changes one whole lot of changes, don't ever assume that you can control your anger against white people. Never assume. You'll have to work at control. Racism and segregation are terrible things, and from time to time, they'll make you so angry you'll want to hurt somebody, but never let it make you that mad. I can't explain it all to you now, but promise me you'll be slow to anger and to hate, especially slow to hate, no matter how mean white people are.

174

What matters . . ." he felt his emotions about to overcome him so he coughed and caught his breath. "What matters, don't you see, is that you hold on to your humanity. That you remain sweet with life and honor and all of the things that good people all over the world, from Africa to Cheriton, Virginia believe is right and true. Promise me this and remember this for me if you don't ever remember another word I've told you."

"Don't ever get angry?" She thought of Shorty chasing her and she knew Earl must not understand how hard keeping such a promise would be. She was fully awake now. "I can't promise. It's too hard."

"You're going to get angry," Earl said, his voice full of passion, "but you don't have to hold onto it. You don't have to hate and then live out the hate. Promise me that no matter what happens, you won't let hate rule you. You'll throw it out of your heart as soon as you feel it there."

Carrie nodded her head and wiped some of the sleep from her eyes. She felt so tired, but if Earl was asking, she had to try very hard. She thought of Shorty King and figured she knew what Earl meant about hate. Even now she could feel hate wanting to live inside of her forever against Shorty King. She looked around, bewildered. It seemed like ages since she had left home. She recalled how fearful the day had been, how close she had come to never returning home again.

"Promise me," Earl said. "Say it."

For no reason that she could fathom, tears filled her eyes and her voice broke as she said, "I promise."

Telling him about Shorty was on the tip of her tongue, but she knew she could never tell him.

He hugged her close and smiled through his worry. "You've got to be exhausted." He wiped at her tears with his shirt tail. She sat patiently on the seat before him, trying to listen while her eyes were half shut, the present clutched in her arms.

"I love you, Carrie." Earl hugged her again. "I love you more than you'll ever know."

When they entered the hall from the stairway, they peeked into the kitchen, and then into the dining room. Miz Rosie, bless her soul, had ironed two tall baskets of clothes. She was sitting by the ironing board, at a lean in her chair, fast asleep. The coast was not only clear, but snoring.

"See you, Rabbit."

"See you." He reached out and hugged her once more, like he was going away forever, then he thumped down the stairway and headed out of the house.

As tired as she was, and beneath that, exhausted, for sanity's sake, as silent and controlled and still frightened as she was, Carrie stood by the front window, his gift clutched in her hand, until Earl pulled out of the driveway. As the truck disappeared, she waved good-bye, wishing he could see her to wave back. When somebody you loved was leaving, it always felt more comforting when they waved back.

Chapter XVI

There is a creek called Cherrystone way back from the coast that winds its way into a small marshy green. Oyster beds lie in abundance all along the way, always carefully watched and replenished after raking by men long ago given to the ways of the Chesapeake Bay. There are nights, like this night, when the gloomy shadows of the deep fir woods, falling partially on solid earth and partially on cattailed marsh, cast eerie shapes with the coming of the faintest moon. The tallest trees, all of them long needled pine, standing high above most in the stillness of that glow, form the shadows of jagged edged tents against the plowed ground of Jesse Togan's fields.

When he was a child, Jesse preferred to play in their shadows. Second to the darkness of night, he relished the small spaces of pitch blackness that fell from the woods during the peak of the moon. Months after he met Eliza, he articulated this fondness. He told her, "When I were a boy, tiny little ole thing on up 'til the middle of my teens, I hid away from time to time, hour on hour, under trees in the woods dark. Don't know why the dark was so warm. But Lord, I loved it. The night you said yes to me marrying you, girl, I went and sat smack under an old sycamo'e tree and thought up some stuff." He laughed and laughed, remembering.

Now Jesse lay nestled comfortably in bed with his wife in his arms. The sounds of crickets and frogs down creek and the soft whisper of Eliza's breathing were gradually lulling him away. He had known her in the darkness and smiled unaware of himself as he cuddled closer to her.

He floated and soared and turned over in his dreams as his sleep grew heavy. His body rubbed against her nakedness, still as soft as cotton. As his head drew down beneath the covers, his face came to rest upon one of her breasts, firm and moving up and down with her breathing. He breathed deeply as the sweet fragrant aroma of her body drifted into his dreams. In his dreams they were very young and he was making love to her. Jesse's arms closed around Eliza. There was for him nothing else under heaven like making love to his wife. Eliza in his arms, lying beneath him one minute and astride him the next.

Eliza, a strong, brown, gentle woman who took her love and her devotion to no other but himself, as it was meant by God to be.

The alarm clock near the bed rattled the silence and shook him awake.

"Lord have mercy," Jesse groaned under his breath as he sat up in bed. He squinted at the clock as he turned its alarm off, holding it near the nite-light by the bed stand. Three o'clock.

"Lord, have mercy."

As he put the clock back on the night table, he turned to look at his wife barely visible in the dark. The noise hadn't made her budge. How many times had he left her for his work? She had gotten used to his climbing out of bed, turning off that fool loud clock alarm, easing away from her when he most wanted to sleep that good sleep shortly before dawn. She was used to it, though she always said she missed him in her sleep after he was gone.

Funny thing. He usually couldn't remember his dreams, but this dream was still with him—the mood of it. He had learned halfway into his life after reaching manhood that he didn't have anything halfway stable to count on in the world more precious than Eliza. There were the children, too, but they were grown and out on their own now. She was *all*: all, and in so many ways, everything!

She got sick once. Nearly left him, and he knew clearly after that that she was the one thing in the world necessary. It was Eliza and him and all of the time that they didn't know they had which gave his eyes their light.

Her face wasn't young looking as it should have been. She had worked much too hard most of her life. She was still beautiful, though. To him she was. Dark, dark brown, the look of her skin a kind of satisfaction in and of itself. Her features reminded him of a picture he saw in a book one time of an African woman standing breast naked with a basket on her head. Could have been Eliza's twin sister. He didn't know much about Africa. It was a foreign place to him and he felt he didn't dare tell Eliza about favoring that picture. But maybe he could one day. Their son, Earl, was going to be a lawyer and was studying at Columbia University, and he loved to talk about Africa. He knew a lot about its history and he made it sound so much better than Jesse and Eliza had ever imagined. All they had ever known was what they saw in the Tarzan movies, and that didn't strike Eliza very well. Jesse chuckled to himself. That Earl was something. He was going to change the world.

Jesse moved quietly to the bathroom where he washed himself and dressed. Eliza turned over in bed as he opened the loudly creaking bedroom door to leave, and he thought for what must have been the millionth time that he must oil the hinges. Eliza didn't seem to hear a thing. Jesse smiled. That gal could sleep through a hurricane and never know the roof was gone.

He sure could have spent an extra hour in bed if he hadn't promised to go hunting with his sons. That space in the bed he'd left was almost calling his name.

Jesse stood on the porch of his house and breathed the morning air deeply into his lungs. He was in pretty good condition, he thought, for an old man of fifty-six. No fat anyplace. Of course, he'd always been lean. Good muscles, but lean and tall. Eliza said nobody could say it was because he didn't eat well. He ate plenty. But he was always reminding her that he'd nearly starved to death as a boy.

The fields of his one hundred acre farm were covered with corn, green-black in the darkness and waving back and forth like heavy-topped furled flags. The ears were well formed and plentiful. The yield would be mighty fine. Twenty acres away from the house his little barn seemed a blank space against the woods. It sat so close to the blacktop road he could scarcely see it.

What was left of the full moon was slipping down behind the woods. There was a half decent breeze going. It made the corn tassels rattle and whisper. It was almost picking time and the market was good so he'd enjoy harvesting this year. Planted mostly cabbage the year before and had had to plow it up in the field, the price was so low. It wouldn't have paid to crate it.

Jesse stretched long and noisily and felt every muscle in his back tremble comfortably with the strain. He tightened his belt and then walked crisply toward his work.

He was one of two blacksmiths left on the lower Eastern Shore, and heaven knew how much back bending work he had to do. He was rather pigeon-toed from all of the shoeing that he had done over the years. There had been many a season when the money he made as a smith made it possible to keep the farm going. Though his skills were in heavy demand, white folks refused to pay beyond a certain rate; practically all of the tracks and breeding farms had fixed the price no matter the rise in his costs, so he couldn't afford to lay off. He knew they would quickly bring in another blacksmith if he pressed them. The racing season was in full swing now, and every track in Northampton County and Accomack, no matter how small, was clamoring after him, at rates they wanted to pay.

Yet, he loved his work, hard as it was. He put in long, sweaty hours. Loved shoeing horses and pounding iron. Loved to feel the muscles, lean as they were, bulging and straining in his arms and across his shoulders, over his back and down his legs right on down to those great big lanky feet of his. He loved making all of those hot-minded horses stand quiet at his hand and voice as he laid the iron to their hooves. He wouldn't trade his job for anything. He just wished he could raise the prices. Jesse smiled at the thought and looked around appreciatively as he walked.

"Man, the day's just sharp for hunting," he said aloud. It never ceased to amaze him how good the world was just before the light of day. Sometimes it made him forget his troubles and all of the things which weren't right and weren't near to getting there. He often wondered why it took so much effort to get out of bed when he knew how pleasant it would be once he was awake and up and out and breathing in the dark day's mist. He had owned his farm for five years now after half a lifetime of paying on it. He was glad he had never gone to the city to live. It was a terrible place to bring up children compared to the countryside.

Tim and Earl had grown into fine men: Tim married and working steady and Earl a big college man. Jesse frowned. Earl had been mighty upset when he came home yesterday afternoon. Something had happened between the time Earl left with Carrie Allen and the time he got back, but he had closed up tight about it when Jesse asked him what was wrong. He had only mumbled something about "a crazy white woman," and then he had said nobody would harm the Allen family again if he had anything to do with it. Especially Shorty King and his kind.

Jesse figured he was referring to the efforts to organize. In a few more days, several key Negro men would be meeting with Turner Allen to see what to do about the white folks' latest threats. The idea of meeting worried Jesse. In fact, it made the hair crawl on the back of his neck. It was hard to know who to trust, and he wasn't sure if they could do anything worth the time anyhow. But Earl had insisted. He and Tim were big on getting community support for busing the children to integrate the schools, but that was one more school year away. The court-ordered busing situation was a time bomb. That, on top of what had happened to Turner's boy, had brought all of the quiet racial hatred to the surface. Lord, he hated thinking about it.

Jesse stepped on, stopping here and there randomly to inspect the corn. Some of his joy in the morning was gone now that unsettling thoughts had entered his mind. He forced himself to think about hunting with his sons. He hadn't toted a gun since the rabbit season went out at the end of January. As he opened the barn doors, he realized he had left his shotgun up at the house. No matter. He could get it later after his boys arrived.

Jesse stepped inside, looking around critically once his eyes adjusted to the strong overhead lights. The barn was old and small, but strong. He had built it himself, thirty years ago, long before he even knew that he had the capacity to finish the payments on the farm. It was an act of faith to build something as sturdy as you could on ground owned by somebody else. He'd felt that when he laid the foundation. He and Eliza had been determined, and with Christ's help, they had kept the promises they had made. The roof didn't leak and the floor was hard earth, packed by hundreds of hooves and countless men's feet. There was an indoor toilet and a tiny kitchen for heating mash and poultices and washing up in times of foalings. The whole place smelled of fresh hay and alfalfa, oats and molasses bran.

The dappled gray mare in the back stall, aged many a year ago, nickered in welcome, tossed her head and daintily pawed the ground. Everybody in the world knew she was old but herself.

"Mornin', Run-a-Rye," he said. The horse nickered again, anticipating her feed.

Jesse took her a pail of oats and corn and watched as she eagerly nosed into the feed bucket, blew in strong puffs of air through her nostrils, causing the oats to scatter, and then sucked in the good aroma. Her lips opened and gathered the grain, then she lifted her head and chewed like she'd never tasted anything so fine in all her born days. Jesse ran his hands over her withers, gave her a good pat and then backed out of the stall. He shook himself and sighed as though to cast off a spell.

"No time to mess around this morning," he said. "I've got me a whole lotta work to do so's I'll be ready to out shoot Tim." He laughed. "That Earl is a mess. Says he only shoots at targets these days. We'll see, once that ole rabbit gits to running, if he can stand to jest watch."

A coal fire was soon banked hot in the forge. Jesse dressed in an old leather apron, picked up the farrier's clamps and hammer, heated a shoe to glowing red and began pounding it to fit Run-a-Rye's near forehoof. That foot had been malformed at birth so the shoe would have to be thicker on one side than the other. He had to get it just right or she would soon go lame. He bent down over his work in serious concentration.

Jesse looked much younger than his years. He gripped the hammer handle like he gripped life, relaxed, firm and with a hint of jubilation, and beat out a rhythm of tones perfected by years of practice. Sparks flew, spun in the air, fell toward the earth and died away in an instant fury. He spoke to Run-a-Rye, "That's how I wants to go, horse," while the hammer sang. "Like them sparks there. Shine bright and hot and burn with light-a-fire, and then die like sparks going out. No messing around." The hammer sang on like the counter measure beat in some holy gospel choir's band.

He was eager to go hunting, especially out of season. It had been that way off and on all of their lives. Had to, just to eat many a time. Old game warden never knew about all of those rabbits in Eliza's stew pot. Shot the fool all around that white man and he never knew a gun went off. Jesse laughed aloud and laid the steel hammer in a steady beat against the iron shoe. The hammer worked like a flat headed demon. He had a pile of other work waiting for him and planned to spend most of the day at Hankle's track. They were getting ready for a racing meet somewhere in Maryland and he'd be there all the blessed week.

The hammer pounded loud, pounded hard, pounded steady.

The hounds outside began barking like they were holding a coon at bay. With him up so early they were probably frantic to hurry him up with their breakfast. They'd just have to wait. Then he heard a light truck engine coming on the farm road. Couldn't be either of the boys. No matter how they arrived, the dogs never barked when Tim or Earl came. Even when they were in somebody else's car, they just seemed to know when it was the boys. Jesse figured it was somebody wanting horseshoes or bringing a horse or wanting racing tips. One way or another, they'd find him by the racket his hammer was making.

Steam rose as Jesse dipped the hot shoe into a water barrel. The doors opened slowly, quietly, until they were swung back wide. Curtis Brewer, the white man that Tim worked for, Brewer's son, and three other white men stared in at Jesse with shotguns in their hands. Jesse removed another shoe from the forge as he replaced the first one. His hammer took up the rhythm again and set the hot metal sparks jumping in a spray. The men moved slowly forward, Brewer in the lead. Jesse caught sight of them out of the corner of his eye. He looked up with a start, his face registering both surprise and puzzlement, and then the barest trace of alarm as he focused on their guns. He rested the clamps and hot shoe on the anvil and wiped his sweaty hands on his apron, all the while staring back at the men. Guns? Crackers? No wonder the dogs were kicking up such a fuss.

"Mr. Brewer?" Jesse said uneasily.

Brewer, without speaking, stepped closer to Jesse, the men a few paces behind him. He looked around suspiciously, glancing to his left and right as though looking for something ominous. He stopped a few feet away with his gun resting across his right shoulder, his eyes narrowing before he spoke through an arrogant mouth.

"Jesse. We come to get Earl. Where is he?"

"To get Earl?" Jesse repeated the words, not understanding. Brewer's face was impatient, mean. Jesse spoke slowly. "What you want with Earl?"

"Never mind that, nigger. Just show'im to me. We already been up to the house and he ain't there."

Jesse stiffened and picked up the hammer. The other men leveled their guns on him and stepped up beside Brewer. Jesse stepped back a little, eyeing them and suddenly desperate to clear his mind. The dogs had just started barking a moment before and he'd just heard their truck a second ago. Unless they'd walked up there, they hadn't had the time to enter the house and be here at practically the same instant. Nothing made sense. This kind of thing hadn't any right to be happening, yet he sensed that he was playing out something which had happened to his father's father and his before him; like nothing had ever changed. Jesse shuddered and spoke after wiping his hand nervously across his dry lips.

"You ain't got no right going into my house." Jesse was trembling inside with anger, now. He could hear it in his own voice, which sounded strange to him. "You bother Eliza?" He turned his head to the side, bracing himself for Brewer's answer.

"We ain't bothered her, yet. Now, you better tell me where that black son of a bitch is or we'll go back and see Eliza. Won't we boys?" The men traded glances and a couple of them laughed.

Anger and disbelief showed openly on Jesse's face. He glared at Brewer with a familiar hatred and disgust and inside he felt a fear as old as slavery creeping down into his stomach. The anger building in him was the worse he had ever known, perhaps more than anything because he had been caught off guard.

"Brewer," Jesse said through his teeth, trying with all of his strength to keep his rage down," I don't know what you wants or why, but it ain't here. And them guns has no place here, neither. Why don't you jest leave me be and get on home where you belongs." He had to get away and get to his gun and Eliza. Tim had a phone, now. If he could only get away and call over there to warn them and to get help.

Jesse stepped around the anvil and raised the hammer a little. It seemed that just standing there would be the most useless and maybe the most dangerous thing he could do. There was nobody in the world that got him as mad as a racist cracker redneck. He didn't know how in the world he had managed to swallow so much from them in his life. He had stayed away from them was what he had done. And there were too many of them now to lose his temper. He was afraid for Eliza. Lord, what had they done to her, and Earl and Tim would be coming along any minute, totally unsuspecting. Jesse swallowed, forcing the rush of saliva and fear in his mouth back down his throat. One of the men jabbed the barrel end of his gun against Jesse's belly. Jesse stepped back, strangling the hammer handle like he would kill it.

Brewer nodded. "That's better, boy. Now, I'm gonna ask you for that nigger boy of your'n one more time. One more time is all."

One by one, the dogs outside ceased their barking, whined and yelped like they'd been kicked, until it got so quiet that even a deaf man might have heard Jesse's breathing, as soft and as uneven as it was. Jesse glanced toward the doors, panic beginning to crowd his senses. He wiped at the heavy sweat pouring off of his face. What did they want with Earl and what were the guns for? And the dogs. What was wrong with the dogs? Maybe he was acting too much like a man for these white bastards. He'd always hated playing coloured. He hadn't acted coloured in a long time; not since he was a boy and hadn't known any better. Maybe if he did they'd go away. Maybe he was dreaming. Maybe his only chance was to fight his way through. Brewer looked like he had killing on his mind. Better himself than Earl or Tim. A sobering, sickening thought crossed his mind. 'Like sparks, if it had to be. Like sparks flung up and spun with light-a-fire ...'

"I told you," Jesse said, raising his voice. "You got no business here! Now ..."

"Nigger," Brewer spit into Jesse's face as he reached for his shirt collar. Jesse closed his fingers hard on Brewer's hand, bending the wrist and the arm painfully down. He shoved Brewer backward and saw him go stumbling until he fell on his backside.

"You'se the nigger, white man! Now, you git out of my barn and you stay out. I can't stand this here." Jesse shook with rage. "Git out, damn you. Git out ..."

The youngest of the three other men, Brewer's son, turned to help his father up. Brewer's face had flamed scarlet as he pushed his son's hand aside and rushed to his feet. He had fallen, Jesse's words screaming past him, and was up in one motion, sucking breath through his teeth and raising his shotgun like an ax. Jesse's hand caught the brunt of its force and his hammer drew back. Then it was on its way down, the hammer coming down and Jesse's other hand holding and pushing the gun cleanly out of the way.

"Look out, Pa." Chuck Brewer saw the descending hammer, saw his father's unprotected head. He jammed the barrel of the gun into

Jesse's stomach and pulled the trigger. A roaring blast echoed through the barn, mixed with a hideous scream, half muffled with the flow of blood that gushed from Jesse's open mouth. His eyes closed against the pain. The hammer dropped harmlessly to the ground and the mare whinnied and snorted at the terrible sound of his dying. Jesse's hand reached feebly back for the anvil, red and slippery now, and then he fell dead at their feet, half his mid-section blown away and splattered behind him.

Eliza raised her head from her pillow, her mind eased to the edge of waking by first the dog's barking and then the gunfire. But then, without ever opening her eyes, she recalled her men were hunting. She turned over and snuggled warmly into her pillow, dead to the world asleep.

Chapter XVII

The men were frozen. It had happened so fast. They hadn't come for Jesse. That fool hotheaded Chuck Brewer had killed him in the kind of stupid panic that got men strung up. They looked at each other, and all looked a breath away from running. The mare whinnied deep in her throat, stomped about and pulled at the rope holding her to the stall. She was terrified.

"Shut that damn horse up, somebody," Brewer shouted.

One of the men said, "That don't make no sense, Curtis. We already made enough racket to ...."

"I said shut that horse up! Damn fool noisy thing, I kain't think!" The man did as he was told. He put his hands around the mare's mouth and talked to her soothingly in an effort to quiet her. Chuck's hands opened slowly and dropped the gun. He spoke like a man returning from the dead.

"I killed him, Pa. I killed a man."

"Shut up, boy," Brewer said nervously, trying to steady himself. "You killed a nigger. Just a nigger. To hell with 'im! It don't matter none. I want Earl and I want him now. We know he was headed this way. If he ain't here then we'll go back and tear that house and Eliza apart until we find him." Brewer turned around, fighting confusion, and looked into the fear-gripped faces, one by one. Two other men, one of them Shorty King, had joined them since the shooting. They had poisoned the dogs and were busy loading them on the back of a pickup when they heard the gunfire. Now they were gaping at Jesse's body.

"It's done, so to hell with it. Stop acting like a bunch a damn fools and search this damn barn for Earl. There's no way out but the front." He paused for breath.

"Bill, you and Tom better run up to the house. One a you get to the front door, and one to the back, and if Eliza come out, you bring her down here to me."

"Now, if'n I know that nigger, he's hiding somewhere behind some hay or in one of them barrels." Brewer spoke so Earl could hear him; he was so certain he was there, somewhere. Coming to his father's to hide would be the natural thing to do, he figured. "We gonna treat him to some fun, huh boys? Find him."

The men didn't move. "He's got to be here. You heard JoBob. He lef' that beer garden with Tim. JoBob called me they was headed down Cherrystone Road. Tim don't live nowhere near here. He's got a place on t'oher side of Cheriton, so's he had to of let Earl off here. He's here, somewhere. Now look for the Goddamn son of a bitch!"

Brewer didn't know about Tim's house two miles through the woods, nor that Earl had gone there instead of returning to his parents' home to sleep.

"Well, git on with it!" Brewer shouted, and leveled the barrel of his shotgun at the nearest man. In exasperation he pushed the man back into a barrel. The man went sprawling and the barrel tumbled over and rolled noisily into the wall.

Lacey Haynes got to his feet, and although he hissed under his breath, he led the men in the search.

Chuck moved in a daze. He couldn't keep his eyes off of Jesse lying dead and mutilated on the floor. He knew Tim well; worked with him at the grader. He knew how much he loved his father, how proudly he talked about him. What was going to happen now? God, he'd heard about lynchings—he'd heard the terrible stories and hated it that men did such things to the coloured, and now he was helping. God! He stood off to himself, staring.

They searched for a good ten minutes, but found no sign of Earl. "Not a damn sign of that nigger nowhere," Shorty King said, a look of vicious hunger in his eyes.

Earl was walking up the five hundred odd yards of sandy road that stretched between the corn on either side. He walked easily, casually, and whistled as he walked with a slight, what he called, New York City dude, bad get-down, bop. He carried a twelve gauge semi-automatic Browning shotgun across his shoulder. His foot hit a tin can and sent it bounding loudly among the corn stalks. A rattle-trap car passed on the hard surfaced road behind him and he turned momentarily to look at it. He couldn't tell who it was. During the height of the racing season, as it was now, people showed up at the most ungodly hours to have their horses shod or their sulkies repaired.

It was probably just some farmer up early and getting busy. The car traveled to the curve, looked like it would hit the barn and then slid around the bend. He was sure that one of these nights some jackass was going to ram a hole in Jesse's barn from missing the turn. Jesse said it hadn't happened in twenty years and it wouldn't ever, unless it wasn't an accident. That was that.

The sandy road stretched ahead through the morning's blackness toward the barn like a silver carpet. Earl recalled how he, Tim, and his father had hauled that sand from the Tower boys' farm late last summer. They redid the road every two years. His Pa hated pot holes and swore he'd be rid of them; he'd worked the shirts off their backs, shoveling and hauling sand on that dilapidated half ton truck of his, and telling jokes that made them half fall out with laughing. It had taken them several days, but it sure looked good and it sure beat mudholes when it rained.

The wind alternately whispered and hushed away among the corn tassels as Earl passed along the road. It was during a lull that he heard it: little feet skittering away just ahead of him. A cottontail came to a jittery halt up ahead. Earl stopped whistling and squinted through the dark at the two beady little eyes looking dead into his from the grass. He couldn't really see it, but its form was there in the shy moonlight.

"Get on, Brer Rabbit," he said stooping down. "You're getting way too far from your briar patch. You better scat long gone before we get those hounds after you." The rabbit sat breathing hard, fast, and scared, its whole body heaving up and down.

"I tell you what," Earl said. "If you promise to run like hell, I promise to set the dogs on one of your brothers instead of you. Well, what you say? Isn't that all you can expect, seeing as how the world is?" The rabbit moved a little and Earl thought of how silly he must look. He shooed the creature away and stood with a feeling of satisfaction as the spared bit of fuzz hopped away, turning and bobbing from side to side down the road. It finally showed some sense and took to the cover of the field.

Earl fell back into stride and commenced his whistling again; a tune Lester Young was always playing. He loved that man's music and had considered himself close to heaven on the two occasions when he had caught him in concert in New York. There was so much more

189

freedom in that city. It was nothing like Cheriton and Cherrystone. The sickening image of Lynn Brewer flashed across his mind. Everything he'd done over the past thirteen hours or so had been in an effort to get her out of his mind—to rid himself of thinking about the implications of his encounter with her. He hadn't quite faced up to telling Tim about it. Tim had never in his life owned a possession like Sweet Georgia Brown, something brand new without scratches or something else wrong with it. The truck was his future. It would break his heart and maybe his life to lose that truck, and the thought that it would be his fault for not keeping his mouth shut when Lynn messed with him made Earl's stomach turn over.

He closed his eyes and shook his head as he walked, making an effort to cast off the ache of despair which had been with him ever since Wednesday when Lynn had first set him off. As he stepped past the high corn into the yard, he switched his gun to a cross carry and began whistling again. Tomorrow he would call Peggy, and in that prospect, he found much hope.

They were listening. At first they thought it was somebody passing along the road when the whistling stopped, but there it was again, just audible and coming toward the barn.

"It's somebody," Chuck said in a shouted whisper. "They gonna see him. They gonna see the body ...."

"Shut up!" Brewer cuffed his son across the mouth. The boy reacted slowly, bringing his hand up to comfort the hurt only after staring into his father's anger-distorted face for a long second. Brewer saw the pain and amazement, and the loathing in his son's eyes. He looked away.

"Now, everybody hide," he whispered. "I don't know where that nigger's been, but he's coming now, I betcha." Brewer crept to the barn doors and tried to see through the crack, but couldn't. "Calm down, Chuck, and come over here with me. Whoever it is, you men jump 'im good an' fast when he come in."

The men vanished behind stalls and huge barrels, waiting and ready and scared and feeling bold and murderous at the same time. Chuck moved to the barn doors and waited, scared and hoping the whistler would keep on going. Curtis Brewer was hoping for Earl.

Earl glanced down at his shotgun as he switched it under his right arm with the barrel pointed downward. Hunting again with Tim and his father would be great. That was if Jesse had the time. By the looks of all of the vehicles in the barnyard, that might not be the case. Jesse was working already and had customers aplenty. Horses were hard to get out of the blood, and men on the Shore had long since lost that battle. They were, so many of them, harness horse racing fools. Earl stepped through the barn doors. "Hey, Pa."

His eyes hadn't focused beneath the bright ceiling lights when he heard a mocking voice behind him.

"Come a hiding, huh, boy?" Brewer grinned maliciously. Earl turned and was jammed in the belly with the blunt barrel end of Brewer's shotgun. He bent over double, all of the air knocked out of him. Hands grabbed him from behind, covered his throat and mouth, and dragged him to the floor amidst grunts of approval. The gun, still in his hands, was snatched from him and thrown aside.

"You gonna git it now, black boy," Brewer said. "You gonna git it real good. Git his pants down."

The men held Earl down tight against the dirt floor while Shorty stripped him down to his skin. Sweat broke out all over Earl's body as he squirmed and tried to wrench himself free. Brewer pulled a long skinning knife and waved it in front of Earl's face.

"See this, boy?" he said, laughing under his breath. "See this here muther of a blade, nigger, all cold and sharp an' all. It's gonna git real hot, real soon."

Earl tried to shake his feet and legs and head free. Sweaty fingers stuck into his eyes and held him tight.

"I'm gonna take your parts and throw 'em to my dogs, boy." Brewer waved the knife like he used to wave the flag when he was a boy and they had a parade once a year in May. He waved it as though there was glory attached to it. Earl twisted and grunted savagely. There were strong hands all over him, digging viciously into his flesh.

Bill and Tom came back into the barn. "Every-thing's quiet up to the house. Nobody there but Eliza and she's dead asleep." Tom spoke out of breath from running and excitement at the scene before him. He'd heard about lynchings, but he'd always managed to have the bad luck of missing them for one reason or another when he lived down in

191

Georgia. He was too young to remember the one in Princess Anne, Maryland, just north in '33. There'd been a few where he lived in Mississippi when he was much younger. Eastern Shore whites had practically never lynched niggers. Sure as he was born, he wouldn't miss this one.

Brewer turned on them, alarmed. "What the hell you doing down here?"

"It's all right. Can't hear a thing up to the house. Jon come and got us." Curtis hadn't even noticed that Jon had left. It scared him that he might be losing track of things.

"Well, git on back up there and keep a watch!"

"Shit, Curtis now, I'm staying. It ain't gonna take long." Earl got free for a second and screamed. Brewer turned back to his work as the men regained their hold on Earl's twisting efforts to get free.

At first he didn't know what was happening to him. That blow in the gut had nearly blinded him. Then he began seeing them. White men everywhere, holding him down and punching on him and cutting off his breath, squeezing his mouth and nose shut, taking his clothes off. It had happened so fast. Everybody was blurred, sweaty and w-h-i-t-e, all over him full of heat and the smell of liquor. At first he couldn't hear anything, there was such a roar in his ears and his heart was racing so. Then he saw the knife and lost what little control he had. Dreaming; a damned nightmare! He had to be in the middle of a nightmare! He still didn't know who they were. Sweat was stinging his eyes shut and the pain from their punches and kicks seemed to be coming from everywhere at once. He had to be in the middle of a nightmare. This wasn't real. It couldn't be.

And then reason crept in—faint, old, shaking its head sadly. It whispered so that he heard it above the din of his attackers, beyond the terror and the blinding rage, which now inflicted such a sense of finality upon his heart. "No," old reason said. "No, it didn't happen so fast. Same thing's been happening, same thing's been going on, for hundreds of years, son. You knew that and you didn't take sufficient warning. How many times does this white man have to kill you over whatever he takes a mind to, simply because you exist, simply because God made you, before you set yourself, every inch of your being, against his racism ahead of time? You told Carrie not to hate, but

192

maybe you should have told her not to trust. You've been naive and now they're going to take you apart, like that other boy you heard of a time ago, that Emmet Till. The one the fate of whom you swore you would never share. You should have been ready!" Faint, old bloody-headed reason came and went away.

Jesse? Where was his father? And Tim? Thank God Tim was still at home in bed with Alice. Maybe he'd get here in time and get help. He had to! He had to!

Earl's mouth wrenched free. "Poppa!," he screamed with all of the strength and fear in him. He screamed "Jesse" over and over again until they trapped his mouth shut again. He screamed and prayed that Jesse and Eliza were still alive somewhere and out of danger; prayed that somehow his father and brother would come and help him get white off his back like they used to do. What did they want? Why? He had done nothing that any man didn't have the right to do.

A fist knocked blood and teeth into the back of Earl's throat. There were two more pairs of eager hands on him now, holding him and sinking their nails deep. There seemed to be a hundred pairs of hands, gripping at the very center of his life as he fought and kicked and cursed and jerked in a desperate effort to get free. Earl gagged and screamed in a spray of blood, teeth, and pain that throbbed down to his feet and back. One of the men hooted with excitement, his eyes wide and ringed with white.

"Hey, Curtis. Git that knife agoing," Shorty grunted eagerly. "Yeah, git that knife agoing. Let's see this here nigger dance on his black ass. Maybe we ought to treat Turner Allen to a party like this, huh, boys?" The men grinned and hooted their agreement.

Earl opened his eyes and saw the knife, shiny and clean and twinkling in the light before Brewer's face. He focused on Brewer, recognized him, got his head loose again and spat blood on Brewer. Brewer sneered, hit Earl a hard backhand across the face and then landed a fist in his groin, beating and cursing and wiping his blood smeared face on his shirt sleeve.

Curtis stepped back, his shoulders heaving from lack of breath. "Nigger, this is for you forcing yourself on my little girl." Brewer's face twisted with rage. He made himself imagine the scene: Lynn's clothes all torn and dirty and bloody and this nigger on top of her. He brought it up to his mind's eye over and over again to make himself enjoy the torture more. Spit oozed down the side of his mouth. "No shitty nigger gone rape my girl or any white woman and live to tell it. You gonna die slow for this nigger. You gonna ....."

There was a numbness over him, despite old reason, made more out of fear and an ancient incredulousness borne way back in the naive hospitality of his ancient, long lost African homeland. He simply, up until now, could not believe that there was a race of men who could and would inflict such horror upon another for no reason. Despite all of the seeing of clear hard-headed fact, despite all of the preaching, he had actually remained naive, and now, he could see it was lynching him as it had taken so many others. He could see the dying, feel it through his skin, hear it beneath all of the shouting. His mind was on how to get free. How to put an end to Black Death. How to wake up from the awful truth of his situation. Only the last words from Brewer came fully to his mind. Rape? His girl? From out of a daze, Earl heard and knew and understood old stern reason.

"Rape?" He found a strength beyond his knowing and got free enough to scream his outrage. He suddenly saw the sense of it. The nonsense of it. Brewer. Little girl. Lynn. Oh, God. It was a lie! It was a terrible lie!

"Yeah," Brewer said low in his throat. "I said rape, nigger."

"He's making too much noise, Curtis. Gag him, Joe."

"Naw." Brewer said. I want to hear him. I want to hear him dying. I done talked to my girl. You black stinkin' nigger." Brewer felt wave after wave of righteous anger rising in a rage inside of him, mounting to such proportions that he was close to bursting from it.

Brewer's fist landed full on Earl's nose. Earl felt the bone crack and shook his head, stunned, the blood streaming over his mouth and down hot and sticky onto his chest. He was almost unconscious, but his body continued to squirm and to kick, every nerve determined to fight for as long as he was alive.

Brewer slapped Earl's face back and forth, trying to stir him into consciousness. Slowly, Earl's eyes opened to the pain. He looked into Brewer's face, made himself focus on that face; on the narrow slit of a mouth spewing words and spit and telling him about raping Lynn. She had been his friend when they were children, and no more. He had tried to defuse her anger, her insanity, but hadn't understood. Instead of feeling stupid, he suddenly felt a terrible sadness for Lynn and for himself and for the future. There was no future if people didn't stop the hatred. It was all so absurd. He couldn't help it. He couldn't help laughing. He felt helpless and mad and suddenly arrogant and couldn't stop laughing out loud through the pain and the hurt and the whole damn thing. It was weirdly funny; dying for raping a poor little girl of a woman he'd never touched, and at the hands of a fool who abused her into believing she was inferior while chasing her to all the black men in the world by bringing her up to believe that black men were sexually superior. God have mercy. It was funny and the saddest thing in the world.

The men looked at one another, dismayed. The laughter was clear and genuine. Earl struggled to get his head free again. There was no other purpose left in his mind. He wrenched and kicked and bit and finally spoke the words just loud enough to be heard. "I don't hate you, Curtis Brewer. I don't hate you even a little!"

A moment of hesitation seemed to flow through the men. They looked at one another in disbelief.

Brewer cursed, reached down and grabbed Earl by the throat, dropping the knife. His hands closed and the thumbs pressed in violent jerks against Earl's windpipe. "Shut up. Stop that laughing. Shut up!"

Earl felt a startling coldness rippling through him and a hot helpless anger flashing as his breath was cut off and given back to him and cut off again. He couldn't breathe, and he suddenly wished it would end here. End without the knife. He kicked and squirmed harder than ever, wanting it to end before they cut him, and refusing to give up.

One of the men lost his grip on Earl's leg. Earl's knee shot forward hard into Brewer's groin. Brewer screamed, "Go-dd-dd," and fell back holding himself, bent over double almost to the ground. The men wrestled harder with Earl and wished Brewer would get it done. He was wasting precious time. But Earl wouldn't lie still. Seemed like he should have been dead already, but he wouldn't lie still. If Brewer didn't have the sense to know to hurry, they would do it!

Tears streamed down his bloody face as he started laughing again. He laughed and cried all together. It was all he could do now;

laugh at every bitching one of them. Tim. Jesse. Eliza. Where were they? Laughing and crying all together. God would surely damn Lynn. God would surely damn her to hell or else he'd forgive her poor self for all the abuse that surely had turned her into such a monster. Sobs came heavy through the laughter, a crazy high-pitched wail, which tore through Chuck Brewer, standing helplessly by his father's side. The men spat on Earl and cursed him and knew deep in their hearts, somewhere hidden away, how wretched they would one day be in hell.

"Git on with it, Curtis. Git on with it," somebody screamed. Brewer stumbled back toward them, picked up the knife and came at Earl, his face a livid white.

"Pa," Chuck said timidly. "Pa you ain't gonna really do that? We done enough, Pa. You cain't ....."

Brewer's arm swung wildly under Chuck's face and knocked him to the ground. "Goddamn you, shut up." He turned on his son, sweat draining down into his eyes. "You spineless piece a shit. Get outten my way!"

Chuck tried to get himself together. He wiped at his mouth, Earl's laughter still coming and fading out and beginning up again. He could go get help or pick up a gun and make them stop. He could do that and give Earl the keys to the car so he could get away.

Chuck shuddered, and finally he walked to his father's side. He had to be a man like the rest of them. It was too late to change things, now. He had already murdered poor Jesse. Now he had to rip this damn nigger to pieces for raping his sister. But he knew Lynn. There was no way in hell that Earl Togan would have wanted to touch her. He had always had too much going for him. Nobody had to rape Lynn, anyhow. She'd laid down with half the men in the county by now. And his father knew that. But even if she was a virgin, Curtis didn't really care. He'd never more than looked at Lynn sideways. It was his pride he was protecting. That and money were all that he cared about. Making money and ordering people around.

Already there was too much blood, and Chuck's stomach wouldn't hold. He grabbed his mouth and vomited as he ran to the back of the barn where he fell crying in a heap. The mare whinnied and reared, but the rope held her fast.

They taunted him with the knife. They beat him, fists taking turns, pounding and battering his body and face. Somebody pulled him upright.

Earl saw the blade—coming. He kicked and tried to scream, but they had his mouth shut tight. Peggy. She would never really know how much he had wanted to marry her, how much he loved her, except for that one short letter. He'd let too many things get in the way, thinking he had plenty of time. His vision was going. Brewer grinned, gathered Earl into his hands and sliced the blade down deep into him, stripping him away.

Earl's body straightened out so hard, doubled up so tight, the men couldn't hold him. His voice tore, half strangled with blood and white hands, ripped from the insides of him as the blade turned to fire and a scream full of his life tore away. He slumped, still drawing breath, his life bleeding, spurting out. His eyes opened and closed, not seeing, except where his last thoughts lingered, infused with a kind of eternal hope against hope that his parents and brother were still alive and free. That Carrie, sweet little Carrie, wouldn't hate . . . wouldn't hate . . . wouldn't hate . . .

"Dear Jesus," were the last words he said aloud.

Chapter XVIII

Timothy walked through the woods along the old Accomac Indian path that led from his house, a double barrel shotgun broken over his arm. He stepped slowly, ambled along, thinking and chewing on a twig. The trees were thick, but he could still see a few stars sprinkled over their tops and blinking and sometimes looking as though they were moving when he knew they weren't.

Pine scent was heavy on the warm breeze as well as that of honeysuckle. Tim was thankful the weather had cooled off some since nightfall, but mostly he was thinking about Alice. He sure hated leaving her for a rabbit, five dogs, and two men who shoulda been in bed just like him. He must have been crazy to ever get up when Alice was snuggled up in bed and warm and they were still honeymooning. But on the other hand, his father had a way about him when he picked up a shotgun and yelled, "Geet-own, gals, geet that rabbit, geet-own." And the dogs put their noses over and under everything and whipped their tails and yowled. When they got on a trail, they chased like the devil in a churchyard full of sinners 'till that ole rabbit was dead in his sights. One shot! One shot was all he required. Hell, yes!

Tim hopped a ditch and continued along the path. Another half mile and he'd be out of the woods.

He felt good. Damn fine. He knew Earl was at the farm by now. Try as he might, Tim had hardly ever managed to beat Earl anyplace. That boy was usually two years earlier than Father Time. It was a shame the younger brother had to be the one to set the example for the older, and Tim had agonized over this kind of thing on many a day. Time just had a way of slipping by him. The same with school. Earl had been the brilliant one, the one bent on becoming a gentleman. Tim had never felt any jealousy, as best he could remember. He was proud of Earl and had worked hard to help him earn expense money over the years. Earl had always been special.

Tim knew that he knew himself, and what he most enjoyed was long haul trucking. There was something about getting out on the road at the wheel of a big rig that just plain turned him on. And Sweet Georgia Brown was a dream come true. He had only had the truck a few weeks, but already he had waxed the cab three times. It was sweet to see water beading up on that pale silver blue paint. Yes, indeed. Alice was making him some special curtains to put at the small porthole windows, which were high on either side of the sleeping compartment. And he planned to begin putting a coat of wax on the chrome trim along the base edge of the trailer later in the day. But before he did that, and after the hunting, he was looking forward to coaxing Alice back into the bed with him. She had the day off from her job today, too. The lady she worked for was off on a trip, so the two of them could spend at least part of the afternoon getting reacquainted. Lordy, he loved that woman.

Tim removed a handkerchief from his hip pocket and wiped at the sweat on his forehead. More popped out almost immediately. "Man, it's gonna be a scorcher, today, once that sun rises," Tim said to himself.

He switched his gun to the other arm. It was strange hunting in August. It was just that the three of them practically never got together to hunt anymore, with Earl away in New York now most of the time. And Jesse thought it would be fun to let the dogs have a go. He figured they could get away with it as long as they stayed on his farm. The game warden wouldn't know the difference.

Now Earl had gotten rather strange about rabbit and quail hunting. He said he loved to hear the dogs run and he loved to watch a good bird dog ranging and then going to point, but he hated killing game. He said he didn't want to shoot another critter as long as he lived. Tim didn't mind one bit, since that meant he would have more chances to do some shooting himself.

If it hadn't been for Alice, he would still be asleep. Alice was a fine cook, and she dearly loved rabbit. He knew he had to go hunt up some for her.

He had told Alice when he came in around one this morning, "That Earl was still playing it cool and partying when I left the beer garden. I just talked to the guys, of course; didn't look at none of the women." And he winked at her and grinned.

"Oh, yes," Alice said in mock attitude. "I know you're gonna go get me some rabbits for cookin' now," she said. "I betta not hear anything about you and a rovin' eye, neither. You hear?"

Tim laughed sheepishly. "Baby," he said. "Have a little sympathy. Here Earl goes out to celebrate me being hitched and he leaves me at the card table so's he can party with a whole bunch a strange people, dancing and singing and cutting the fool. Bet you he won't get hisself in here until time to go hunting, and then he'll be as ready to go as if he'd slept all night."

And sure enough, Earl had come in and had shook Tim right out of bed. Said he was gonna get a shower and then go over to Jesse's place a little early to chew the fat while Tim took his slow time getting out of the house from all the honeymooning. Earl said that he should get his butt up right away and follow. Well, Tim had decided to do just that, but it had taken him another half-hour to get out of bed. Hell, it had been 3:00 when Earl woke him. They wouldn't be hunting 'til 5:30, when the sun put some light on what they were doing. Sleep was precious, especially when you were a man lying next to a woman as fine as Alice.

Tim passed the last of the trees at the edge of the woods, amused by his thoughts, and crossed the asphalt road. Way up ahead he could see the shadow of the barn's roof. His feet touched the firm sand of the farm road and then he slowed his pace. There was no need to hurry now that he was so close.

Tim figured he'd give all of his rabbits to Earl to tote. He chuckled to himself. That would leave him free to shoot. Lord, he loved to tease Earl about him not shooting, and getting himself labored down with everybody else's game. Tim was about to laugh when a hideous sound stopped him halfway in his stride. A scream, like somebody's very soul had been cut open, shot across the stillness from the general direction of the barn. Tim searched the darkness, a chill running over him like he had stepped outside from a warm bed without any clothes on in the dead of a damp winter night. The chill seemed to come from the center of him, causing the hair to rise along his back, arms, and legs. The twig fell from his lips and another chill played up his back and over his shoulders.

He ran forward twenty feet or so when he saw a short burst of light come flooding from the barn doors. In an instant the doors closed again. Something had changed forever in Tim. Never in his life could he have created that sound, which still seemed to linger on the air. All

201

of a sudden the darkness was thick like pitch and mean. Breaking again into a run, he sped up the road as fast as he could.

He stopped short when he saw the pickup and cars. They were off to the right side of the yard, mostly hidden from the sand road by the corn. That scream, if that's what it had been, felt like it had lodged in his throat. He felt a cool emptiness there, which made it difficult to swallow. It was now a different night, sinister, a different place in the world. Tim dropped two shells into his gun and snapped it shut, covering the gun with his large hand so the click wouldn't carry. Jesse might have hurt himself working, but Tim didn't really believe that. All of his instincts sent him into a cautious running crouch across the yard.

Inching up close to the barn doors, slightly off to the side, listening, he heard unfamiliar voices raised in shouted whispers from inside. He backed off, holding his gun vertically in front of him with his right hand gripping the trigger guard at the ready, the left just above it on the barrel stock, expecting someone to come out at any moment.

The voices ebbed to a mumble and after standing for several minutes, listening to his own heartbeat, standing frozen and scared with his back pressed up against the barn in the darkness, he looked cautiously around to see if anyone else was about. It seemed like the darkest night in history, that slip of a moon no help at all, and everything was shrouded in an eerie quiet. A haze was over the corn, milky white and elusive in the way it curled like smoke and then seemed to lie flat against the tips of the tassels.

He wondered why the dogs weren't making a fuss with strangers around. He had never known them to stay in their houses on nights when visitors were about. He found that the lock was gone from the pen and the latch was broken. Not a dog was inside of the houses or pen. A wave of terror, infinitely faint, moved through his mind against any will to obscure it, and then Tim crept forward again and looked through the crack between the doors, his gun ready in his hands. His vision was blocked. Someone was standing in the way.

".....to worry 'bout nothin'. And don't you go getting panicky again, Chuck," an angry voice bellowed. Curtis Brewer. That was Brewer talking. His next words were softer, as though he had suddenly remembered that he wanted the talking low. What was Brewer doing in his father's barn at 4:00 in the morning?   He didn't own any horses or farm equipment that might need repair.

"Now, like I told you, we can hide 'em without anybody knowing any different. You'd best go see if anybody's outside. Be careful, boy."

"Ok, Pa," the voice sounded young and shaky. It was Chuck; he was sure it was. Tim scrambled from the doors and ducked behind the corner of the barn. He peeped around the edge and watched for Chuck. He knew the boy's voice, had received orders from his father through him. He had always seemed a decent, sensitive boy. Why was he here now, and what were those white men planning to hide?

A slice of light spread over Chuck's shoulders. He nervously tugged at the door, alternately opening and closing it, as he stood in the doorway, looking halfheartedly out at the night. He could still see them killing Earl, could smell the blood and feel himself pulling the trigger on Jesse. He felt weak and molested of mind. But strangely, his was a guilt without shame. He might never in his life be able to understand why he felt no shame. A metamorphosis had come over him. It was a state, a condition, unlike any he might have imagined. Lynching was a dreadful thing, but now, he was a lyncher, and to be ashamed would mean he would never be free again to think clear thoughts. He could go insane, and he was determined to hold onto his mind at all costs. Better to be guilty, for he was guilty of the crime, and to transform such a terribly troublesome burden as shame into annoyance. For now, for a long time, he would be annoyed that Earl and Jesse had been such obstacles in his life as to cause him so much worry. They had caused him to hate them by their very natures, by their very existence. He was sure of this now, watching the night from the barn's open door. He took a few hesitant steps into the abyss beyond the wooden walls and then eased back to the cover of his father's scrutiny, locking the door behind him.

"Nobody's out there, but we gotta hurry, Pa. The sun's gonna be up."

"Ok! Ok! Now start putting dirt over the blood and cleaning up." Brewer was frightened and trying not to show it, thinking of the rushing sunrise, holding back his impatience with his son and himself for raging so long that now they might be discovered by somebody.

"Joe, you git them big burlap sacks over there. We'll put the bodies in 'em."

Tim had returned to the doors. He lowered his head, still trying to piece their words together into some binding thought. Sweat rolled from his hairline into his eyes. Where were his father and brother? What did Brewer want? And all those other men? What were they doing there, talking like they were? And why had everything in the world slowed its pace so that he seemed to be crawling, to be clawing with his mind at sense.

Only a few minutes had passed since he heard the scream, but a million images had rushed through his mind. It seemed more like all of his life was waiting to understand what it was he was hearing. His heartbeat shook in his ears like an old broken drum, pounding like his father's hammer on a cold day when the barrel held ice and the hot curved iron had to force its way to find substance for steam.

In desperation, Tim moved to the window at the side of the barn, taking the chance that no one would come around the side of the barn and discover him. It was a small window and he had to stand on tiptoe to look over the ledge. He peered in, not really himself anymore due to the breath of fear on his neck. Fear was sucking his breath away with its own, creeping up behind his ears so he could hear nothing outside of himself.

In front of the window and on the floor; a man, a big man dressed in overalls ... lying in blood ... as still as death. Tim gasped so loudly that the sound surely traveled through the wooden walls into the barn. He backed away from the window and shuddered. In seconds he was trembling out of control, stumbling into the trees and branches and cob webs, and grass was in his mouth mixed with the dirt of the woods floor. He let go of his gun and covered his face.

"Poppa." He crawled further into the woods as a heavy wretching started. He wretched and vomited so hard and deep that he thought he was drowning. The gagging stink shot through his teeth in waves as he put more distance between himself and the barn and tried to keep the sound down inside of him, his stomach aching.

"Poppa!" He breathed a labored and fast and hollow agony and tried not to make any noise as he choked for air. He finally leaned back against a tree, eased to his knees and dug his fingers into the ground, trying to clear his mind, yet momentarily mindless.

When had he, in his memory, first met his father? Had he seen him as a face leaning above him, as hands tossing him upward? Or was that a dream from some far gone time? He would never hear his voice again. His father always laughed so much like a stranger; a wonderful stranger who refused to stay long enough, to laugh often enough.

The woods floor floated above Tim's head, then the treetops. He was losing consciousness, it seemed to him, and he couldn't seem to stop it from happening. He was entering eternity and above him, in the tree, something was moving the limbs, bobbing them, sending leaves down into his face. An opossum? No—a coon, with eyes green from the spare light from the barn window; masked black and always ripe prey for hunters and dogs.

Tim wiped his mouth and came back into the world. He took several deep breaths, steadied his nerves with resolve and rose to his feet, leaving the coon and the fear and every other consideration save the men in the barn way behind him. How much time had passed he didn't know. That there would be enough time, he was certain. He would make it so if it took the rest of his life.

He crept closer and looked once more through the glass. He strained himself into an understanding with himself that his brother had long left him and would be, like his father, dead among his murderers. As he looked, he prayed to find him a hostage of some kind. He prayed, his lips moving, but his eyes open and searching, moving with the men who carried his father toward the back left stall. One man was scattering dirt on the floor to hide the blood, wiping part of his father up off the anvil with a rag so nobody would ever see. Tim looked on bewildered and praying until he saw Earl. He stood paralyzed. If only he'd come when Earl first called him. How many seconds might have saved them? He rested his face on his arm and cried and fought a bitter trembling struggle for control so single-minded that his fingers pressed into the barn wood until they were on fire with pain.

Tim moved away and found the gun. He was vaguely aware that he would have created enough racket walking about by now to have alerted the men had the ground not been mostly covered with soft pine needles. He considered a shotgun useless under the circumstances. There were seven of them. Tears rolled down his face with a wearisome sadness. What could he do with two damn shells against seven men and no damn time to reload?

"Shit............" he groaned.

The light from the window glistened shiny black off of his sweaty face. He clutched the gun, his fingers pressing violently, while his mind searched for an answer. Slowly, he took it all in, turned it over and set it to boiling, blending the horror with a dark-headed reasoning. His lips moved as though in prayer.

He watched them and suddenly understood their plan. Brewer had said something about hiding the bodies "without anybody knowing any different," and at the time it had made no sense. But now they were bunched together a couple of feet away from the back wall of the barn, digging a gigantic hole. It was already waist deep and almost broad enough to hold the Togan men. The men dug frantically. It wouldn't be long before they could do the burying, and then Tim guessed that they planned to strew the floor with straw, and if he had been the one trying to cover up, he would walk the horse all over the area so no one would think to look there for two men who had disappeared without a trace. If they had any sense, they would put shoring under and above the bodies so the earth wouldn't sink in as they decomposed. Cinder blocks and several flooring planks were stored along the far side wall and could be used for that purpose. If they were thinking and moved quickly, they had the time to do it, but then, he didn't know if they were thinking that clearly.

The men paid no attention to the mare as she stomped about in her stall, the smell of fresh blood unnerving her. Time was too short, their situation too menacing. They were intent on their digging, Shorty and Curtis in the hole, the rest removing the loosened dirt to the sides, each one a jumble of nerves, stopping to listen at the faintest sound, yet digging for their futures, digging away with no knowledge of Tim's broad grin in that little pane of barn glass. He knew all seven of them. He knew every last one and they were bound to die. He propped his shotgun against a tree and walked away.

"HOLD ON, WHITE MAN!" Tim screamed within himself. "HOLD ON!"

His face was pitch, his eyes wide and blaring out at the unlighted morning. His feet crushed everything they fell upon as he ran the long two miles through the woods back to his house. He was driven by one thought; to kill, to kill brutally and unmercifully, even if the cost was his own journey to Glory. He knew he couldn't ask God for help, so he asked for forgiveness as he ran.

Everything got into his way: the trees, the brush, the distance, the dark, but the pain of running, in his lungs and in his legs, soon numbed to no feeling. He was running free, with an ironic jubilation, one hand holding tightly to a ring of keys. This was a hunting morning, the real hunt just starting, and he needed only one thing to make the kill.

The big diesel cab sat in the middle of Tim's yard like a mean grinning giant. Tim rammed the key into the ignition, knew its shape by heart, like an extension of himself. He turned the key hard and listened as the engine started loud, hard, and the sky showed a brilliant pink. He sat in the cab, impatient to start, but restrained by the time it took the huge diesel engine to turn over and hum. Then they were together in their purpose. They were moving together, Tim and Sweet Georgia Brown. He ran his right hand over the fine leather seat and shook his head one final time in regret. He looked back at the house where his bride was sleeping and said good-bye, for whatever the outcome, he would not be returning home.

"Brewer," he said grinning and fighting for breath. "You never thought my pretty produce hauling truck would kill your ass, did you? Did you? She's coming for you, white man. Sweet Georgia Brown and me is coming."

Tim laughed bitterly. The sound traveled angrily out through the truck's open window. He laughed and choked back tears. He couldn't get them out of his mind, lying dead and all cut to pieces and not one of those bastards giving a damn. This time white folks were going to pay. Not near enough, but they were going to pay on this night. It wouldn't be long. He'd take the toll right straight. That hole would have to go deep to hide what they had done. They'd be digging a little while longer. God. If they left that place without him nailing them . . . He would find no rest in eternity if he didn't.

Curtis Brewer and Shorty King looked up from the digging. They were down in the hole loosening the hard earth with spades. Their shovels had run into a few scattered rocks, so their progress had been slowed. Still, they were chest deep and just a few minutes from stopping. Chuck was still over against the wall behind them, all curled up in a knot. Curtis hadn't given him more than a glance. And the others were placing cinder blocks just in front of the hole so they could shore things up as fast as they had to. Curtis had insisted that the hole had to be deep so they could rest easy in their beds at night and not worry about somebody discovering what had been done. Once the Togans disappeared, it might be a long time before they could sneak back in the night undetected to fix up any mistakes they'd made.

"What's that noise?" Brewer asked. They all looked at each other, scared pale. They looked toward the barn doors some sixty feet away. They were stuck to the ground, too scared to move, waiting, wanting to check the roar that was drawing closer, afraid to approach it. Just a farmer on the road. The hard surfaced road ran right up to the barn before it veered into the turn. They'd heard other vehicles since they'd started the digging and every last one sounded like it was headed straight for the barn. That's all it was. They had to keep on digging. The sun was coming up. It was just a truck going by the barn on the road out there. That was all.

The mare's ears pricked up, listening, twitching at that roar of something powerful getting closer. She trembled and put all of her weight against the halter rope, pulling to get free, panic and the whites showing plainly around her eyes.

The truck drove at high speed off the highway onto the sand of Jesse's farm road.

FIVE HUNDRED YARDS

"God, don't let 'em move."

THREE HUNDRED YARDS

"Soon I'll see 'em damned to hell."

The diesel rolled up dirt and sand and belched out smoke like a locomotive running through a plate of dust. The corn stalks laid down stiff to the wind as Tim and Sweet Georgia Brown whooshed past them. The corn stalks laid down and swung back up like they'd been drinking all day and long into the night.

BARN DOORS DEAD AHEAD

"Right here, Poppa. I'm with you, Earl boy! I love you, Momma. . . "

The hole was done. Brewer placed his hands along the front edge and hoisted himself up with his arms, intent on climbing out of the hole.

When the nose of the diesel entered the barn, the speedometer was past registering. Tim held the wheel like his hands were welded to it. He saw the uplifted faces trapped with no place to run, felt the bodies gnash into the bug screen, felt one wheel crush racist Brewer into the hole he had dug for black.

Tim laughed; laughed pain and tears and hopes and dreams; laughed caring and America and white folks and life; cursed them all and swore them to hell as the screams met his ears, as the wall met the windshield and its wood splintered away; as his body catapulted over the steering wheel through glassy spikes into the tall woods pines which always kept the storms out on the Bay from reaching the barn.

They lay silent beneath two-by-fours, hay, and metal. They lay unmoving among the pine needles and fallen trees. The barn leaned down broken upon them, around them, within them. Run-a-Rye tried to get up, but couldn't. Her hind legs were severed, her side crushed in. She heaved and shuddered and died.

Chapter XIX

The way down was long and the darkness was tepid. The walls were close upon one another, a circle of brick oozing slime. There was a smell like earthworms and the sky was a narrowing oval, dwindling below her feet, an opening she thought she would never see again. The top of her head, her face, then her neck, chest, legs, and feet went under as cold water assaulted her, detaching her from herself. A hand reached down, pulled her up by the hair, righting her again. She took a deep breath as an overwhelming feeling of relief came. But it was a trick, an illusion. Her nose filled with water. She panicked, suffocating, and then gasping and spitting, air filled her lungs and she thought she was finally truly saved from drowning in the well.

When she opened her eyes, she saw that the hand was white. It was just a hand held out toward her. No face or body hovered above its attention. Just a white hand beckoning her while another held her by the hair and dragged at her weight in the water. She began to be suspicious, though faith in whiteness had been taught to her and was a hard thing to break, that she was not really safe. Before she could fully grasp the thought, the beckoning hand reached, took her by the feet way beneath the water and dangled her upside down again. Progressing slowly, ever so slowly, both hands lowered her to the well's liquid mouth until her nose was covered and she was gone.

"Lord. What we gone do? She's died in her sleep. That poor chile. First she lost her poor little mind. I was afraid a-this soon's I heard Earl was kilt. I know'd she'd get sick, and now she's died in her sleep!"

It was Miz Rosie, saving Carrie from drowning. Only her old loving voice, raised in fright at the split second when Carrie couldn't have held her breath any longer, had brought her back from death in the well to the mellow soft quiet of her own bedroom in the late afternoon. Carrie's mother was helping Miz Rosie down the hall away from her room. She could just barely remember that a few minutes earlier, the old woman had been sitting in the rocking chair by her bed, keeping watch. And then, because Carrie had been so still for so long, Miz Rosie had reached out to touch her forehead and had found Carrie's flesh as cold as death. It was then that Miz Rosie had begun screaming. Carrie hadn't known Miz Rosie was there until the old woman screamed, "Lord ..."

It seemed to Carrie that every time she closed her eyes and opened them again, hours had gone by. She looked around and struggled to understand the changed quality of her room and discovered her father standing near her bed.

He leaned down.

"How do you feel, Sweetheart?"

She could feel the worry in his eyes. Trying to answer brought on desperation. She was still under water and when she opened her mouth to talk it was impossible to breathe. Still, she tried. She opened her mouth despite the water and the fear, and moved her lips, forcing the remaining air in her lungs over her vocal chords. Her father's facial expression was expectant; then amazed. Disappointed, then blank. Then frightened. His frightened look terrified her. Where was her voice? In the well. Down the well. Turner caressed her cheek, cupping her head gently in his two hands, trying to calm her, as he looked at her face.

"Carrie."

She screamed and had to be held down. Didn't he see the danger? Why didn't her father understand what she was saying? Even if her voice wasn't working, surely he could hear her thoughts, they were screaming in her head so loudly.

"You'd both better let her rest, Turner." Dr. Reynolds placed an empty hypodermic needle on the table. She could still feel the punched place on her arm, like the needle was still way in deep, but she couldn't remember seeing the doctor enter her room, nor give her the shot. Neither could she remember her mother walking up to the foot of the bed.

"She's irrational, and the sight of you seems to trigger hysteria." Doc Reynolds thought better of what he had said. "I mean, she's upset to the point where she can't seem to handle seeing anybody right now."

Turner started to object, and then shook his head, agreeing reluctantly. He seemed to be in a great deal of pain, all of it showing in his eyes. The room went empty, but their voices floated through the wood of the door. When she couldn't hear anymore, she crept silently down the hall and listened at the kitchen door. Her mother's voice was grieving, shrill.

"What's happening to her?"

Her father answered. "I don't know. Honest to God, I don't know. I just don't understand. She reacted to the news the way I expected. She cried hard. I held her, stayed with her. Then she seemed to be all right. You remember, Stella, she ate a pretty good meal last night. We put her to bed and took turns reading to her. She went off to sleep. She was sad, but she seemed fine."

Doc Reynolds said softly, "It's shock. Sometimes a person reacts to news like this hours after they've been told."

"I know, but she was so different this morning," her mother said. "I came into her room to wake her up and she was balled up on the floor in the corner, staring. She was just staring and she wouldn't say anything. I couldn't get her to talk at all. She hasn't said a word all day and every time she tries to talk she ends up screaming." Stella was close to screaming herself.

Turner took Stella into his arms to comfort her and Dr. Reynolds patted Turner on the shoulder in an attempt to comfort him. He spoke calmly, in a voice full of hope struggling against fear.

"She's a little child. She's lost her first love, outside of the two of you and her brother. Even I knew that she had a crush on Earl. She's in shock. And it could lead to all kinds of deep seated problems, but if you take it patiently and care for her, as I know you will, I'm certain she'll come out of it intact."

Stella cried softly into Turner's arms and Turner nodded that he understood.

"Now listen. You've got to disguise your own anxiety for her sake. Give her all of the love and care that you can. Spend time with her. Reassure her. She'll be fine. It's only a matter of time."

Their voices sounded mechanical. Carrie had a feeling they were all saying things differently from the way she was hearing the words and tones. She crept back down the hall, closed the door to her room and got well under the covers of her bed. Everything was bland, bordering on somber, unreal. She couldn't feel her skin or her breathing or her heartbeat. She reached over to the night table and touched Earl's gift, which she had unwrapped in the quiet of her room on that last afternoon after he brought her home. It was a book, THE SOULS OF BLACK FOLK, by William Edward Burghardt DuBois. Earl had penned a note, which he had placed inside.

> August 9, 1958
> Dearest Carrie,

> This man, who wrote at the turn of the century, like you, was of mixed blood. His relatives were European (white) from France and Holland, as well as African. He was light-skinned as you are, and there was no American who was more black in his love of African people, especially African American people. Ask your Mom and Dad to read this to you and to discuss it with you until the day when you can read it with clear understanding alone. I love you.

> Earl L. T.

Carrie pulled THE SOULS OF BLACK FOLK onto her pillow beneath her face, closed her eyes, tears wetting the cover, and slept without knowing she was asleep.

Carrie closed her eyes and slept without knowing she was asleep.
her father was angry, and he and the men had been meeting. she wondered what they were going to do about Shorty King. her father was talking to her. trying to tell her something. she didn't want to hear it.

instead, she heard Earl's voice. he was alive. thank goodness. he was alive. she could hear him, just like yesterday.

"Listen to me, little girl. Don't you ever deny yourself knowledge of who you are. Not for anybody. So you're light-skinned and the kids called you yella. You're a Negro, a black girl-child, and whites call you nigger. So you called Beanie a nigger, too. So now you feel you have no place. Bull. Look at me. We're a rainbow people. We're fat and tall and skinny and pretty faced. We're bold and scared and humpbacked and straight. We're light and night colored. We're us. Black folk. YOU AND ME. Don't you ever again question your right to be who you are. You are an African American girl-child, and that's many many things at once. We're all swimmers of the same faith, baby, not a one of us in the boat."

he wiped her tears away. never let her cry. wouldn't stand for crying when there was a sun and good folk to see. And he was gone now. Carrie shut her eyes tight and felt her throat closing on bitterness. Why was there such a thing as dying? Where did he go and how he must have screamed and agonized to be free of that terrible knife! She'd seen him. Last night, after everybody in the house had gone to bed, she'd crept down there and opened the morgue door and turned on the light. If her daddy hadn't been an undertaker, Earl's body wouldn't have been there to see. But she saw. He was cut. They had cut him. What she saw would stay inside of her, screaming at her, pulling at her insides like rats gnawing and clawing their scratching feet, tearing, red-eyed, until she was dead and gone like him to Glory. He would wait for her forever now.

"Listen to me, little girl. Love yourself and your own because they are your own, even when they don't want you to claim them.... See that man over there? That's a man who's lost everything. Fire burned him out of what was a shack to begin with. He was born poor and tired. Lost it before his momma's womb let him breathe air. Lost it before his daddy gave him meaning. Lost it all because a sense of loss was passed on to him from so many down the line. But he's standing there praising God. He's there loving a woman and fathering a child. He's eating and working when he can find work and sometimes he sees something to laugh about. Don't you forsake him. He's all of us. And in his poverty, little girl, is your need. When he makes a dime, you've got to praise the Lord with him, even if he can't believe in you . . . and maybe one day you'll know how to teach him to make more money than he's ever dreamed of. You who went to school when you grew up and got skills and passed them on—back to him and on up to your children.

"Lord, you're gonna be a fine black woman some day. I can see you, grown up and making old brothers wish they'd been labored later and young brothers wish they'd come sooner and the right aged brothers, Lord, you gonna make 'em wage war . . .

215

"Hush your sorrow and be the best you can be. You belong here; first to yourself and then to all of us."

back. how many days now? a long time ago. the room was foggy, fuzzy, as her eyes blinked open and closed again, still sleeping. she saw him in that half second, standing in a haze above her bed. his head was high up—way up high, his face looking down at her. she loved him. there was no father like him anywhere.

he looked strange in the face: a paler tone than she had ever seen except for the nose. his nose was flushed; a pink brown nose like hers got when she'd been crying a lot. his eyes were narrowed; wet, just a trace. his hands seemed extremely large at the ends of his long arms and his chest was more broad than she could remember. it was sunday morning; two mornings after the afternoon when Shorty King chased her as she was riding her bike to Earl's. maybe her father knew. he had told her and told her that she couldn't leave the yard to go bike riding anywhere and she had disobeyed him and now he knew and he was going to give her a whipping. she was really in trouble this time. she could tell by the way he was looking down at her. he was going to whip her with his eyes and his mouth and his disappointment, and then he was going to take off his belt . . .

"Earl's gone, baby..."

maybe if she apologized ahead of time, he'd understand, and she could beg him not to go after Shorty King because white people would kill him if he did, even if Earl did say that justice must be done. she wasn't hurt. just a few scratches. she got away . . . gone where?

". . . so, you see. . . Jesse and Tim and Earl were killed early Saturday morning. . ."

Carrie sat forward, her mouth open and her eyes pinned to her father's face, asking him, begging him to say he hadn't said what she knew he had said and she had seen for so long now in her dreams. All the sound in the room left and whined into a suspension of feeling.

"What?"

The word came in a hush from her mouth and was half swallowed back. And now she heard everything her father had been saying to her when she wasn't listening so long ago; two days ago when he first told her and she had heard him without quite knowing how to feel or what to say. His voice had crammed words into nonsense about the barn and seven lynchers, and that night she had gone down to the morgue and the next day she had no voice, and the doctor had come and then she had eavesdropped and crawled back under the covers and slept off and on for what seemed like forever.

So many things had happened that she would never know about or understand. Some had torn holes through her heart.

Chapter XX

Days and days on top of days passed. People came and went and she saw them through a veil. She remembered Mr. Pat bending down to talk to her. He looked so sad, so lost in the face when he bent down to her and told her how sorry he was. She heard him saying something to her father about Lynn Brewer, but she wasn't sure what he meant. He said it was her fault. Said if she ever came into his store again he would . . . Carrie had turned away from all of the people in the house and had gone back to her room, not really understanding much. She had only seen Lynn once or twice and she didn't know what Mr. Pat was talking about. She didn't think it had anything to do with Earl, or she would have listened further. The people frightened her. They all could die, like Earl had died. They were all black people and they could die.

Never in her life had she felt such loneliness, aloneness. This was no seclusion for crying beyond the prying eyes of friends or strangers. She was solitary, alone, afraid, and speechless. Literally speechless. Everything of meaning in her life seemed to have left her. She reacted to everything as though it bore evil and cringed in the shadows of places and was beginning a deadly stalk against her.

Then Beanie came. Stella had decided that Beanie might cheer Carrie. Everything else had failed.

Due to her condition, none of the services for the Togan men had been held in the funeral home downstairs, and no one realized that Carrie had seen Earl in the morgue. Stella had filled the house with music and laughter, which she found hidden somewhere, and with children and games and pies, cookies and cakes. She had watched as three specialists had tried to get Carrie to speak. She carried Carrie to Norfolk, then to Richmond, then to Petersburg, and they all said the same thing—that she and Turner should give Carrie the time to get over this trauma, but if in a couple of months she still was unable to speak, perhaps the Allens should seek help for her from a psychiatrist. Stella was determined that a psychiatrist would be the very last resort. There were no black psychiatrists anywhere nearby, and Stella didn't trust anyone white at this point in time. Her trust might never return. For now, her reward for coming to more fully trust her own people was to fully embrace their distrust of those who had set the whole mess in motion hundreds of years before.

Beanie had been afraid to try to see Carrie. She knew how much her friend had loved Earl. They had talked long hours, sitting in the grass near the tadpole pond at school and on the school bus and behind the teacher's back in the middle of many a rest period. It had been Earl this and Earl that.

She had thought a lot about Carrie; her lying in bed or sitting in the sun on the porch where Miz Rosie said she always was, just sitting and not saying a word.

When Beanie entered the room, Carrie turned away toward the far wall. The room was bright; pretty colors dancing in loveliness, which any girl would have given her heart to have. Beanie wondered how Carrie could be long unhappy in such a room. She sat for a long, awkward time, looking and wondering what to say while playing nervously with her fingers.

"Almost time for school."

Carrie closed her eyes and remained silent.

What could she say, Beanie wondered, more than ever perplexed by Carrie's silence? What would interest Carrie to make her say something? Mrs. Allen said not to say anything about Earl. "Your granddaddy's coming. Be here tomorrow. Your momma say he bringing a carloada presents and your horse for a visit ..."

Beanie walked down the hall, listless. She met Miz Rosie. "She won't say nothin'. Do she know Shorty King got out the barn? Do she know about the inque. . .?"

"Inquest," Miz Rosie said. "Yeah, Baby. She know much too much. She saw the headline in the paper and she come to her daddy and spoke for the furst time since she heared Earl and them was killed. Her Daddy was overjoyed that she was talking again and he hugged her and was shouting for Miz Stella and M.T. But they was out in the yard and before he could go get 'em, Carrie screamed and made her Daddy tell her what happened. An' when he explained 'bout Shorty King being found alive under the wreckage down in that hole, she got the funniest look on her face. She looked right pitiful and she cried so hard it made her Daddy almost go crazy trying to get her quiet again. She ain't spoke a word since.

The day went by and the room was soon dark. A strange lady was suddenly there, dressed in white, sitting at the foot of Carrie's bed, so black that in the darkness Carrie could only see the white uniform. She screamed and rushed from the bed, tearing at the door as the lady caught her by the waist and wrestled her arms down against her sides.

"Carrie, it's me. Nurse Slocum from Eastville. You knows me, child. You'se had a fever. Hold fast, baby and hush now. I'm with you. Hush now. Hush now."

She helped Carrie back into bed and the child fell into an exhausted sleep where she remained unmoving until well into the next morning. Her grandfather was coming today. He was late. It was way past her birthday. She was born August 17th. Why was he bringing the horse, now? She didn't want it. Not now. She wanted to talk with him. She wanted to ask him why they weren't just going to try Shorty King and get it over. Lord, he should have died for killing Earl and Jesse the way he did. For making Tim have to kill all those men and die doing it. Shorty King should have died. How could mean folks like him keep on living?

Granddaddy Lawrence came into her room and smothered her with a hug and a soft cheek against her face, holding her cradled in his arms the way he had whenever he was around and she had troubles. "Aren't you gonna speak to your ole granddaddy?" He pleaded with her.

She tried, but was unable to say an intelligible word. Everything that she wanted to say was locked away. Even the arrival of her beautiful bay filly made no difference. She didn't even want to go see it.

Carrie continued to move in silence, waiting to hear the news about the inquest. She was missing school. She couldn't stand the thought of school.

September 30th was the day the judge had set. He was guilty. Her father had hired a detective and lawyers and they had found, had proved, the truth. They got to the evidence before whites could stop them or destroy the crime scene, and they showed to everybody that Shorty and the rest had lynched, first the dogs and then Jesse and Earl, and had been caught at it and Tim had given his own life avenging his family. The only just thing was to indict and to try Shorty King for two counts of murder in the first degree. She heard her father say so and she knew it was the truth.

The whites were acting like there was some question about Shorty's guilt. She couldn't understand. He was guilty. Even white folks could see that. They'd have to try him. The inquest was just a ceremony or legal stuff. They'd go to trial and find Shorty guilty or she'd kill him herself. She didn't know any words to describe her hatred for him. His living on would mean the end of everything right. There was no right if white people let him go free. And there would never be any right if black folk didn't make the law come true. Somebody black had to see that Shorty was punished if the white people didn't uphold the laws they had made.

The entire community was poised on the brink of an abyss wherein further violence might explode. The vocal whites took Shorty King to be a symbol of their threatened supremacy; the silent whites simply remained silent. The black people wanted justice, pure and simple, and their anger was a threat to peace. They did not possess the power to make things right, but they could make peace impossible for whites. And suffering in the middle of this gulf of tension was Carrie. Turner and Stella were considering sending her to stay with her grandfather. A conversation with Dr. Reynolds convinced them this might help.

"Turner, I sincerely think she's better than she was, but Stella's father has a point. It'll be almost impossible to keep her from hearing about the inquest if she remains here. The tension is building so hard, I think she needs the stay at his farm. It should only be for a month or six weeks, and under the circumstances, her schoolwork is much less important than her mental health. She's not up to school, anyway."

"Yes. I guess you're right," Turner said. He kissed Stella and Carrie good-bye two mornings later, wishing he could go with them and leave his worries behind. Carrie had kissed M.T. good-bye earlier, before he left for school, and now she hugged her father hard, clinging to him with small arms, as thin as rails. The robust child was gone out of her. She was a stranger. Turner squeezed back his tears. He didn't want his grief to infect her. She already had enough reasons of her own to cry.

When they were gone, Turner walked and half ran until he reached the vault yard. He should have killed Shorty himself, but it hadn't been in him. Murder was wrong and the odds would have been in favor of his being caught and punished for life, causing him to abandon his family. Yet and still, he wished he had acted. Every time he thought of Earl and Tim and Jesse, and he thought of them often, he felt an anguish unparalleled in his life. And poor Eliza and Alice. Eliza was still hospitalized. Within an hour of discovering Tim's body and calling him to come right away to help, she had taken ill. By noon, he and others of his secret group, whom he had called to the scene, had confirmed that Jesse and Earl were also among those lying dead in the rubble of the barn. Eliza had collapsed and was diagnosed later that day as having suffered a massive stroke. She wasn't expected to leave the hospital alive.

Alice had moved in with her mother, and though she managed to attend the funerals, it was obvious that never again in her life would she be the same.

As for Lynn Brewer, well, Pat was the one who knew the part she had played, but nothing could really be done about her. She had lost her father and brother, and based on rumors about Curtis Brewer's debts, she and her mother were going to lose everything. That, in and of itself, was a hellish punishment. Lynn had no skills, no legitimate way to earn a living. Her mother was a hairdresser, sometimes, and an alcoholic. Along with Chuck, they were three more people wasted by the vitriolic Curtis Brewer.

Turner's anger and indignation took control of him as he moved through the vault yard. Everything was the same. He could sense it; that Shorty would go free and racism would continue to be king, with nothing essentially changing. Nothing had changed except for the destruction of the Togans and the fact that his daughter might not ever speak again or recover her emotional health. And he didn't know how to stop such a thing from happening again to some other black family.

Turner looked around in desperation. He wiped the tears from his face as he picked up a long handled spade. He turned in a circle and slammed the spade into the side of the vault house, the tears coming in a long ache from deep in his gut.

Miz Rosie, standing on her porch across from the vault yard, raised her hands to her face in fear as she saw Turner turning with the shovel in a run. He raised the spade again and again and brought it down in a rage against the side of the vault house, slugged it hard against the wood again and again until it shattered in his hands. He fell to his knees with the last blow, and across the distance she could hear him crying, an angry, helpless sound which came to her sorrowfully, rending her heart.

She was about to climb down her steps and go to him when her brother urged her back. "He got to do somethin'. Don't bother him now."

Miz Rosie turned around and her brother walked with her into their house. If she couldn't help, she didn't want to watch.

Chapter XXI

Carrie's mother bathed her every night at Granddaddy Lawrence's home in water as hot as Carrie could stand, and rubbed her body in lotion and sometimes in witch hazel. She sang to her and read to her from all the stories with happy endings. She held Carrie in her arms, rocking in long-departed Grandmother Lawrence's rocking chair, folding her child away from terror with all of the love she could fashion or find.

Yet, with all that was done to occupy Carrie and to raise her spirits, she thought about Shorty King and the inquest anyway. No matter how long they kept her away from knowing, she would know one day soon, and she was determined that if the white people were lost to justice, she was going to find a way to bring final justice to Shorty King herself.

She wanted to believe in all the stories, the ones in books and on the television. Surely the law wouldn't set the guilty free. Even when it was a white man, surely they'd do right. White people weren't that hopeless and astray from the rest of the folks in the world that they'd lie on themselves before the whole world about the credibility of their own laws.

Roy Rogers knew the truth, and Gene Autrey. Hoot Gibson knew, and Hopalong Cassidy. All of them knew. Even Lassie knew. Even though there were no black heroes on TV, the white heroes knew. They were always there and watching for the good people of the town so that if the sheriff or the judge was scared or crooked, the real crooks would be caught by the heroes and made to pay. She could be like them. Even if it meant she'd have to grow up first. But even the child stars were able to make justice, Shirley Temple could, sometimes, and why else did they show those movies and shows if that wasn't the way it was supposed to be.

It got so Carrie spent practically all of her waking time seated before her grandfather's TV set. Stella had noticed with concern the interest which Carrie had been taking in the television here lately, so, unsure of what it meant, if anything, she let her watch somewhat against her better judgment, hoping it would help her to speak again one day soon. Carrie had shown practically no interest in anything since the killings. Maybe her new interest in television was a good sign.

One night, Carrie stayed up quite past her bedtime watching a mystery show. Television programs seemed to soothe her as nothing else. Stella called to her to remind her to retire to her room. Carrie leaned closer to the set and stalled. She was determined that she must see the remainder of the story. Something important was happening on the screen, and she needed to understand every detail.

A man was doing something wrong. He hated his wife and was trying to decide how to kill her. He thought of many things, but decided they wouldn't work. So one day he went into a store, and when he came out, he was carrying a small, thick cardboard canister that had a small drawing on it.

A few days earlier, Carrie had seen such a design in her grandfather's barn. She pointed to it where it sat way up high on a shelf and he explained that it was a poison, arsenic, which he used to kill rats, but which certain Negro cooks had used during slavery to kill their masters by mixing a little here and there in the white folks' food. He explained that slow poisoning with arsenic caused an illness that was difficult to diagnose if the doctor wasn't looking for it. Carrie's great, great grandmother had called arsenic "Slave's Remedy." Carrie had been forbidden to touch any container bearing a skull and crossbones. She forgot about it until the Alfred Hitchcock episode.

Her eyes bright, she turned off the television before the program ended. And when she was tucked into bed, she lay awake well into the early morning. All kinds of things were brewing in her head and deep in her spirit so that she felt a kind of exquisite pain from the effort, as though her whole self was adjusting for what was to come. She called for every word she could remember Earl saying to her. She conjured up his face so that he seemed to be standing by the bed. He was saying, "It's a long row to hoe, this trek for Black Folks' Freedom, and we'll lose many a soul before the struggle is over. But you've got to keep a stout heart and a keen eye so you'll know what part you can best play. And when you know—when you have it for certain in both your heart and in your mind, do what you have to do, girl, and there'll be no shame. No lie."

Carrie fell asleep, fortified and determined and full of understanding.

December was on the verge of giving the world another Christmas when the right Sunday rolled around. Carrie had been back home for almost a month now. She was back in school but was still unable to speak. Turner and Stella had decided that if she wasn't speaking by the first of spring, they would seek psychiatric help for her. It was a decision that weighed heavily on their minds.

Carrie had known for almost a month now, in fact, since her foot had touched the door sill of her house and she had looked into M.T.'s face. There would be no trial. Not enough evidence was what the white folks said. And they had sent Shorty someplace. Gave him money to take a month's vacation because the black folk were in an angry mood, acting rather unlike themselves according to the way they'd acted over the years. It was suspected that the coloured might try to harm the battered and worn Mr. King, who had suffered a concussion and a broken arm when the truck knocked one of the men's bodies into him on its way through the barn. He had been saved only by his presence in the hole. His story was that he and Curtis and the other men had heard gunshots while playing cards down Cherrystone Creek at the home of Tom Hines, just down the way from the Togans. They'd just gotten in the barn to see what the trouble was when the truck ran them down. The evidence that countered Shorty's story was somehow judged as inadequate to warrant such a grave charge as murder, or anything else, for that matter. Mr. King had surely suffered enough, through his injuries and the loss of six of his close friends.

Miz Rosie was ironing. Carrie slipped away, like on one Friday before when it was summertime. She was warmly dressed and carried a small jar full of white powder in a brown paper bag.

Her mother and father were at church—another funeral. She would get back home as soon as possible, but it wasn't important to her if her parents found her missing, as long as she was able to carry out her mission. She was certain she would be back home before long.

Shorty was back from his grand trip to Florida. He had been back for two weeks now and this was her first opportunity to leave the house alone. The deacon who brought the news to her father had spoken louder than he knew. She was downstairs playing in the showroom and listened with ease as he talked. White folks figured the coloured had cooled down, though Shorty was a little nervous. They figured Christmas would ease the coloured into warm hearts, and since trouble could make life messy for all concerned, a whole lot of Christmas bonuses were being given to the poor coloured folk this Christmas for the first time, ever.

Carrie heard her father say, "We've filed an appeal. We'll take it all the way to the Supreme Court if we have to. I'll be talking to you."

She wanted to ask him what an appeal was, but she couldn't get the words out, and she knew she wasn't supposed to be listening.

Carrie walked at a fast clip, bent forward in her coat against the cold. Through the vault yard, around through the woods to bypass the Line, one half mile into the woods behind the eastern side of Cheriton. Good. The way was clear. Shorty's pickup truck was gone. If Shorty had been home, she would have returned another day. One day she knew he would be away just long enough.

The air was moist, promising snow, but the ground was dry, the woods floor crackly with leaves. She watched for him, crept a few feet at a time toward his house over the noisy woods ground. There were lots of bushy evergreen cedar trees to hide behind.

Onto the porch, she listened and inched closer. There was no sign of him. The kitchen window was shut. She waited and worked her way to the next. It was shut tight. She saw no one inside and continued to look through every window that was not too high. She waited, her heart racing in heavy thumps, and finally she decided to risk entering through the front door, if it was unlocked.

Opening the door put a strain of fear into her back. The door cried like some creature from another world. She stepped into the living room ready to break and run. There was no sign of anyone.

The bedroom was empty. There were empty whiskey bottles on the bed and everywhere she looked, and a brand new suitcase was standing at the foot of the washstand.

The kitchen was dirty, empty food cans all over the table, the counters, and the floor. A small pot of stew had been left on the back of the stove. It was still warm. She lifted her jar, unscrewed the lid and carefully sprinkled in a very small amount of "Slave's Remedy." She stirred the pot vigorously with its own spoon.

She left a dash in the sugar dish and the salt shaker received the very tip of a teaspoonful, shaken well. The white powder blended and almost looked the same. She even spooned a little into the small one pound bag of flour and the fresh quart of milk, which she found in the icebox.

She was about to leave when she thought she heard a voice behind her. Her heart skipped and she turned around with a jerk, scared out of her wits.

"Carrie?"

It was Earl. Earl's voice.

Carrie walked slowly back into the kitchen, unafraid, but full of dread. She knew why he had come. Since she learned that he had been murdered, she had remembered every word he had ever said to her in her life, as best she could, but on that last day, when he brought her home in his truck, he had made her promise and she hadn't wanted to remember. She hadn't wanted to, but she had and she knew he would be disappointed.

There was a large, crumpled, brown paper grocery bag on the counter. As she reached for it, she began to cry.

"No. Please. He should die." She could talk to Earl. She had to talk to him now, but not with her voice. He could hear her without her using her speaking voice. She knew she would never use her voice, ever, to speak to him again. He was a spirit now.

"Carrie? Remember? Not to hate?"

Tears welled in her eyes so she could barely see. She took the bag and into it she placed the smaller bag containing the poison jar with its spoon. She loaded in the milk carton, the salt shaker, the flour, and the sugar dish, and as she folded down the top of the bag, she struggled for breath, she was crying so hard.

"I promised, I know. He isn't good, for anybody. He's a killer. Please, Earl. Please, don't make me."

"I can't make you. You know right from wrong. You made that promise to yourself and to your children. You know right from wrong."

She shook her head, the tears coursing down so she could barely see.

Jamming the bag under her arm, she lifted the small pot of stew from the stove and walked back through the house, crouched over with the weight of her burdens.

"I know right from wrong." Her voice was barely audible in her mind. "I know right from wrong. I promised. Not to hate." She couldn't see, the tears were so heavy, a crying like the end of everything.

She walked and stumbled, reluctant yet determined despite herself, back, well back into the woods, tears falling silently. She placed the things down and found a good sized broken limb, not so long, but broad. She dug a hole where the ground was soft loam, thawed by a day that was cold but not freezing cold. She seemed frantic, the way she attacked the ground, digging with no regard for dirt on her clothes or in her hair.

It took a while and she was tired when she was done; she didn't rest, couldn't rest or stop for fear that she would go back to the house despite Earl's voice and do what she had come there for. She placed the items in, one by one as though at some ceremony. She poured the milk in first, watching it soak the ground, and before she laid the carton flat against the left side of the hole, she made a space for the small pot of stew. Then she put in the small brown bag, its jar inside, and then the sugar, flour, salt shaker, and spoon, and covered them over with dirt and then with leaves and pine needles.

All the while in silence, tears that blinded her eyes kept coming down her soiled face. She was so tired. It was cold, but if she rested awhile beside the grave and pulled her legs up under her coat, she would be warm. As she drifted off to sleep, looking for a place inside of herself where she didn't hurt so much, she heard Earl's voice, soothing, and she felt all of the grief for him rising up so that for the first time, the sounds of her grieving came into the world. For a long time, the sounds rose up out of her as she hugged the small grave where nothing had died. The sound of her grieving caused a hush in the forest, a calm. She cried and cried and hugged the earth and finally slept in the cold, warm and bundled up as she was, by something beyond what she wore.

Feeling the sweet press of life in the wind on her face for the first time since before August 10th, when Earl died, Carrie walked home. It was a brisk day, different in its brightness from all the other days, even from when she left home three hours before. It was like another day long ago, a year before, when she was a little child and she and her mother and Granddaddy Lawrence and M.T. had gone Christmas tree hunting.

As she approached the vault yard from the rear of the lot, she heard her father's voice calling, worried, "Carrie! Carrie!"

"Carrie!" Her mother was calling frantically.

Carrie pitched forward into a run, running now like in the early spring when she was excited about May Day and the dance around the May pole. She pushed through the bushes and tangle vines and rounded a row of vaults, panting, running, anxious to let them know they shouldn't worry anymore.

"Carrie. Where are you?" It was her brother calling.

"Here!" she yelled, over and over again, astonished. "I'm here! I'm here!" through tears of joy, now, lifting the old and the reclaimed sound of her voice above the new freedom in her heart. Her task was done now. For Earl's sake, her true task was done. She could hear him laughing, cheering her life on, telling her what a wonderful thing her life was going to be, how so many good changes were coming if she would only love her people and not look back in hate. As doctor Reynolds had said, "She'll be fine. It's only a matter of time."